MW00898363

Two Lives
One Life

To Scott with much
love From your Mother,
Gail

(signature)

Author

Two Lives One Life
Copyright 2012 Charles Pitcher

Cover Design Copyright Laura Shinn
Book Design by Maureen Cutajar

ISBN-13: 978-1478240990
ISBN-10: 1478240997

Two Lives One Life

CHARLES PITCHER

CHAPTER ONE

Mark Hill is a small town in rural Georgia, near the Atlantic coast. The population of the town and county is about ten thousand, more or less.

A two-lane highway runs into town, around the square, and then North out of town. A courthouse occupies the square and it is a place for old men to gather for lively discussions, which usually result in heated arguments. Each person has a firm opinion on the topics of the day. Great debates with no solutions are common.

The trip between corporate limits takes less than five minutes, except on Saturday, when most outlying residents come in to shop and buy provisions for the coming week. Cotton, tobacco and some row crops support the economy. There is a cotton gin outside of town. The same families have possessed much of the farmland for generations.

The town has one main street occupied by small retail businesses and a co-op store for the farmers. Most are farmers and small business people who live in close relationship with one another. There are no strangers in Mark Hill. Many of the families are either interrelated or are life long friends.

The church is the mainstay of the community and the center of social activity for the people. They are all intent on being good neighbors. If one has a need then many will respond. It is a way of life in Mark Hill.

The summer of 1936 was a particularly hot one for the region. The school year would be over in two weeks and Henry Jimson, a seventh grader, could hardly wait. Henry was a tall, lanky boy with a shock of wavy blond hair that usually matted around his ears in the humid climate. He liked school, enjoyed reading, and had no problem learning. Summer vacation would be a change of pace for him.

His family was of modest means. Henry, and his Mother and Father lived in a small one story, frame house outside of town. His Dad owned a forty-acre tract, which his Father helped him buy before the depression. He built a pond, dug a well, installed a windmill, and built the house and a barn on the property. He also fenced and cross-fenced the property and raised and sold a few cattle and horses. This was our home. Mr. Jimson farmed part-time and worked full-time at the local cotton gin. He was a general foreman on the day shift and had upwards of twenty men under him, processing cotton during the harvest season. It was a noisy, hot and dusty business and Henry often filled in when it got busy. It was either that or pick cotton in the hot sun, dragging sacks behind him and rushing to keep up with more experienced workers.

Families all struggled to make ends meet. The effects of the Great Depression reached into the local economy and everyone was anxious to provide food and shelter for their own. For some the accepting of charity was the only way to survive hard times. Jobs in Mark Hill were almost nonexistent. Henry was fortunate that his Dad had a good job at the gin.

Mark Hill Junior High had a scheduled field trip by school bus to the local county home. There were about fifty residents there and all of them were permanent. Workers employed in the 1930's had built the home under the depression era, Work Progress Administration (WPA) program, enacted to provide for construction of public works by the unemployed. The building was constructed and occupied soon after completion. The initial residents were the aged and infirm, some with non-life threatening disabilities and Veterans of The Great War and a few from the Spanish American War. Some of the veterans were older when they enlisted and were advanced in years when they later entered the home. None of the school class wanted to go there because it was so depressing. The county home was too realistic to cope with, for thirteen and fourteen year old children.

Henry was particularly disturbed by the trip because his Grandfather was there. Grandpa stayed in the Jimson's home until shortly after his nine-tieth birthday. He had become increasingly senile and was a danger to him-self and the family. Often he would disappear, only to be found miles away, walking to his old homestead. A passerby would see him on the road and drive him to the old place, and then later, call us so we wouldn't worry. Everyone knows everyone in Mark Hill and Grandpa was loved and looked after by all.

He rolled his own cigarettes and on too many occasions would smoke in bed. For that reason Mom would hide his tobacco and papers at night. One night he found his tobacco pouch and pad of cigarette paper, rolled and lit one, and set his bed on fire at two o'clock in the morning. That was the last straw. Everyone was sad and Mother cried as we left the county home two days later. He was confused and very agitated, but Dad and Mom knew it had to be done. It was hard and the routine visits became more depressing with the passage of time. The family all loved him and hated the whole situation.

The school bus pulled up in front of the school at ten o'clock a.m. and we were led out single file and assigned seats with boys on one side and girls on the other. Usually bus trips to basketball games and other school events were fun, but today was different. No one wanted to go on this trip. The home was on the east side of town and the road that led there was gravel and washboard rough. Dust flew everywhere; outside in billows as the bus lumbered along, and drifting into the open windows and onto the seats and our clothes. One of the girls was sneezing, trying to stand in the aisle of the swaying bus and pounding her dress to get the dust off. She only made her plight worse with her vain attempts to stay clean. Agitated and self-conscious she fell back into her seat and rearranged her dust-covered hair. Girls sure are peculiar about little things like staying prim and proper under every situation, and are often comical for boys to watch. The boys on the bus took great delight in her failed efforts.

As the county home came into view everyone stood and the boys began to jockey for position to get off the bus first. I stayed in my seat to avoid be-ing trampled and to be obedient to my upbringing. "Girls should always go first and assisted in their times of need," my Mother often reminded me. So when everyone was outside, I got up and moved outside behind the driver. He smiled and thanked me for my behavior. He knew I was shy and not pushy in crowds. Once again, single file, we proceeded up the steps and into the long, dark hall to wait for instructions. Cattle and children are doomed to be herded in groups and stragglers were not tolerated.

The teacher in charge of our group instructed us to not move and wait where we stood as she went to find the administrator of the county home. In about five minutes she returned with a guide. We were again lined up single file to tour the home. I stayed in back and tried to pretend I was invisible, so as not to be seen by Grandpa. He had become more detached and some said he was now in advanced senility or perhaps had developed Alzheimer's disease. Whatever the case, he no longer knew me or would confuse me with Dad and that really bothered me. We moved down the hall, past the bulletin board that contained government regulations, letters, notices, schedule of activities for the residents, and a meal menu for the week. I stopped to look at the letters and became separated from the group; a fact I noticed some minutes later. No one was in sight, so I went in the direction I last saw them. As I turned the corner I almost fell over a wheelchair containing an elderly lady. She wanted to know why I was in such a hurry and that I should watch where I was going and would I find her dog. No pets are allowed in the home. I excused myself and saw my group as I passed the library. Everyone was standing in a semi-circle and gazing about as the librarian was explaining checkout procedures and the Dewey Decimal System of filing. I decided not to go in and slipped past the door unnoticed.

I wondered if all these homes smelled alike. It's the first thing of notice when entering. Disinfectants are used constantly in all public ways as well as the resident's rooms and the odor is very strong. But there is another smell that I think is that of the dying. It is almost sweet and seems to hang in the air. At first one thinks the place is filthy, but that's not the case. Cleanliness is necessary to prevent the spread of disease just as in hospitals, but here the whole atmosphere is different than on a hospital ward. A nurse attendant approached me and asked if I was looking for someone. Not knowing what to say, I told her my Grandpa was here and I was going to visit him. Satisfied, she left me to my wandering and I moved past the cafeteria toward the rooms where residents stayed.

As the hall turned to the right and I rounded the corner past a door to one of the rooms a voice yelled out and startled me. "Who is that out there skulking around? If you think you can sneak in here and steal my stuff, just try it! I'll blow your head clean off at the neck and your ears will fall to the floor in a bloody mess! Do you hear me?" I jumped back against the wall and froze in fear. Some of these people were not all there and might be dangerous. Minutes passed until I mustered enough courage to move back in the direction I had come in order to rejoin my group. Just as I was going to move past the door, a head appeared from the room and the man said I should be ashamed of myself for invading his privacy.

I blurted out, "My name is Henry Jimson and I meant no harm. I was passing by and intend to go back with my class now."

He told me that I had to come in and sit down so he could size the situation up. Why I did so is beyond me, but in a moment, he had me sitting in a straight back chair. He sat down in a rocker not three feet from me and began to slowly rock back and forth in deliberate fashion. I began to feel panic, but then, as time passed, the rhythmic rocking took hold of me and I became fascinated with him.

"Are you going to hurt me?" At that very instant he got up, went to the only window in the small room and with his back to me he began to shake. Turning back to face me, he let out a loud and melodic laugh, and continued to laugh until he again sat down and began to rock again.

"So you are one of those skittish ones are you." I made no reply so as not to agitate him. Instead I began to notice things about him. He appeared to me to be younger than Grandpa and he still had all his hair. It was jet black with flecks of gray, was well oiled and slicked back on both sides, parted right down the middle and cut very close. His height must have been at least six feet and weighed probably 160 or 170 pounds. I guessed he must be in his seventies, but it was hard to tell. What struck me most were his eyes. They peered out from under heavy dark eyebrows, were deep blue and gazed through narrow slits in a manner that pierced right into your mind. I could not take my gaze from those eyes. Suddenly he released me from his intense stare and looked back out the window.

The nurse attendant came into the room and inquired, "Are you Henry Jimson? Boy they been looking all over for you. The bus is loaded and waiting. You are in a mess of trouble, I declare." As I jumped to my feet the man asked me where I lived. I told him on the south side of Mark Hill. "When you come back here to see your Grandpa I want you to come in here so I can tell you some things that might interest you." "Do you know about my Grandpa? I don't remember telling you about him." "I use my ears boy and heard you tell the nurse," he replied in a matter of fact fashion. "Yes sir, but I have to go now so goodbye and good luck." Why did I say that? He grinned and laughed again, nodded at the door and replied, "Get out of here, but remember to come back like I told you."

As I boarded the bus in a dead run, the teacher asked me how many weeks were left in school. "Two weeks, I guess." She said that my guess was correct and also happened to be the number of days I would be staying after school to clean erasers and blackboards as punishment for disappearing and holding the whole class up by being irresponsible. As I sank into my seat everyone around me were giggling and kidding me. It wasn't a good day for me for I knew that when I got home, no amount of explaining would save me from the wrath of my Father. I was right.

After two weeks of chalk dust and late suppers and early bedtimes my punishment was finally complete. Now with the last day of school and the summer vacation at hand my life would again return to normal. I was wrong.

The large double doors, framed in steel and paned with thick glass, flew open and children burst forth, running down the two-tiered steps of the Mark Hill Junior High School. Henry led the pack. He felt good about the beginning of summer vacation and no more school for three months. When he reached the street he stopped and turned to watch the bedlam. Kids were throwing their books in the air and screaming with glee. We were free from teachers and rules and homework and classes and punishments and getting up early to rush to school. As he started toward home he sat on the curb and removed his shoes. The ritual was about to begin. Every summer a boy shed his shoes and walked on the hot pavement until the heat became so intense that he would break into a full run and holler at the top of his voice to distract himself from the pain. This was done in order to toughen the soles of the feet so that the rest of the summer could be spent under any and all conditions without injury. It was amazing to me how blisters would quickly turn into calluses and feet became immune to the discomfort of rocks, stickers, hot pavement and most of all, shoes.

Summer attire consisted of bib overalls, a denim shirt or none at all, and a handkerchief, which Mother said every gentleman should possess. I kept it deep in my pocket for that very reason.

Every summer started with great expectations of adventure and fun. That attitude usually vanished after a week, and was then replaced with routine. When Dad got up at five o'clock then everyone got up. If I failed to respond at the first call of, "get out of that bed, get dressed and do your chores", he had a sure-fire way of getting you up. He would come to the foot of the bed and pull all the covers to the floor, leaving you fully exposed in your underwear. Next his big hand would make a giant fist totally encapsulating your big toe, at which point, in a tugging relentless motion your toe, foot and attached body would follow the hand until your body hit the floor with a thud. "Ow! ow! ow!" would be the immediate response, followed by his repeated command to get dressed and do your chores. I learned to lie quietly and listen for his footsteps before jumping to my feet, but on occasion because of the stupor of twilight sleep, I'd be too late and always regretted my tardiness.

My summer chores were not bad and in fact I enjoyed most of them. First I'd go to the old pitcher pump, prime it with a small can of water, and then pump the handle furiously until the clear, cold water would flow forth into the waiting pail. With several trips I'd fill the chicken water feeders, water the row garden where the vegetables were grown for our use, fill to half full the hog trough, and skim and top off the water tank for the horse and cattle. Next came the milking of two cows, and then releasing the livestock to pasture. Then I'd check the chicken nests in the roost for eggs. This was done in a gentle and stealthy manner, because chickens were irritable when laying and, if disturbed, could peck the fire out of you. If one started squawking, then all would join in; at which point the rooster would run up out of nowhere, fly in your face and attempt to spur you. This was not a good thing and required a hasty retreat to the house with rooster in hot pursuit. All the while the dogs were following me at every step with tails wagging and paws climbing and tongues licking. They were begging to be fed table scraps and watered also. Then it was off to the corncrib to fetch enough corncobs to feed the animals. Chicken feed was tossed in the chicken run and then the horse and cattle stalls were shoveled and the manure carried by wheelbarrow to the garden for the vegetables. Nothing on a farm goes to waste, including your time. Please understand that we are not farmers but rather, farm to live off the land. Did I mention the five acres of corn and row crops that had to be tilled, planted, weeded, cultivated and harvested in season? The rest was pasture for the horses and cattle. I often wondered what city dwellers did with all their spare time.

When the chores, which were my responsibility, were completed, I'd fill up the washtub on the back porch with water and Mother would add a kettle of boiling water to warm it. A little lye soap which she made, and a lot of scrubbing was necessary before I was permitted to sit down for breakfast, which usually occurred just as the sun broke over the horizon.

Now breakfast is worth more than a little mention, as it was my favorite meal of the day. You should know that my Mother was always up before me and often before Dad. In the winter she would stoke the cast iron, pot bellied stove that stood in the middle of the kitchen with wood or coal if we had any, and fire it with pine knots, lighter, and paper. In about an hour the house would be warm as the stove cast a reddish glow. She also had a cooking oven of the same construction on which she would make the coffee and cook in her skillets and pans. Breads were prepared in tins on baking sheets in the oven next to the adjoining firebox, which opened at its door with an iron handle, hooked on the end and coiled to dissipate the heat of the stove. Oven pads were always nearby for handling the skillets and pots.

Dad would always say Grace and thank God for sustaining us in hard times. He would then serve himself. We would follow in turn, Mother first and then me. We would usually have fresh milk from the ice cooler out back, bacon or ham, grits, eggs fried or scrambled, biscuits with brown flour gravy, churned butter, and home made jam.

After breakfast I'd clean the table and put the table scraps in the slop bucket and feed the hogs. Then the bed was made with fresh sheets and pillowcase if necessary followed by teeth brushing, hair combing and an outhouse visit to complete the morning schedule. By this time Dad was on his way to the gin and Mother was beginning her household duties. The rest of my day was filled with play and fanciful activities of my choosing.

Days progressed into weeks until Saturday, three weeks since my school outing to the county home. A trip to visit Grandpa was at hand. As we drove through town and east along the gravel road, my thoughts centered not on the visit, but on my chance encounter with the man there. It suddenly occurred to me that I didn't even know his name, much less anything about him. My first inclination was to stay with the family and not see him. We parked, went into the building to check in and then to the cafeteria where they were feeding Grandpa.

The people there did not seem to change and most of them reacted very little to their surroundings. A few were detached mentally and seemed to crave the touch of another human being over conversation. Others were either stoic or by comparison, were argumentative and even aggressive. I noticed more men than women, but the women were more visible; in the library in small groups, sitting together in the cafeteria, in the hall and usually in wheelchairs, wandering about or in rooms talking to each other. The men were more inclined to be on the porch or in the yard, usually walking alone or in pairs, sole figures in the library, in groups of two or three eating and usually alone when in their rooms.

Every activity there was planned with military precision and always by the clock. Nurses would be at their stations on the men and women's floors managing charts and counting and preparing medications. They would all snap to when the local doctor made his daily rounds, keeping a respectful distance behind him as they went from room to room, juggling charts and making notes. Attendants were always busy moving residents from place to place, as schedules required. Some were in charge of the rooms, busily making beds, changing linen, cleaning basins, emptying bedpans, picking up clothing for the residents and putting closets in order. The home also had staff assigned to maintenance, cleaning and disinfecting, stores and inventory, personnel, food service, laundry and activities for the residents which involved the library, games, movies, outdoor gardens and walking trails. The home operated around the clock with three shifts. Some of the help were truly interested in the residents but most performed their duties with mechanical disinterest. I think many of the latter type disconnected themselves to insulate their feelings. The environment was emotionally draining for all concerned; staff, residents and visitors alike.

As we walked into the cafeteria all the ambulatory residents were eating lunch at bench style tables. Today it was milk or water, breaded cutlet, collards, mashed potatoes, cornbread and gelatin. The meal was served on metal trays and looked and smelled pretty good. I thought my attitude about the meal might be different if I was confined here. We noticed a nurse over in the back corner helping Grandpa eat. As we approached the table it was evident that something was wrong. He spit a mouthful of potatoes on the floor and cursed. Grandpa never cursed. Then Mother saw that her Father was tied to the chair with a bed sheet around his waist and she completely lost it. I had never seen her in this state before. Her eyes were white with rage and she threw her hands to her head.

"What is this?" she screamed. "He can't stand to be held or tied down. He has claustrophobia." As the attendant tried to offer an explanation, Dad intervened and demanded that everyone calm down. Mother and I went outside so Dad and the attendant could talk about the matter. The other residents had all quit eating and were watching the scene intently. One lady exclaimed that she was a prisoner there and was often tied to her bed. As I left I told Mother I was going to the library until we left. She said she was going outside to the truck to calm down.

As I rounded the corner, there he was. He was just leaving the library and saw me at the same time. "So you decided to return and visit an old man."

"We came to see my Grandpa but there was some trouble in the cafeteria with him so Dad told me to leave and I decided to come here," as I pointed at the library door. "Do you like libraries?" "Yes sir, I do and reading is one of my favorites things." He leaned back inside the doorway and told the librarian that Henry Jimson would be in his room when his people came looking for him. Then he turned to me and asked if I would like to go to his room to pass some time.

Upon entering his room, he directed me to the straight back chair and he sat in his rocker and began to rock. After some period of time had past, he asked me why I liked to read. "Because stories take me to far away places and I like to see what people do in books. Also I learn things I didn't know or had never even thought of before. Sometimes I feel like I'm almost in the book and part of what's going on if you know what I mean."

"Are you smart Henry?" He caught me off guard because I usually don't like to seem smart to my friends. They all think kids and book learning mix like oil and water. "Yes sir, I think I am," I exclaimed without thinking. "Why?" he queried. "Because school has never been hard for me like it is for most of my friends. Because when I hear or see and read I always remember most of it." "What was the last thing I said to you on our last visit?" he inquired. "Get out of here, but remember to come back like I told you," I replied with no hesitation.

He smiled and paused, looking away from me and out the open window. "I can not abide stupidity and I greatly respect intelligence. What do you think of that?" "I think it depends on your definition of stupid and intelligent." "That answer is acceptable."

I thanked him and we again sat in silence looking out the window at a beautiful day. Early summer rains and rising night temperatures had brought the trees into new leaf and most flowers were in full bloom. The flowerbed just outside the window was a multicolor sea of bedding plants. I think some of the residents tend them. Overhead puffy clouds barely drifted along West to East; so white they seemed to glow in the sunlight. The sky was littered with birds. Robins were now in abundance, and the infinite variety of the mockingbirds' songs delighted the ear. The crows were all in one tree, appearing to be black fruit hanging from the branches. Their loud and constant grating calls could be heard for miles away as they seemed to communicate with one another. Suddenly they moved in flight in unison as if of one mind, circled higher and higher only to dive earthward and light in graceful formation in a nearby field.

"Sir, I don't know your name." He looked back and his blue eyes fixed on mine. Staring intently, he replied: "What do you know of me?"

I pondered that question for several minutes while he continued to gaze at me in anticipation of my answer. I thought somehow, that my response was critically important to him. "I know that you are old and that you live in this home. I see that you are well groomed and the state of your room tells me you're organized and you have a place for everything and everything in its place. I haven't heard anyone in our presence speak your name. I don't see it on your door and see no writings or pictures on your table or dresser that contain your name. I think you are kind, very smart and ask a lot of questions. Why you spend time with me I have not reasoned out. Beyond that I know very little of you that would reveal your name to me."

He stood and laughed as before, a deep laugh, pleasant to the ear, very real and sincere. It was as if he really enjoyed what he had just heard. "That is an astute answer, and for that very reason you may call me 'Old Man.'"

My first thought was that this was a game, but he was somber standing there with brow knitted, fixing me in his continuous stare, and seeming to have completed his thought on the matter. "I think that my calling you

'Old Man' would seem to others to be disrespectful and I'd be uncomfortable with it." "Why?" he asked. "You are my elder and I'm still a young boy Sir."

"Do you think that all old people should be respected? Should they be revered and given a place of honor in society?" Now he had me perplexed and at a loss. Thinking furiously, I responded: "I think that people in positions of honor either by age or position generally should. But I believe that to whom much is given, much is required. So I feel that some who are old may not deserve respect and reverence because of their actions." Now it was obvious that he was deep in thought, mulling over and digesting my answer in order to take it all in. My well thought out responses and articulation surprised and amazed me, as it was far beyond my past art of conversation. This old man seemed to draw me out of a shell of my own making.

"Do you respect me?" he asked. "I don't have any basis to do so but, yes, I do." "Then it is settled. You shall call me 'Old Man'."

My Father entered the room. "What are you doing in this man's room?" he asked. "We've been talking. I met him three weeks ago and decided to visit him again." Not even looking at him, my Dad asked what his name was. "Old Man," I replied, without thinking. "Boy, you wait outside in the car so I can talk to this gentleman."

As I left I waved goodbye and he acknowledged with a nod. At the truck I found Mom. Her eyes were red from crying but she had regained her composure and told me not to be upset about Grandpa. She said she and Dad had talked to the administrator and the reason for strapping Grandpa to the chair was a good one and would only be done when absolutely necessary. She was satisfied and so was I.

Dad was in the home for almost thirty minutes before coming out and into the drivers seat. He had a funny look on his face and I thought I was in for it and would never see the old man again. We rode along while Mom looked out the window and Dad drove deliberately along the dusty road. As he turned onto our path to the house, he looked at me over his shoulder and said the most surprising thing. "Henry, it is all right with me if you want to visit Old Man from time to time." "Yes Sir!"

Two weeks later after finishing up at home I asked Mom if I could go to the county home for a while. "Will you check on your Grandfather?" she asked. I said I would and that I was taking some bread and a piece of fried chicken we had left over from last night for my lunch. She checked me over as mothers often do and asked, "Are you going to visit the old man?" She knew the answer but was mildly curious at my fascination with him. "Henry, don't get too involved with strangers." Some of my shyness came directly from her and so there was very little understanding of this developing relationship between this man and her boy. "Tell Grandpa we will come to see him next week. Perhaps he will understand what you say to him." There was really no need. We saw him every two weeks when possible and he never seemed to know us or with what frequency we visited. "Yes Mam." I left the house and raised the kickstand and began peddling my bicycle along our path to the road. "Watch for cars!"

Our two hounds ran along with me to the road at the end of the driveway and then sat with heads cocked in curious fashion as if to say, where are you going and when will you be back? How do dogs know property lines? I've often noticed them walking the side and back lines of our property sniffing and marking as they went. They would stop to spray a post or tree and then on they would go, never crossing the line. Animals know things that we don't, I believe.

Dogs are the best friends a boy can have. Have you noticed how they watch your every move when they are with you? They will bark and snarl at anyone who intrudes upon their property. You can beat them when they kill a chicken or run after a visitor, snarling so as to scare them half to death, but afterwards, all is forgiven. They are loyal, often one-man dogs, and constant companions. When you leave they seem to mourn and upon your return they jump, wag and lick as if they had not seen you in years. They do this every time. It doesn't seem to matter if you don't return the affection, although it usually is. They watch you in periods of inattention and seem to say that it is all right and they forgive you and would never hold it against you. Do you know a single person like that?

I got to the home just before noon and took my sack lunch and jar of lemonade to the old live oak tree in the side yard, and sat there to eat. It was Wednesday and no one came to the home while I ate. I finished, put the paper sack in the trash barrel out front, my jar in the bicycle basket and went inside. The nurse at the desk recognized me and told me that Grandpa was in his room. The door was open and he was in bed. Quietly entering so as not to disturb him, I leaned over to see if he was asleep. His eyes were open but he was perfectly still, stretched out under one sheet and rigid as a board. His fists were clinched tight as was his jaw. He did not seem to be in any pain as I spoke to him.

"Hello Grandpa, its Henry." There was no movement or response other than his eyes darting to me and then quickly back to the ceiling. Then he had a bowel movement and I realized why he had been straining and rigid. He immediately relaxed and his eyes closed. This is not the way life should be lived I thought, as I searched for an attendant. "My Grandpa had a bowel movement in bed." "It is no problem Mr. Henry. We been putting him in diapers for some time now." She went down the hall toward his room as I proceeded to Old Man's room.

"Good afternoon Old Man," as I walked into the room and sat in my chair. He was looking for some article in his dresser and grunted as a greeting in return.

"Henry, did you ever put an item in a particular place, every time in the same place, and then find later that it was not where you always put it." "No Sir."

He spun around with a look of total disbelief. "Never?" "Well Sir, I don't have much stuff and what I do have is all out in the open where I can see it." "There is a lesson to be learned there Henry. Do you believe in gremlins, elves, fairies and the like?" he asked with some degree of sarcasm. "I believe in spiritual beings as portrayed in the Bible," I replied.

He chose not to pursue the subject and asked instead if I knew the time. He said it was cloudy or he could look at the sun, but couldn't look at his watch because an elf had hidden it. I asked him what the object hanging from his dresser knob was. He spun back around, snatched the watch from the knob and remarked that elves were creatures of mischief. He noted the time and then pulled his rocker close to my chair. He leaned near to me and asked the most curious question.

"Henry, do you see the tallest oak tree on yonder hill?" He pointed out the window over his shoulder without even looking. "Have you ever climbed such a tree?" How could he know of one of my most embarrassing and frightening experiences? "Yes Sir." He responded, "Tell me about it."

I recollected that a huge live oak tree occupied the bottom behind our house. I was ten years old when I decided to climb to the very top of it to discover how far I could see. The oak had a diameter at the trunk of about eight feet. Its limbs were very stout and stretched out from the trunk parallel to the ground, often as far out as thirty feet or more. Spanish moss hung from the smaller, secondary limbs branching from the main limbs. On the tops of limbs and usually on the north side of the trunk lichens grew, knit tightly to the tree bark. The bark was thick, with deep groves dividing it. As the tree grew upward the limbs became progressively smaller and the tree rounded at the top. The leaves were dark green, oval shaped and of glossy appearance. The tree bore acorns in season by the bushel basket full. And so, there was the description of my "Everest" as I recalled it.

My climb began quickly on the lower main limb branches and the going was fairly easy. As I continued upward the limbs grew smaller and my efforts greater. My attention to this point had been constantly upward. A few feet from the top and probably ten minutes later I stopped to rest and felt a little tired. For the first time I looked down through the foliage to the ground below. I must have been thirty or forty feet off the ground. My stomach tightened into a little knot as my arms and legs locked in a death grip around the limb I had reached. The lichen under my arms and legs suddenly felt wet and slippery. I was wet with sweat from the climb and it began to get in my eyes and burn. A wave of nausea overtook me. I closed my eyes to shut out the reality of my plight. I was so scared. It was more than I could bear. I imagined my certain fall to the ground. I supposed that the limbs would cause me to tumble rather than break my fall. The ground would race up to meet me with incredible force. My life would probably flash before my eyes. So there I was perched some forty feet off the ground, hanging tenaciously to the limb, paralyzed with fear and afraid to even move or look.

After what seemed like forever I heard a curious sound just in front of me. I opened my eyes and there, in the midst of my calamity, was a gray squirrel not five feet from my head. He was perched on the limb with me, sitting upright on his haunches and busily shelling an acorn to eat the meat inside. He was watching me intently but showed no fear of me. I was absolutely of no threat to him in my present state and he seemed to know it. After finishing his snack, with bushy tail flagging furiously, he groomed his face, eyes and mouth with his front paws. He took one last glance at me as he leapt from his perch. He landed on the limb below me and scurried out to the end of it, grabbed another acorn and began to eat once more.

My fascination with the squirrel coupled with his obvious agility and climbing ability eased my fear somewhat to the point that I was able to loosen my death grip and slowly sit upright. I regained my senses and carefully scooted backwards along the limb until I reached the trunk. I then felt with my foot for the limb below and slowly lowered myself to it. After a brief assessment of the move I mustered enough courage to repeat it to the next lower limb; and so I progressed, backing down, crab like, until at dusk dark I reached the ground and fell prostrate there and lay for some time until I regained my composure and contemplated my brush with death. Until that time I was immortal, but now, mortal indeed.

Having completed the recounting of my tale for him, we both sat in silence, reliving the experience in our minds. Then he inquired, "Have you been back up the tree?"

"No Sir, and I don't plan to do so!" "When you reached the top did you look out and around to see what it looked like from way up there?" he asked, even though I believe he knew the answer. "No Sir, I was too scared to look," I replied. He leaned forward and in an accusatory tone said, "So you did not accomplish what you had intended, did you? And therefore the climb was for naught, was it not? And your fear overcame every part of your being didn't it?" This was too much to take in all at once. I arose and told him I was going to walk around for a while, and did so as he rose and moved to his window.

I cannot explain why his statements angered me. Had I done something wrong? Was he unimpressed with my life threatening experience? Was he right to question the outcome? I went back and confronted him with a question of my own. "Old Man, what would you have done if in my shoes?" I have you now, I thought to myself. "That is not the question to ask Henry. The question is what will you do when, in the future, you are once again confronted with fearful things? Will you confront the fear head on and conquer it, or will the fear always control your life?" He paused briefly and then said, "Most of our fears or either imagined or blown all out of proportion to what is reality. In any event, to grow in wisdom one must learn to use and control ones' fear and not let the fear control you." "What should I do?" I asked, anticipating the response but not wishing to hear it. Old Man moved back to the rocker, fixed those blue eyes upon mine and sternly exclaimed, "Go and climb the tree again and look around this time!"

Three days later I climbed the tree again and looked around. It was beautiful up there. I could see the water tower on the other side of town, cars passing along the highway in the distance, flocks of birds gliding along at eye level and clouds that seemed so close that I might reach out and touch them. The climb down was easy. That afternoon I made a special trip to his room and told him. He smiled and said softly, "Good." With that affirmation, I left.

A nearby creek was one of the favorite destinations for families in the latter stages of summer, when the temperatures often exceeded 100 degrees in the shade. This summer was no exception. The city fathers organized the first annual Mark Hill picnic in conjunction with the County Fair celebration.

The fair was held each year for one week at the local fairground. The grounds contained a gymnasium size building cooled by big fans mounted in eaves at each end. The fans circulated the hot air and made it more bearable for those manning exhibit booths. The workers and booth owners were usually there most of the day and appreciated the breeze the fans created. The spectators were in and out all day long looking at all the handmade objects, crafts of various sorts, jams and jellies and other interesting things exhibited there. Sales were made on a regular basis.

On the opposite side of the fairgrounds were individual booths, built, organized and manned by members of local churches and civic organizations. A long row of booths lined a wooden platform walkway, with ten booths on either side. The top front half of a booth could be raised to perpendicular for service and then lowered and locked at night. There was running water and electricity supplied to all the structures on the grounds by the county. In addition, there was an outdoor arena for rodeo events, an open sided shelter for livestock exhibits and a small stage for live performances.

People attended the annual event as far as two counties distance. Often a carnival would make a circuit stop and that really pulled in the people. There were rides for small children, a ferris wheel, a carousel with its brightly colored horses and mirrors and several other fast rides designed to disorient, scare, sicken, jerk around and generally delight the riders, for a price of course. Equally popular were games of chance, which could quickly and efficiently separate you from what little money you might have.

The food at the booths was first class simply because each group tried to outdo its competition and thereby gain the most customers. Fried catfish and hush puppies were a big favorite, with an unbelievable variety of mulligan stews a close second choice. Homemade lemonade and sweet iced tea were the beverages of choice. Alcohol of any kind was strictly forbidden. Anyone so foolish as to bring it on the premises was soon found out. There were always a few partakers who did so. A deputy would haul them away, and they would be given a hearing at the next available court term, which always occurred on the Monday after the completion and closing of the fair. Ten dollars or ten days in jail was the standard punishment. Homemade lemonade or sweet iced tea was provided once a day free of charge to all inmates.

My family stayed all day until the ten o'clock closing and had a grand time. Mother worked the Methodist Church booth, which had by far the best mulligan stew that year, or so she said. Dad entered a sow in the livestock competition and it won second place. He allowed as how the sow would sure yield some good ham and bacon that winter. He was kidding at the time, but I swear, that sow fell to the ground, rolled over and refused to get up for some time afterwards.

I had written a poem and, much to my delight, it won first place in the writing contest from among nineteen other entries, all female. I stood out like a sore thumb up on the stand with all those girls and mothers glaring at me, as my blue ribbon and two-dollar cash award was presented. What I had not counted on was the requirement that the winner had to read the winning entry out loud and in front of everyone. I was petrified, but got through it somehow. I must admit that it was a most pleasant thing to be the object of applause.

The fair closed on the following Saturday night and a picnic at Toms Creek took place after church on Sunday. Blankets were spread out on the ground and food appeared in abundance from among the thirty or more families there. The creek was slow running, ice cold and crystal clear. Everyone prepared their picnic spots by spreading blankets and setting up folding chairs. Galvanized washtubs filled with block ice were placed in the shade and the ice chipped into chunks with a pick. Cold creek water was then added and big striped watermelons were submerged in the tubs to cool.

Ice cream freezers were prepared and set up for homemade, custard ice cream flavored with peaches, plums or blackberries to satisfy every taste. Older boys and men were in charge of hand cranking the churns in the five freezers there, each taking a turn at the labor. Ice and rock salt were added as needed by the younger children who wanted to help, but more to the point, wanted to lick the paddle when the ice cream was ready.

Children also played Red Rover, Hide and Seek, Dodge Ball, King Of The Mountain and took turns swinging out over the creek on a long rope tied to an overhead branch, with a board tied to the other end for seating.

Finally, the time for eating arrived and everyone moved to their blankets for the meal. Reverend Hill, a direct descendant of the town's founder, said Grace and thanked God for sustaining us in mind, body and spirit in these hard times. At the conclusion of his rather lengthy prayer by my observation, he got several emphatic "Amen's", and we all proceeded to gorge ourselves. Families moved among each other to sample each special dish and it was wonderful. Afterwards the men stretched out and took naps, while all the children protested loudly at not being allowed to swim for one hour after eating. When the hour finally passed many of us stripped to our waists, while others went into the bushes or vehicles to change into swimsuits, and headed for the creek.

There are basically two types of creek swimmers. There are those who dash head long with a long dive and rebel yell into the ice cold water and then instantly climb out, shivering and dashing to mothers for towels. The other type of creek swimmer cautiously eases up to the creeks edge and gingerly sticks a hand or foot in and yelps and screams, "Too cold!" They are the ones for whom medieval torture was first devised, as they slowly walk in to knee deep only to back out and then slowly to waist deep, trying to gather nerve to splash small portions of cold water on their upper bodies and then slowly submerging with water coming only up to their necks. They then rocket upward, turn and retreat from the frigid water. They scamper, lips blue and noses running to the blankets for towels. The creek was very, very cold but once you became numb it was great fun.

The younger children were taking their naps as the men awakened to distribute watermelon and ice cream. I don't believe there is anything on this earth better than ice cold, red meat, juicy watermelon and homemade, churned ice cream flavored with fresh fruit of your liking. The kids had watermelon all the way around to their ears as they buried their faces in the cool slices. Watermelon seed spitting commenced with great enthusiasm and some lesser degree of accuracy. When no one present could eat another bite, the sun was setting on the horizon, and mosquitoes were beginning to swarm in the cooling evening air, we left our paradise, and to a family, all agreed to attend the picnic every year.

I had invited Old Man to attend the picnic with our family. He was gracious in his refusal. "I get real nervous around a lot of people," he explained. "Besides, I am not accustomed to the outdoors." He went on to say that he was a creature of habit that children made him very uncomfortable, that loud and boisterous conduct upset him and that only food from the county home agreed with him. Then he quietly watched me as I formed a response. He was fidgeting in his rocker and appeared ready to jump out of his skin. This was a brand new side to this man of mystery. "Okay." I left it alone.

It was Wednesday following the festivities that I next paid him a visit. I knocked on his door that was seldom shut. The door flew open and he grabbed me forcefully and pulled me into the room and placed me in my chair, all in one fluid motion. I had no time to recover as he began speaking in an excited manner. "Did you go to the County Fair? How about the picnic? Tell me everything and don't leave out any details. I want you to be my eyes and ears so I can experience the whole thing through you. Do you understand?" I did not understand at all but nevertheless, spent the better part of an hour relating each event with as much detail as I could recall, until I finally finished and leaned back in the chair. "That is what I remember Old Man." "Excellent," he exclaimed as he rose from his rocker and began to pace back and forth from one wall to the opposite wall. His eyes were shut the whole time but he never faltered or ran into any of the furniture. He would pause at a wall, turn around and nod his head as if in agreement with some thing unspoken, and begin his trek to the opposite wall. Then he returned to his rocker, sat down, leaned forward, as was his custom and with those eyes riveted upon my face he said, "Recite the poem."

I didn't want to and told him so. He would have none of it and insisted. "Recite the poem now Henry." I offered another excuse. "I don't have my writing with me. I may not remember it all." "When you recite you must stand erect, fold your hands at your waist and look your audience, that is me, in the eye and with great confidence and emotion as you deliver your work. Do so with pride and confidence!" He would not let me go. "I do this under protest. Now give me just a minute." He gestured with a wave for me to rise. He lifted his shoulders back and raised his chin in a mocking manner and nodded twice for emphasis. I dutifully folded my hands at the waist and assumed the position as he instructed. At that point he closed his eyes, began to rock with his lips pursed as if pouting.

I began. "Gray clouds racing along, casting fleeting shadows upon the deep, moving with purpose to an unheard song.

A figure stood alone upon the shore, watching and waiting in concert, for the shadows to reveal their form.

Swooping down and across the winds, see the speck against the sky; wandering, why, and for how long?

A solitary man sat there upon the sand, searching sea and sky, watching and dreading the coming of the storm.

But wait and see, the sun breaks through and bright light colors earth and sky with golden hue.

Could this be the reason for the speck up in the heavens, swooping to and fro?

Or, is it impossible to know the reason for earth and sky, wind and speck away up high. Or is it possible to know."

"The end," I concluded.

He continued to rock with eyes closed and the faint smile still upon his face. "Henry, what depth you have; far beyond your years." He rose again and walked to the window. Turning to me he began to interpret the poem. When he had finished, I marveled at his insight. "That is uncanny," I exclaimed. "It is as if you were in my head when I composed it. Thank you Old Man." He told me to write a copy out for him, which I later did. Without telling me, he anonymously sent the copy to The General, a newspaper with statewide circulation and it was published. He showed me the paper on my last visit of the summer. It was a wonderful thing he did for me and it made my family proud.

The next several years were filled with new experiences for a young boy in close relationship with an old man. My visits with Old Man were uninterrupted and always full and mutually beneficial. I had become like a son to him. He remained a source of knowledge and wisdom for me.

Henry was now a senior in high school and preparing for college. With the school year over and admission to the university with full scholarship assured, he had to face leaving Old Man for extended periods of time.

CHAPTER TWO

The week before leaving for college on the bus, I made a final visit. He was on the front steps as I drove up in Dad's truck, which I had been driving for some time now. I'd be on foot at school, but I was told the campus was small enough to walk where I needed to go.

"Hello Henry. Great to see you college boy!" I ran up the steps and he grabbed me in a big bear hug and actually lifted me from the ground. "Now Henry, you will be home on holidays and summer vacation and we will have a lot of catching up to do." He stood to my side as he spoke, never looking directly at me, as was his usual manner. I could hear the strained tone of his voice as he continued. "Take paper and pen and write to me at least twice a month. Promise me."

"Old Man, I'll miss you and promise to write." I almost choked from the emotion welling up in me.

"Good and goodbye." He turned and without looking back, disappeared into the home.

As I entered the path to the house, I had to stop, and gather myself. Not since Grandpa's funeral had I been so moved. I thanked God for delivering me into the life of Old Man. I moved along to the house and stopped. Tears were streaming down my face and I did not want Mother to see me in this condition. After a few minutes I composed myself and went into the house and to my room. Several hours later we ate supper.

I'd received offers from several universities and colleges around the South. My grades in high school were perfect and also, I had won the school citizenship award, was top finalist in the state debate competition and was appointed to serve as a page with one of our legislative representatives at the age of sixteen.

One school, in particular, was most attractive because it offered a full scholarship for four years. It also allowed me to select a course of study. The fact that the university was out of state concerned me, but there were none close anyway. I'd be responsible for my spending money, food and incidentals, but everything else was covered.

The university sent an envelope to me by mail. It contained a tremendous volume of material and I took several hours one evening attempting to digest it all. The cover letter was a welcome to the freshman class of 1941. Next was a checklist of things to do upon arrival. They informed me of the campus bus that ran from town to the campus and its schedule. I was assigned to a dormitory and would share a room with another freshman student. I was advised that the dormitories would be ready for occupancy on Saturday, September the sixth. Registration would take place the following Monday, at nine o'clock in the morning.

A map of the campus was enclosed for my use. I was glad to have it, as I had never been on the campus before. A brief description of location and hours of operation of the office of financial affairs, cafeteria, medical clinic, hospital and registration followed. A campus directory and a catalogue outlining the degrees offered, and offerings for each course of study were there for review.

Next were a listing of names and locations of contacts for my use.

The dormitory manager to whom I was to report on arrival, my faculty advisor who would assist me during my orientation, an upper classman to hold my hand I suppose, the financial aid officer assigned to my case to explain my scholarship procedure (a certificate of eligibility and acceptance form was enclosed for presentation to him), and a directory of names and telephone numbers of all university departments and personnel.

Included was a book setting out rules of conduct for students. It also identified all the on campus extracurricular activities available and a multitude of programs and activities for students. Included in this publication was a statement of purpose of the university and a personal message of welcome from the Chancellor to incoming freshman.

There was a sheet explaining meal plans, laundry facilities and fees, student activity fees for various events and sport schedules.

A list of recommended personal items including toilet articles, bedding, room accessories not provided, articles of clothing and general school supplies followed.

In conclusion, I was advised to bring no more that two pieces of luggage on campus for storage. I was completely bewildered and wondered how many freshmen dropped out of school during the admission process.

Friday, after a brief time of silence over lunch, I went to my room for the suitcases which Mother had carefully packed the night before. Dad was at work, but planned on taking me to the Greyhound bus station at two o'clock. The bus to Atlanta was scheduled to leave at three. I put the luggage in the back of the pickup, walked back in the house for one last look and then to the front porch where the hounds were resting in the shade. The days were still very hot and there was no breeze. When I stepped off the porch they both came to their feet and moved to the waiting truck together and watched me. I approached one of them and he whined as if hurt. Both dropped their heads and stood motionless before me. They knew somehow that I'd not be back that night. We drove away in the afternoon sun, with a dust cloud in pursuit, again in silence. Looking over my shoulder, the dogs were still in the same position and motionless.

Neither of us said a word during the trip to the station. Mother stared out her window and was detached from her surroundings, watching the horizon far away. We arrived at quarter past two, and after parking and putting my luggage inside I went to the counter to get my ticket. I had fifty dollars in my wallet, which was the most money I had ever carried at one time. I should have felt independent with that much on me, but to the contrary, felt almost helpless and somehow abandoned. Mother sat on the bench out front and stared across the street at nothing in particular. She had not smiled in several days and was really out of sorts. I slowly began to realize, with some guilt I might add, that my leaving was very hard on her. What could I do, I wondered, as I sat beside her to wait for the bus? "Mother, I'll miss you terribly but don't worry, for I'll write and call at least once a month. If you need me I'll come home." She leaned into my shoulder and placed her head there. "Thank you Son, I love you." I choked with emotion as I replied in a trembling whisper, "I haven't told you often enough that I love and honor you and would be willing to give up everything for you." Through her tears she smiled and threw her arms around me. "Thank you Henry. A Mother who loves you thanks you."

"Mother, he will come back you know. It's not the end of the world." She smiled once more and nodded in agreement, as the bus pulled into the station. Suitcases were stored and I sat on the half empty bus next to a window and waved goodbye as we pulled away. Atlanta came into sight about five and one half hours later and we pulled into the terminal.

I got my luggage and asked the person at the ticket counter about my connecting bus. He pointed to the schedule board and continued his paperwork. My connection would depart at ten thirty, so I put my suitcases in a locker and walked outside to find a place to eat. Directly across the street was a diner and I was starving. The hamburger and fries were equally greasy, and the sweet tea was weak, but I devoured the meal and finished it off with a Baby Ruth and some water. I thought the meal was not at all like Mom's cooking, as I went back across the street to the waiting room.

I had just dozed off when the loudspeaker announced the arrival of my bus. I hastily removed the luggage from the locker, checked them through and boarded my bus. It seemed to me to be brand new and had a pleasant fresh smell, unlike the smoke laden and musty transportation on the first leg of the trip. The cloth seats were bright blue with gray accent stripes and were hardly worn. Now I'm really traveling in style I thought, as we moved away from the terminal, away from the lights of the city and into the darkness. Dim lights were on inside and you couldn't see anything outside, except for the headlights of an occasional passing car. The driver turned out the interior lights and we sped along the highway as I listened to the whine of the diesel engine and the singing of the tires on the pavement.

I sat in a seat by myself, so I raised the center armrest and curled up in fetal position with my legs pulled up tightly and closed my eyes. The driver was gently shaking me when I awoke. "The next stop is the university if you want to use the bathroom," he said. "Going to the university?" he asked quietly. "Yes, Sir," I replied. I jumped off the bus, went to the restroom and washed up. The mirror reflected a groggy face with a shadow of a beard and wrinkled shirt. I did the best I could to freshen up and then boarded the bus for the last leg of my journey.

We were forty-five minutes late arriving and I gladly left the bus after thanking the driver for the ride. "Good luck Son and study hard!" An hour later the campus bus pulled up and fifteen of my fellow adventurers and myself hopped aboard for the short trip to the campus.

From the time we drove through the stone gated entrance until we stopped, I am certain that my mouth hung ajar and my attention was riveted to the sights and sounds of the campus. We rounded a large, flat, grassy area covered with gargantuan oak trees, lined up in canopy fashion and allowing patterns of sunlight to drape the grounds. How beautiful, I mused. Then a large, stone building came into view with the road circling in front of it and continuing on back to the entrance along the opposite side of the grove. The building was in the Corinthian style, three or four stories high and very old. Massive scrolled doors graced the entrance at the head of the stairs. The driver commented that it housed administration offices and served as a hospital in the Civil War. He said Civil War in reverent tone. "Next stop, freshman dorms," he exclaimed. "Good luck, my friends," he said as the bus pulled away. Five of us stood there looking around as if some thing would jump out of the hedges and grab us. "Over here boys!" The fellow across the street was seated at a desk on the sidewalk, which supported a printed sign stating "freshman dormitory assignments." The giving of my name resulted in a piece of paper and key being placed in my hand with building name and room number along with my name imprinted on it. "Lunch is served from noon to one," he stated as he pointed up to a long, low building with front and side entrances. All the buildings I had seen so far were of the same light gray, stone construction and most were multi-storied. "Where is this dormitory," to which inquiry, he pointed over his shoulder, directly behind him. "Thank you." I proceeded up three flights of stairs to the landing and glanced down the long hall. Numbers were on all the rooms and I found mine near the end on the right. I used the key provided, and the wooden door squeaked on its hinges to reveal a spartan interior. There were two iron-railed beds on opposite walls, each supporting a thin mattress and pillow and two gray metal, office style desks, each with a metal cushioned chair. The wood framed window with glass panes raised from the bottom and was open. There was a tan, paper like, pull down shade, for privacy and to block the sun. On either side of the door was a small open closet with a clothes bar and wooden shelf. Under the window was a radiator for heat, equipped with a control valve and a pop off valve for safety. A white, porcelain sink was mounted in a corner with a mirror on the wall and storage cabinet underneath. The floor was concrete and painted gray. Be it ever so humble I thought as I threw my suitcases on one of the beds. I found my towel, washrag and bar of soap and went to the bathroom and showers I had noted going to the room. Almost seventeen hours of road grime, and weariness washed away, I went back to the room, unpacked one suitcase and hung its contents in one of the closets. I put clean clothes on and left the door locked as I exited for lunch. The rest of the day was spent walking the campus and taking note of the ever-increasing number of students doing the same, until dusk was upon me and I returned to the room.

My roommate had arrived and was hanging clothes in the unoccupied closet. "Hi, my name is Johnny Milstead and you must be Henry Jimson." As he reached out his hand to greet me and size me up. "Yes, I hope it is all right that I selected a bed, closet and desk. I got here this morning but have not done much else other than put my belongings where you see them," Johnny replied, "Fine with me. Have you eaten?" "I had lunch earlier," as I looked at Grandpa's pocket watch. "Nice timepiece, as he held out his hand for further inspection. Handing him the watch, I told him it was my deceased Grandfathers. He told me that both sets of his grandparents were dead and that he was sure it meant a lot to me to have the watch. What a nice thing to say. "I did not realize the time until you asked, but I am hungry." "Lets go then and we will visit over supper," he replied and we left for the cafeteria.

As we ate we shared our backgrounds and got to know each other. He made a good first impression. Our lives had very little in common however. Johnny was raised in south Mississippi, and his family had lived in that area for twenty years. His Father worked in a local shipyard and his Mother was a schoolteacher. He told me that he was the fourth generation of his family to attend the school and that he had often been on campus over the years, usually for football games. Consequently, he was no stranger to the campus and knew several upper classmen, as well as five other freshmen from his hometown. I was very interested as he described university life from his perspective. He said he would help me adjust to campus life and learn the ropes.

When we returned to the dormitory afterwards, I told Johnny that I needed to call my parents and he directed me to the phone booth on the first floor. There was a line of students waiting to use the phone and I stood along with them for a short period, until it was my turn. Dad had instructed me to call collect when I got settled. Mother answered the phone and was so excited to hear from me. "It's Henry," she exclaimed to Dad, who I was certain was listening to the radio in the living room, as was his custom at this time of night. "The Shadow" or "Amos and Andy" was probably on, I thought. We talked for almost twenty minutes and the students outside were impatiently waiting their turn in silence. They all understood as I answered question after question. "Go to church tomorrow Henry," was her last instruction and I consented and hung up. "Sorry," I told the next in line as I exited the booth. "No problem," he said as he moved past me.

Afterwards, I emptied the remaining suitcase, arranged the clothes in the closet and made my bed. I sat at the desk for a while and we talked some more about school and our expectations concerning registration. By now it was almost midnight and I was tired and asked if would be all right to go to bed. He agreed and went down the hall to make his phone call home as I prepared for bed. He came back in just as I was about to turn off the lights and asked what I had planned for tomorrow. "Church, I guess." "What denomination are you?" he asked. "I was raised Methodist. How about you?" "How about that," he remarked, "two back sliding Methodists in the same room!" We laughed together, and I sensed relief at his being involved in church. He then said he would go with me and knew where it was located. Lights went out and I lay there in the darkness and thought about all that had happened to me in such a brief time. I felt good so far but wondered what next week would bring.

A few students were up when I went to shower the next morning but most were still asleep on our floor. Johnny was still asleep as I prepared to dress for the day. "Johnny, are you still planning to go to church?" He rose up on one elbow and looked around. He appeared confused about his surroundings and looked as if he was lost. He squinted at me. "Henry?" His feet hit the floor and he stretched and yawned and walked to the window to look out. "What time is it?" "Seven-thirty," I replied and he turned with a look of utter disbelief on his face. "You mean to say that I am on my feet and awake on Sunday morning and it is just seven-thirty? This has got to be a record!" He stretched again, gathered up his morning toiletries and bath stuff and trudged out the door. Upon returning, now awake and alert, he recollected that he couldn't remember the last time he was awake this early on Sunday. "What time do you usually get up?" he inquired. "Oh I don't know. At home I'm usually going by five-thirty." "That's incredible!" he exclaimed.

Most of the local churches sent buses on campus to provide transportation for students to attend church. I learned later that not many students went to church with any regularity and some not at all. Johnny admitted that he had not intended to go and that I may be a good influence on him. I sincerely hoped so. After breakfast at the student grill (Johnny introduced me to this place that served as eatery, gathering place and rest stop for students between classes) and a quick trip back to the dorm to brush teeth, we met the bus and boarded for the First Methodist Church.

Once exiting the campus it was less than ten minutes to the church. There were four students on the bus with us and one had a Bible. I brought one to school with me but had forgotten it. When we pulled up out front Johnny said to me, "This is the Methodist Church, Henry. They have a coffee counter for students in the assembly room." The church provided a way to meet people. All churches really pursue the student population. "I believe the Bible refers to us as fertile fields." Johnny broke out in a big grin as we walked into the church by a side entrance to find some twenty or more like-minded students present for worship, fellowship, coffee and doughnuts.

The comparison between Mark Hill Methodist and this church near to our university was of great interest to me. The sanctuary here was grandiose. There was carpet down a center aisle that flowed to the front and up and onto the kneeling step. There was a dark, ornamented rail across the kneeling area, separating it from the choir section. The choir area contained five rows of cushioned bench seating, arranged in an oval, with organ pipes stretching almost to the ceiling and mounted above and behind the choir section. The pulpit was elevated with a spiral, railed set of steps to the platform. It was white, wood construction with inlaid biblical scenes ornamenting it. The carvings were magnificent. When occupied, only the top half of the speaker could be seen and he had a commanding view of the whole church in front of him. On the opposite side was a beautiful organ. Stained glass windows stretched down either side of the sanctuary and went from knee high and upwards some fifteen feet. There were seven on each side. Each window depicted a religious theme with Christ-like imagery displayed in a unique manner in each one. Outside the rear, double door entrance was a narthex, which served multiple purposes, including exit doors to the entry steps outside. I wondered how many anxious brides and dazed fathers had stood there before entering into the moment of truth.

My home church in Mark Hill was of single story, white clapboard construction. It was rectangular in shape with wooden floors that creaked with every footstep. The pews were hand made, very upright and not cushioned; some said to keep the congregation awake. The windows were paned with frosted glass, eight in number and of standard window height. The preacher stood behind a fixed podium at eye level with his congregation. He was centered on the aisle and directly in front of the choir. Removable benches housed the singers and they were accompanied by an upright piano nearby. In the rear was a storage closet, table and double doors to the steps outside. Up on the hill was a cemetery that contained several generations of Methodist faithful. A small steeple rose above the church and contained the church bell, which doubled as a call to worship and a warning signal when bad weather approached.

This morning I sat in a much different church. The ceilings were elevated and scrolled. Outside I had noticed the slate roof and bell tower that housed two bells. I wondered how the preaching would compare to my home church, as the choir processed in from the rear, singing "Onward Christian Soldiers" until they were seated.

At my church in Mark Hill, we had Reverend Hill. He was a mild mannered man that every person in the community greatly respected. He was scholarly and preached with depth, but very little emotion. He was best known for his stamina, as sermons often approached two hours. Even the hard benches failed to keep some alert and many a wife would bruise husband's ribs during the service. He was especially good at funerals and had performed many because of his age and standing in the community. He would give departed ones a grand sendoff in a relatively expeditious manner. Consequently, many with no church affiliation would request him for their funeral needs.

As I sat in this large, stately church this morning, I watched a robed figure enter from stage left, and climb up into his elevated pulpit. I turned to Johnny and said in a whisper, "I'm not in my Mark Hill church anymore."

While sitting there, dreading a boring and dry sermon, the Reverend Doctor Fleming skipped all the usual order of worship and began to preach on the world condition, imperialist aggression, and how the sovereignty of God applied to such complexities. He never mentioned Germany, but everyone who followed world affairs knew the focus of his comments. It was a riveting and interesting discourse and lasted exactly one hour. Hymns, collections, prayers, creeds, announcements and benediction followed in order and we were dismissed.

After the service, Doctor Fleming stood outside greeting members and visitors alike with a smile and surprisingly, a firm handshake. He grabbed my hand and threw his arm over my shoulder, inquired as to my name and circumstances, thanked me for coming, and turned to Johnny and said, "Bring this boy back with you son, I like the cut of his jib." "On the way back to the campus we walked through several "Old South" neighborhoods with columns adorning two story mansions, set on tree laden, spacious grounds and curved driveways. Flowering shrubs were in great abundance on every property. " This is a beautiful town," I remarked to Johnny. "It's old, and old South," he replied, seemingly unimpressed.

The rest of the day was spent in our room, which that night had become the gathering place for the other students on our floor. Twenty or more students sat on the beds, chairs and floor and we shared experiences with each other until after midnight. It was a good day all around and Johnny also enjoyed church. Tomorrow would be hectic I thought as I dropped off to sleep.

It was Monday morning as I rose up to check the time. The alarm had not gone off, or I failed to hear it and I was late. I sprang to my feet, grabbed the first clothing I could reach in the closet, and hurriedly dressed. The paperwork on the desk was gathered up in a bundle and shoved under my arm as I bolted for the door, outside and across campus at full run to the gymnasium where registration had begun over an hour ago. There were three lines stretching out the entrance. I found a place at the end after asking if it was the line for freshman. After a brief time, I noticed people staring at me. I looked down in horror to see that I had grabbed my bib over-alls and work boots. A red bandana handkerchief was hanging out of my pocket and I looked like a farm boy about to do chores. My face turned crimson as I attempted to act nonchalant and stared up at the sky. Some thirty or so minutes later I reached the head of the line. The woman got my name and requested my paperwork. I did not know what she needed so I dropped the whole bundle in front of her. She shook her head in disgust and proceeded to sift through the pile. She finally looked up and said impatiently, "Where is your form MD916-B?" "That is all my paperwork that I received in the mail," I responded. "You can't register without the required form," as she motioned to the other end of the gymnasium to another long line. I dutifully got at the end of the new line and some thirty or so minutes later I reached the head of the line and asked for the form I needed to register. "Where is your paperwork," the person behind the desk replied. I pointed across the room and advised that my paperwork was at the other table. "I am so sorry. I can not issue your form MD916-B without your paperwork." I broke out in a cold sweat as I contemplated going back to the other table that still had a line that snaked out the door and out of sight. "No, I am not leaving here until I have that stupid form." She glanced over at a security guard and beckoned him to our table. "Is this student giving you trouble?" He grabbed my arm and began to pull me toward the exit.

Johnny was pulling on my arm. "Henry, wake up. It's seven o'clock. Let's get dressed, grab a bite and go register." My head cleared and I shouted, "Hallelujah! I was dreaming." Johnny thought I had lost my mind until I told him about the dream. He thought it funny and, with a big grin, admonished me to bring the necessary form to register.

After breakfast I made a trip to the financial aid office, secured my first check and then deposited it at the branch bank on campus and received temporary checks to use at registration. The registration process went smoothly and we were both out in less than an hour, much to my relief. The processor advised me that an appointment had been made with my advisor for the next morning and that I could complete my class scheduling afterwards. The rest of the day was spent on a guided tour of the campus compliments of Johnny.

My appointment was at ten o'clock and I was fifteen minutes early. I sat in the outer waiting room at the secretary's direction, picked up a magazine, and began to read. The article concerning the unrest in Europe had just gotten interesting when my name was called. The advisor identified himself as Mr. Fountain and greeted me with a hearty handshake and a big toothy smile. He sat behind his desk, invited me to sit down opposite him and inquired, "You are Henry Jimson?" "Yes, Sir." "Well Henry, I've reviewed your high school transcript and also read a note which your Principal had voluntarily enclosed. You are highly thought of, and after reviewing the transcript, I see why." "Thank you Sir." "Now Henry, I want you to give me a family background, your extracurricular activities, likes and dislikes, why you decided to seek advanced education, where you perceive your academic strengths to lie, what you think would be logical choices for courses of study here and what you think would be a fulfilling profession for you." Good grief I thought to myself. I spent almost an hour responding in as succinct a manner as possible. He nodded from time to time, propped his feet on the desk and closed his eyes. At one point I thought he might have dozed off. When I finished, he stood up and asked me to wait in the reception area; that he wanted to make some notes. About twenty minutes later his head emerged from the door and he beckoned me to come in. "Henry, I am going to give you a battery of tests in standardized form to determine your aptitude, strengths and weaknesses and see if we can find an academic fit for you here. The testing area is this way," and we moved down the hall to a room, a small windowless cubicle with a single desk, a clock and an overhead light. "Do you need the restroom or water; anything at all before beginning?" "No, Sir." "Then you will begin with the top booklet. It is a timed test and I will call your time. Afterwards you may go eat lunch and upon return, complete the remaining testing areas. If you need anything I'll be in my office and can assist you. This procedure is not pass or fail, but rather, designed to aid me in advising you. There is no time limit after lunch. There are extra pencils for your use. When you are finished, bring the papers to my receptionist. Do you have any questions?" I had none and began.

I completed the first test in less time than allowed and went to lunch. Three hours and one break later I returned to the office and delivered the balance of the paperwork to the receptionist. She instructed me to return at one o'clock the next day and I left. The rest of the day was spent in the student grill with Johnny and friends comparing experiences to date and wondering what tomorrow would bring.

I returned to the advisor's office at One o'clock, as instructed. Mr. Fountain was very upbeat as we sat down to confer. "Well Henry, you are a very intelligent young man. You scored in the top percentile of your grouping. Your communication and language skills are very advanced for your age. Application of logic is one of your top strengths. I've reviewed your results with a fellow staff member and we both agree on a recommended course. How do you feel about a major in History or English, with perhaps graduate school in a chosen profession in your future?" "How long do I have to decide?" I asked. "Final course schedules must be turned in by Friday. Classes start on the following Monday and, of course, as a freshman, your curriculum is pretty much fixed for the first two semesters." "I'll come by tomorrow if that is all right," as I stood to leave. "We will assign individual classes through this office for you Henry, and give you the schedule." "Thank you Sir," as I left the office. I felt as if I was looking down a long, dark tunnel with a very weak light far ahead of me to point the way.

I awoke the next morning from a restless sleep with the answer. I would major in English and minor in history, if possible. It also occurred to me that law or medicine could be a good fit for me. I felt immediate relief at having made a life transforming decision. I called the folks to tell them of my decision. Dad wanted to know how I could make a living with an English degree and we spent some time on the phone together discussing my pursuit of a post graduate degree. I don't believe he really grasped the concept and I am not sure I could fully comprehend it either. He was uncomfortable with my making this kind of decision without his help, but he had no understanding of college and advanced education and so, for perhaps the first time, told me that he trusted my judgment. I hoped his confidence was well founded.

Thursday morning I returned to the advisor's office and, after further consultation, we decided on a class schedule. A trip to the Registrars office to confirm my class schedule was next. My class assignments and hours and places of meeting were decided and a form schedule was provided for my use. So, I transformed into a bone fide enrolled freshman ready to jump into university life bright and early the following Monday.

The next day started with breakfast at the grill, a gathering place for students to eat and visit. Afterwards I went to the campus bookstore with my schedule and secured all the necessary textbooks, workbooks, supplies and a few other items recommended by the student clerk. She was very helpful and even suggested that I purchase several available used textbooks to save money. I also splurged and bought a freshman hat with the school emblem embroidered on it, and a jacket with like emblem. I wrote my second check and went back to the dormitory with an armload of books and supplies, dropping several items along the way, as I struggled to balance the pile of material in my arms. Later on that day Johnny returned to the room with an equally unwieldy load of books and supplies, deposited them on his desk and flopped down on his bed with a sigh of relief. We rested in our beds for a while, went to lunch and I spent the rest of the day at the library.

The library building stood in the middle of the campus. It was a massive and imposing structure. The entrance was decorated overhead with a literary theme containing books, scrolls and busts of great ancient writers. Inside was the usual reception area for inquiries, checkout and return stations and cataloguing facilities. It was by far, the most complete and extensive facility for learning and research I had ever been in. One of the librarians had a small group of students gathered for a tour and I joined in. She was very informative and took us around to key areas, with a brief stop and explanation at each point of interest. Tables for community use and cubicles for individuals were in abundance. Of course the atmosphere was one of quiet dignity, almost to the point of reverence. There were stacks laid out in seemingly endless rows, and overhead, along the exterior walls were walkways and more stacks, some accessible by ladder. Much dark wood and gold colored metal was used with great taste as well as utility. It struck me as absolutely beautiful while, at the same time, imposing and intimidating. It would be some time before I'd feel comfortable here, but decided to do all my studying at this seat of learning. Perhaps the very spirit of the place where many had gone before in pursuit of knowledge would somehow inspire me to absorb the information I needed for living a productive life. In the meantime, I intended to concentrate here on the task of studying, in order to pass my coursework and do it with success.

With the weekend upon us, the last one before classes, a group of us decided to go into town to the movies. This turned out to be more than we bargained for and very entertaining, considering the cost of a dime for entry and fifteen cents for a drink and popcorn. The feature movie theme was cowboys and Indians all the way, with a newsreel, adventure serial and cartoon piece thrown in for good measure. But as if that was not enough entertainment, we were all privileged to meet the town character. We were later told that he was a permanent Saturday matinee attendee. He was called "Blue" by the locals and was the oldest son of a prominent family. Some say he was mildly retarded. Others claim he was eccentric to the extreme and a few even thought he was a genius. Whatever the case, he was extremely entertaining to the audiences in attendance with him. He usually stayed in the theater from the beginning of the matinee until the last showing Saturday night. His conduct never changed and he chose to watch only cowboy movies.

Blue always sat on the back row. If at any given point during the movie that the hero or heroine was in grave danger, Blue would stand up and with great gusto, yell out a warning to the figures on the screen. "Look out there, he's hiding behind the rock and will shoot you dead! Watch out! Watch out!" In a chase scene he would exclaim with all the confidence he could muster, "Nobody can catch that horse," pointing to the hero's horse on the screen and further exclaiming, "That is the fastest horse in the world and can't be beat by no outlaw's animal!" When the action got tense or the hero seemed destined to die, Blue would bolt from his seat on the back row and run out the rear door into the lobby. He would crack the door and take quick glances at the action until the danger passed and only then, would he reenter the theater. At each performance his behavior was exactly the same. He was tolerated by everyone and even encouraged by students who often joined in with him in like behavior. The first time he yelled at the top of his voice behind me I nearly jumped out of my skin, but as time went by, I found myself giving Blue as much attention as the action on the screen. It was great fun.

Monday found me sitting on the front row with three hole punched, lined paper in ring binder, Algebra book opened to first chapter, first page and eagerly awaiting the first words from the professor. He began to take roll and I responded, "Here," in turn. Upon completion he walked to the window and stood there for a few minutes, his back to the class. He then turned and stated, "Half of you will probably fail this class. Your first assignment is the first two chapters in the text and completion of all problems at the end of each chapter. My name is Mr. Alzwinger. The problems will be reviewed at the next class. There may be a test on the material covered. "Dismissed", he exclaimed as he picked up the paperwork on his desk and left ahead of the class. My head was spinning, trying to absorb what just took place.

My next class was freshman Chemistry. We sat in an auditorium style room, tilted downward back to front with a stage in front for the professor. This class was large; some one hundred students I calculated. An elderly man appeared from stage right and stood behind a speaker's podium. "My name is Doctor John Albright. I'll teach you chemistry in this grand hall three days a week and in the laboratory once a week. This course of study will be difficult. I use it as a means to wash out pre-med students not equipped in this science to an acceptable level to become medical doctors. If you pass this course you will have a right to be proud." At that point he instructed the student on the end of the first row left to sign and pass a clipboard with attendance form attached. He admonished the class not to leave without signing it. He then immediately began to lecture from the first chapter and continued non-stop for the rest of the class. At the conclusion, he assigned work in the lab book for that session, scheduled on Thursday afternoons, and we were then dismissed.

I had one afternoon class in beginning Spanish. "Como esta usted hoy?" he inquired. "Mi llama es Senor Rodriguez." he advised and then called the roll, assigned the first three chapters, and spent the balance of the hour comparing the romance languages and entertaining us with several personal experiences in his native Mexico. We were dismissed.

My first day of schooling was thus completed. No one knew my name or anything about me. I was a number and an impersonal one at that. The professors showed little interest in us as individuals and I had the uneasy feeling that they cared not in the least whether we passed or failed their courses. By the same token, I knew nothing of these teachers. What were they like as human beings? Could they communicate the subject matter in a manner I could understand? Were their tests hard? Would they grade on a curve? What method of teaching would they employ? The homework assignments given today would probably keep me in the library until after midnight. I was correct in that assumption.

Tuesday found me in two additional courses, offered on Tuesdays and Thursdays of duration of one and a half hours each. Mondays' classes were one hour each and offered on Monday, Wednesday and Friday of each week.

My English professor was Doctor Herrington and I liked him very much. He seemed truly interested in our class and spent time orienting us to the textbook contents and what he expected. He invited us to dig in and really study the material and assured us that we would enjoy it. The assignment was to write a descriptive short story of our choosing, no more than five hundred words and based on some personal experience. He then read a poem from the textbook entitled "The Raven" by Edgar Allen Poe and advised that we would discuss it at the next class.

I took a course entitled Physical Geology to fill out my schedule. The professor was Doctor Gilman. He entered class ten minutes late and appeared out of breath. He apologized and explained that he thought the class was being held in another building. His clothing, including his blazer, pants, shirt and tie looked as if they had not been cleaned or pressed in ages. His shoes were not polished. He smoked a pipe that kept going out on him in spite of many long draws upon the stem. He lit it every ten minutes or so and would then set it on the table to once again go out. I believe he was brilliant and also extremely absent-minded. He explained that he adhered to the science of Evolution, did not adhere to Creationism, and that if any of us were of the Christian bent, that we would probably have a problem with the teaching. He invited us to be open-minded and admitted that Geology was not an exact science. He assigned the first four chapters in the text and admonished us to take good notes. He also told us that he would key us in his lectures when test material was covered. He wished us luck and then left the room with his pipe still on his desk. We sat there for a few minutes, undecided what to do, and then left also.

I spent most of the night in the library working on my English assignment. Johnny was asleep when I got back to the room, so I undressed in the dark and slipped into bed as quietly as possible. The alarm announced the beginning of another day. I slept so soundly that my face was wrinkled and I felt groggy and disoriented as I prepared for classes.

Algebra would be a problem even though I had no trouble with it in high school. Mr. Alzwinger came in and immediately walked to the black board, picked up chalk and began to work the first assigned problem. Upon completion, he walked to the window with back to the class and inquired, "Any questions?" Half the class raised their hands. He turned to view the scene with an incredulous look and stated, "You simply put the components of the equation in the barrel and shake it about vigorously and out pops the answer. It is not a difficult exercise." He then erased the problem and immediately worked the second, and so it went for the balance of the hour. He would finish a problem, erase it and go to the next until the assignment was completed. As we proceeded out the door completely bewildered, he suggested that we cover the next two chapters and work the problems at the end of each. "There may be a test next session." He shouted as a parting shot. Chemistry and Spanish classes were interesting and I took extensive notes in each. I would do well in these subjects.

At the beginning of English class on Thursday, Dr Herrington requested our writing assignment and then asked if anyone would volunteer to discuss the life of Edgar Allan Poe and his poem, "The Raven". No response was heard from the class. "Come now, surely some of you researched Mr. Poe and his rather bizarre life and will share with us." No response. "Mr. Jimson, can you enlighten us today?" By some grace extended to me, I had decided in the library to read an article on Poe so that I might better understand "The Raven". "Stand up Mr. Jimson and share with us." As I stood Mr. Herrington began shuffling through our written assignment and seemed to be totally engaged in that activity, glancing up at me only occasionally.

"Sir, Edgar Allan Poe was born in 1809 in Richmond, Virginia to a family of actors. He died in poverty in 1849. His Father abandoned the family and his Mother died shortly thereafter. He was taken in by a wealthy family, but never adopted. He spent his early childhood in Virginia, Scotland and England. He attended the University of Virginia but never completed schooling there and left in a cloud of controversy. In 1827 he enlisted in the Army and later went to West Point but was expelled for reasons unclear. He then met and married his cousin, Virginia Clemm. She was only thirteen when married, and later died of tuberculosis. His early writing career was unsuccessful and he moved through a series of positions in the publishing field with no marked fulfillment. Not until his publication of 'The Gold Bug', a later work, did he gain notoriety. 'The Raven", a part of a book of poems was published in 1845. His life was greatly affected by alcohol and mental illness. He was plagued by bouts of depression and perhaps was addicted to illicit drugs; the totality of all of which resulted in his death at the age of forty. He died a relative pauper and very much alone. His work has been considered the product of genius by some and that of a delusional personality by others. He was a master of the mysterious and macabre. He had the ability to mix the extremes of horror and love so as to evoke a wide range of strong emotions in his readers. I believe he was a genius and yet, disturbed by measure of that considered 'normal'. I enjoyed 'The Raven' very much." I took my seat and sighed in relief, feeling that the presentation was adequate at best. Mr. Harrington thanked me and completed the balance of class time discussing Poe.

I met Johnny at the grill and sat with a group of his friends who were members of the fraternity he had pledged. He was a third generation legatee and even though rushed by four other fraternities, he chose the same one as his family members had, for tradition's sake, I suspect. They wanted to know why I did not participate in rush. I explained candidly that I was not financially able to join a fraternity and that my coursework had to come first. They were not impressed with my explanation, but dropped the subject and I was glad to go on to other topics of the day.

The Algebra class on Friday was unbelievable. Professor Alzwinger approached the blackboard with chalk in right hand and eraser in left. He would write out a problem and the solution, no sooner completing a line and then erasing it. When completed he would turn and inquire if anyone had questions. Of course the board would be blank and had the same appearance as most of the class. No one had a clue. I decided that if I were going to master this subject it would be through self-instruction and many long hours of study. Near the end of the hour, he stood at the window with back to class and assigned two more chapters with problems at the end of each to work and advised that the first test would be given the following Monday on the material covered to date. You could sense the fear and anxiety in the room as he departed. Chemistry and Spanish went well and I felt confident about my ability to handle these subjects. Most of the weekend was spent studying for Algebra. The following Monday, the test was distributed. We did not review Friday's assignment, but rather turned in the problems without review and immediately began to take the test. To my surprise, it consisted of one problem. I worked on it for approximately thirty minutes, placed it on Professor Alzwinger's desk, and left. I was the first to leave and learned later that my grade was "98", with only two other students making a passing grade. I was told that he never gave out perfect scores. I was sure the work was completely correct and when returned, the paper was unmarked with "98" written across the top.

Dr. Herrington arrived in the classroom a little late, assigned in class reading that took up the balance of the period. He then spent his time at his desk reading our short stories. The rest of the class went quickly and without incident. The highlight of the week occurred the following Thursday in English. As we settled into our seats Dr. Herrington announced his pleasure with the short story assignment. "You have all done very well in forming word pictures and descriptive story lines to develop your piece. Now I would like for two students to read their stories and we will then critique them in turn." The first story involved the students experience during her senior year in high school, playing on a girl's basketball team, which went to state finals and lost the championship game in overtime. Not many questions were asked except as directed by our teacher. I thought the story was excellent and said so. Dr. Herrington then called my name and directed me to the front of the class to recite my story. I was pleased and intimidated. What did Old Man say to me, I pondered as I moved to the front of the class to begin the recitation? Stand erect, make eye contact with the listeners, exude confidence and take pride in your performance.

"I've entitled my story 'The Island Adventure'," and I began to read.

"As I made my way to the inner harbor feelings of anticipation welled up within me. Going to the island was my favorite summer activity and it had been two years since I last made the trip. The sailboat was moored alongside the wharf, with lines fore and aft securing it and tied off slack to accommodate the tide. She was sixteen feet in length and carried a mainsail and jib when fully rigged. One man could sail her, weather permitting. The early morning breeze would be offshore today and I could probably make the run mostly fair wind with a minimum of tacking once I cleared the harbor. The gray skies were already giving way to dawn and obscure objects were growing distinguishable as I released the lines, raised the mainsail and drifted away from the dock to begin the journey. I used the rudder to scull the boat around to catch the breeze and then tacked my way to the mouth of the harbor and into open water. As soon as I cleared land I caught a light wind directly off my stern, trimmed the sail accordingly, raised the centerboard and was on my way.

Sailing is not at all like motoring. You immediately notice the quiet sounds of the water lapping against the boat as it slides along from wave to wave, and the occasional raucous cry of the seagulls hovering in formation above. At times a school of mullet would be encountered and as the bow crosses their path they would jump and splash. Some say mullet jump to escape their predators but I believe they do so for the sheer joy it brings them. As the channel passes behind, the murky water gives way to clear and to the trained eye one notes bars and shoals as they pass underneath.

The wind was picking up now and I made my first tack to approach the eastern tip of the island where the beaches were more to my liking. The trip took almost one hour. I felt totally relaxed and at peace as I lowered the sail and drifted onshore. The anchor attached to the bow was buried on the beach and then I paddled away from shore to throw over a stern anchor, thus properly securing the boat in the event of increase in winds and to account for a dropping tide. Failing to do so could leave one beached and stranded until the next tide change, and was an experience I had encountered previously. The sand was white, packed tightly below high tide line and soft and fluffy above it. It was cool in this early morning hour, but that would change to blistering hot in the afternoon.

It seems to me that beachcombers who live by the sea and explore the shores daily for some trinket or treasure live a carefree life. I call the experience, as I sat out doing the same, a grand adventure that requires no thought and very little effort. Personally, my joy comes not in the discoveries I may make, but rather, in the quiet solitude of it all. It must have been this way for ancient man as he plied the shores, looking for food or material for shelter from the elements and a myriad of other purposes, not least of which would have been communing at one with nature in one of its most primitive forms.

If one walks a beach they may see most unusual sights. There is a fiddler crab motionless until approached and then dashing sideways and vanishing in a flash into a hole in the sand. Pursuing him, digging furiously to capture him, one discovers that they are like ghosts, not only in appearance but also in their ability to disappear within the sand.

The waters are churned on occasion by storms and all manner of objects are raised from the deeps and deposited on the shore. Dead sea creatures and man made objects litter the sand in helter-skelter fashion. All manner of shells, some whole, but most broken by wave action are everywhere and many are intricate in form, beautifully colored and wonderfully designed by the Maker. I have several rare finds decorating my home.

After walking several miles I came to a freshwater lake in the interior of the island. In the distance I saw several wild hogs and also an alligator basking at the waters edge, motionless, with gaze fixed on the hogs. They would glance up every few seconds to see what old gator was doing. This is the natural order of living on the island, species versus species, surviving on one another in the cycle of existence. The big ones capture and eat the smaller, and man is often, but not always at the top of the food chain.

As I made my way back to the boat the sun shone directly overhead and it was suddenly hot and still. I pulled a piece of canvas from under the deck and with driftwood, fashioned a lean to. Then I got my lunch pail and thermos of ice water and ate, drank and lay down under my manmade shelter to rest. I must have slept for several hours. I awakened to buzzing sounds and sharp stings. In the later afternoon the wind shifted and brought with its cool breeze thousands of hungry and very aggressive mosquitoes. It was time to leave the island and I made a hasty retreat to the boat. Beach anchor, lunch pail, thermos, several old bottles and shells of interest were secured in the canvas and I jumped on board. The stern anchor was retrieved and sail hoisted as I drifted away from my retreat for the day.

Storm clouds were making up in the North and the wind rose steadily as I neared the harbor mouth some one and a half hours later. My trip was ended at just the right time. Rain began to fall as I finished mooring my sailboat in its berth. That night I reflected on the day. I've never tired of the island trips. They are best made alone. Learn of yourself; go to an island and spend the day in quiet reflection. Time is fleeting so soak it up by the moment. Stop and look around. It will add perspective to your own life. The end."

That night I wrote Old Man. I covered the last few weeks with as much detail as I could muster, knowing of Old Man's genuine interest in everything that I experienced. I doubt that he had any knowledge of college life but I was unsure of anything regarding his past, so I spent considerable time relating my day-to-day life here. I also enclosed a copy of the short story for his critique. His reply was received by return post. It was not what I expected at all and in fact, disturbed me greatly. After quickly reading his letter at the post office, I returned to the dormitory room to sit and re-read it carefully.

October 1, 1941

Henry,

I want you to be knowledgeable in the affairs of war. It is of the utmost importance to survive. It is equally important to be under discipline. Learn to work with your fellow comrades. Try to find a few men that you trust and share yourself with them. Look for the quiet ones who go about doing their tasks with diligence and a sense of duty. Someday those men may save your life and they will have the same reliance upon you.

Take your training to heart. Learn as much as you can during your basic training. Your weapon should be your closest companion. Sleep with it, carry it with you when off duty and learn how to assemble it and break it down until it feels a part of you. Fire it until you can hit your target without thought or effort. Instinct is the key. Be prepared to act as a part of a unit and also to act alone.

You may face fear in its most gruesome form. You will probably want to run or disappear into the earth, but fear in combat will often immobilize you and take away all senses. You will have to learn of your inner self, Henry. Do you remember climbing the tree? We cannot learn of these matters but they will come in war, so be prepared. Dwell on this thing called fear, and pray to your Creator for wisdom, knowledge and courage. I believe in angels, Henry. I believe they hover over battlefields grieving at the horror of the scene below and I believe that they often shield some from harm.

War is an awful thing Henry. Nations reflect the will of their citizens, but not always. Throughout history evil men have risen to take hold of the will of the nation and pervert it. Such a thing has happened in Germany. Adolf Hitler is such a man. He has taken hold of the will of Germany and intends, with its resources, to do evil in the world. God help us.

I have read Mein Kampf and cried. This man is a hater of all peoples except the Aryan race. He considers the Jew to be subhuman and worthy of enslavement and death. He also feels called to expand the "living space" of his "superior" race to the exclusion of other nations rights and territories. His plans are in motion, which he formulated some twenty years ago. We have witnessed his intent in Czechoslovakia, Poland, Denmark, Norway, France, Luxembourg, Belgium and the Netherlands. Now he is spreading his hatred into the British Isles.

I believe that Winston Churchill understands this monster better than any. He does not underestimate his genius, though delusional, and recognizes that Hitler has the ability to completely control the German people with his charisma. They are spellbound by his rhetoric. They still smart from the defeat of The Great War and are a proud people, not accustomed to being subjugated and humiliated. Hitler has a willing audience who likes his talk of rising out of the ashes and fulfilling German destiny to be the dominator of the world. I fear that the world sleeps as he proceeds.

Do not believe that America will remain in isolation. Our enemies are many and would do us great harm. Cruel dictators also lead Italy and Japan and I don't trust them. I believe that we are perceived as a threat to their desire for domination and expansion. After the experiences of The Great War, we have no national stomach for more war. I feel there will come a time when we will be forced to act in order to preserve our own liberties.

I miss you boy and my heart is troubled. Please forgive me as I ramble on. Have you met a girl?

Old Man

I showed the letter to Johnny and he wanted to know why the man was obsessed with war. I couldn't explain it. I put the letter in a box and intended to save all his letters there. I put it there, stored away and out of sight, but I couldn't get its content out of my mind. Hardly a day passed that I did not dwell on his advice. What a curious question: "Have you met a girl?"

Over the next few weeks' school went very well. I had settled into a comfortable routine that pretty much centered on sleeping, eating, classes and study. Johnny and I met many new friends in the dormitory. We all spent late nights in idle chatter and deep philosophy which was a fruitless undertaking, but fun.

CHAPTER THREE

It was still dark outside when I arose for Monday morning classes. I prepared for classes, then gathered up an armload of books and an umbrella and proceeded down the stairs to meet the day. The weather was awful. It had been raining for three straight days and the daytime temperature hovered in the low thirties. The sidewalks were treacherous and covered with water or ice depending on the hour. I raised the umbrella and stepped outside into a dark and dreary pre-dawn mess. It was drizzling and the wind was blowing in gusts, driving the rain at angles. I crossed the street and headed for my first class with head lowered under the umbrella in a vain attempt to stay dry. I was immediately wet from my knees to my heels. I stepped up my pace to escape this predicament and was almost running when, in an instant, I collided with an unknown object and found myself on the ground, in the water and looking up at the falling rain. What could have happened? My books lay all around me and the umbrella had taken flight in the wind. I rose up on one elbow, still stunned and saw another body in front of me in like position. That unfortunate person was attired in an ankle length raincoat with hood and was likewise soaked and surrounded by books lying all about. We both jumped to our feet and hastened a quick glance around to see if anyone else had witnessed this sorry spectacle. Then it began. "Why don't you look where you are going? You almost killed me! My books are ruined! I am soaked and cold and mad! Why don't you look where you are going, you oaf?" Good heavens, I thought. This is a girl and an abrasive one at that. "My dear young Lady, it takes two to form a collision and I shall therefore inquire of you, why don't you look where you are going." I finished with a smug, haughty look for emphasis. She was still looking down to assess the damage when she raised her head and made eye contact. "Good grief, who speaks in such an archaic manner. You are an insolent dolt." I did not reply. I simply stared into her eyes. My surroundings vanished along with all recollection of what had just transpired. I no longer felt the wind and rain. I only felt my face becoming increasingly flush. I believe my mouth had dropped open and I was standing there completely motionless. I was having trouble catching a breath. I couldn't break eye contact. They were a deep blue and penetrated into my mind and held me there for what seemed like hours. All I saw were her eyes.

She finally blinked and released me. "Are you all right?" No response. "Well, the least you could do is retrieve my books", she said, in a much lower voice than previously. I came out of the trance. "Oh please forgive me. I am such an idiot, lumbering along without watching where I was going, and knocking you to the ground. I hope you are not hurt. Look at you all wet; here, take my coat. I can't believe I'm so stupid. Will you please, please forgive me for what I did and for what I said?" "I'll get your books now. I should have done that already. Are you injured? Let me escort you to someplace dry. Will you ever forgive me? I am so sorry!" "Stop!" she exclaimed. "It is not that serious. I'm fine now." As I finished retrieving all the books I could feel her watching me. She asked if I were a freshman as if trying to justify my behavior. I answered her and she volunteered that she was also. She thanked me and said that she had to go, as classes were about to begin. I apologized again. As we both started to slowly walk away in opposite directions, suddenly we both turned and blurted out in unison, "What is your name?" We laughed. Her laugh was infectious and caressed and enveloped me with feelings of warmth and joy. "My name is Henry Jimson." "My name is Mary Blyth and I live in Forrest dormitory." With that she turned and disappeared. I stood there alone for several more minutes trying to regain my full senses. She was the most beautiful girl I had ever knocked down, I thought. Then I started laughing uncontrollably. The rest of the day I could concentrate on nothing else but my chance encounter with Mary Blyth, the girl with the beautiful blue eyes and lilting laugh. I hastened to memorize Mary Blyth and Forrest dormitory.

That night in the room Johnny asked, "What is wrong with you Henry?" "What do you mean?" "You haven't said a word in an hour and seem to be a million miles away." "I met a girl this morning." "Where?" "On the ground outside," I replied. Johnny wanted a full explanation after that response. "Have you called her?" "No, not yet." "What are you waiting for?" That was an excellent question and the truth was that the prospect frightened me to death. The thought of a phone call to her caused my stomach to tighten, my mouth go dry and my palms sweat. "What is wrong with me?" I wondered. All she can do is hang up. With that thought I became lightheaded and began to laugh again for absolutely no reason. "What's so funny? Johnny asked. "I don't know, I guess I'm going to the hall phone now to call her." "Good" he replied with a look of relief.

"Is Mary Blyth in please?" The girl on the other end yelled out "Mary Blyth, telephone. It's a boy." A chorus of giggles and laughter ensued. Then a subdued voice was speaking to me. "This is Mary, who is this please?" "Mary, this is Henry Jimson." "Yes." I could hear more muffled sounds as if someone's hand covered the receiver. "Do you remember me from this morning?" I was so nervous I almost dropped the phone. "Why I believe I do now. Are you the boy who mauled me on the sidewalk and left me for dead in the rain?" More laughter was heard. "All right girls, the fun is over so you can go back to your rooms now." She then turned her attention to me and said, "Henry, the girls in the dorm have really been kidding me about our meeting this morning. They think it was very romantic." "Mary, I can call back at another time if you wish," hoping to somehow escape my feelings of inadequacy. "Henry, I can't think of anything I'd rather do tonight than to talk to you but I missed classes today and have to study. I'd love to meet you tomorrow. When are your free?" "I have English and geology and then I can meet you about one o'clock if that's all right." "We could meet in the student union lounge if that's good for you," she replied. "Fine, I'll see you then. I look forward to talking with you." It occurred to me that I knew little of her appearance other than her eyes. "Mary, what color is your hair?" "You don't know?" she replied in an exasperated tone. "You had a hood over your head," I said. "Well, my hair is brownish blonde, I have warts all over my body and I am actually six feet tall." "Now you are making fun of me!" I spoke in the most indignant tone I could muster. "Good night, Henry. I'll see you tomorrow." When I returned to the room Johnny exclaimed, "Well!" "I talked to her." "And…?" "Good night, Johnny," I replied. I did not wish to share any of this with him now. "You could at least tell me what she looks like." "Well she has brownish blonde hair, warts all over her body and is six feet tall." Johnny turned the lights out for the night and muttered something about my being a jerk. I had trouble going to sleep that night. The name Mary danced in my mind and I relived our meeting several times before I finally dropped off to sleep.

I waited in the student union the next afternoon, sitting and glancing at one of the magazines there. "Hi Henry, I hope you haven't been waiting long. I just took a few minutes after my last class to freshen up." I looked up, stood up and my mouth gaped open once more. My head was spinning as I looked at her standing there, near enough for me to smell her perfume. I instinctively backed up a step and reached out to shake her hand. "Do you remember me?" she quipped with a soft laugh. She was the most beautiful girl I had ever seen. Her hair was actually a golden brown, cut shoulder length and very wavy and full all around her face.

She was radiant as she smiled at me. Her lips were full and her teeth perfectly formed and brilliantly white. I know I blushed as my eyes followed the contours of her body from head to foot. She was gorgeous. She stood there patiently waiting for a reply. I regained my senses enough to acknowledge her presence, but could do little else. I was certain from her glance that she could sense my feelings and that was obviously delighting her. "You are a man of few words Henry," she said in a taunting manner. I recovered. "No I was just looking for the warts," and we both laughed. "Please sit here," as I motioned to a couch nearby. We were alone in the room and I was thankful for that. Next she said in a very direct manner, "Now, I want you to tell me all about yourself." The more I described my life the easier it got. From time to time she would interject with a question or comment and would thereby draw me further out. I found myself becoming more and more at ease in her presence and as we continued to talk I became not so mesmerized by her. Instead, I began to reveal more of myself to her than to any other person except perhaps Old Man.

When I told her about my friendship with him she leaned closer in to me and became intently interested. She was obviously fascinated with Old

Man and the mystery that surrounded him. She observed that I must care very much for him. I related that he was my very best friend and that I could confide in him about anything. I said that he was an amazing source of wisdom and sound advice in my life.

She wanted to know all about my family and what it was like to live in Mark Hill. She asked if I went to church and where. "Yes, the Methodist church." I shared with her about my visits with Johnny to the Methodist Church in town and she said that perhaps I'd take her one Sunday. "Would you like to go this Sunday?" I asked. "I would love to."

"Now Mary, tell me about yourself." She related that she was from the gulf coast of Mississippi, having been born and raised in Ocean Springs. Her Father was an accountant and worked at a ship building facility nearby and her Mother was employed in a local bank. She was an only child. She loved school coming up in her hometown and really missed her family and friends since college began. She loved the water and had her own sailboat. She was a cheerleader in high school. She wanted to pursue a liberal arts degree and then go on to some position in medicine. After some time, I glanced down at my watch. Two hours had gone by and it seemed only a few minutes. Mary inquired as to the time. "It is almost three o'clock." "I am so sorry but I have to meet some friends at the dorm for a study session. My, the time just flew by didn't it?" As we stood to leave, she suddenly placed her arms around my neck and squeezed me tightly. My knees almost gave out on me. I never had these feelings before. I wondered if it could be love. I had no way of knowing. Mary smiled, turned and with a wave over her shoulder was gone.

That night I wrote Old Man.

Old Man,

I've met a wonderful girl. I believe that I'm in love with her. How can I tell, as I have never fallen in love before? I just know that when I am around her I feel funny inside and get kind of addled. Please write me concerning love. I don't want to make a fool of myself. I am totally out of control and really don't know what I'm doing. Please carefully consider what you can tell me because I feel I'm at an important point of decision and need your experience to guide me.

Henry

His letter was a week in coming. In the meantime I saw Mary every chance I could. We arranged Saturday night to ride the church bus to the service and Sunday morning we did so, with Johnny tagging along. He couldn't wait to see Mary as I had refused to tell him anything. They hit it off immediately and spent most of the ride to church talking. I'll admit that feelings of jealousy overtook me and, for the first time, I resented Johnny.

The service was very good and the preacher talked about patriotism. He equated pride of Nation with the pride that God has in his created people. Mary sat close to me throughout and was very intent on the message. We ate lunch afterwards and then spent the afternoon walking and talking. We were growing closer by the day and learning that we had much in common.

Mary was lying on her bed that night talking to her roommate. They had been close friends since grade school. It was no surprise that upon graduation from high school they chose the same college and decided to room together. Mary knew that she could always trust Janice with her most private thoughts. Sisters could not have been closer. They would simply be there for each other for support and comfort. Often they needed only silent friendship from one another. When one of them hurt they both suffered. They had laughed and cried together, shared in their joys and suffered through all their disappointments together. They would never make any decision, large or small, without talking first.

Janice met Henry previously, at one of their many visits to the grill after classes. On one such gathering a group of five students exchanged small talk about a myriad of subjects over the course of an hour or so, as college students are apt to do. The time was spent discussing nothing heavy or meaningful, but definitely entertaining. Henry and Janice hit it off at once and seemed to really enjoy each other. She had a wonderful sense of humor and kept everyone in stitches for most of their time together.

"Janice, what do you think of Henry?" Mary asked. "I have seen the way you look at him and hang on his every word. You can't wait until he calls," she replied. "But what do you think about him. Do you like him?" Mary leaned closer to see Janice's face as she propped on one elbow, eagerly awaiting an answer. "Everybody likes Henry." "Janice Casey, you are so mean. Tell me, now!" Janice laughed and Mary giggled, rolled over on her back and stared at the ceiling, still waiting for the answer. There was a minute or two of silence. Then Janice replied, "I think he is handsome. That wavy blonde hair is so, you know, cute. He seems to be very serious about everything. I believe he is very smart but he doesn't flaunt it. He knows so much, not at all like other boys his age." Janice was quiet for a while, reflecting on her feelings. "When he looks at you I get all tingly inside. I like the way he always holds your hand, and the way he pays attention to you Mary. Not many boys do that, but Henry does. I really believe that he is in love with you." Mary arose, walked over to the wall switch and turned out the lights. They both lay there in their beds, in the dark, considering it all. "Goodnight Janice." "Goodnight my best friend in the whole world," Janice whispered. "I love you."

> *Dear Henry,*
>
> *I want you to carefully consider what I am about to relate to you, mull it over and digest it. Then I suspect that you will come to the conclusion that you know no more about "falling in love" than when you first read this.*
>
> *You just know. Follow your heart and not your head. Feel your feelings. Love is a warmth that glows within you. Love is relishing in the little things. It wants to be with your beloved. It endures all things. It is God's gift to be treasured and cultivated. Love forgives wrongs and rejoices in the right. To a person in love all things are beautiful even when they are not. It is a consuming fire that destroys logic and reason. True love lasts and knows no bounds. Love can make you cry and laugh at the same time. Love hurts on occasion and that is also good. Love gives and gives, expecting nothing in return. Love can break your heart and it can restore it again.*
>
> *Look in I Corinthians 13, Henry. Read verses 4 through 7. Notice the wisdom contained there. Henry, what is love?*
> *Old Man*

I read the letter over and over and wrestled with the words. I applied all of my feelings to those words. What is love indeed?

One night as we sat on the dormitory steps before curfew began, I told Mary that I'd be spending the Christmas holidays on campus, as it was to great an expense to travel home. She told me that I could come to her home and spend Christmas there with her family. I was not comfortable with the thought of intruding at such a special time and told her so. "My parents know all about you Henry, and they are very anxious to meet you and would love to have you in our home. I'd also very much love to have you there with me." She reached out and took my hand in hers and gently held it and fixed me with those eyes. I had no ability left in me to refuse. What happened next was wonderful. She pulled me to herself and kissed me on the cheek and rested her face on mine. Her breath brushed my ear. I turned my face to hers and kissed her gently and whispered, "Mary, I've fallen in love with you and I want to be with you always." "Oh Henry I do love you so." "Mary, I don't understand what I'm about to tell you. Even though we've only known each other for a short while, I feel as if I've known you forever. Before I met you there had never been any other girl in my life. I cannot tell you how I know that I love you. I just know that I'd be empty without you. I only hope that you have the same feelings for me and that we can share our lives together." Mary began to cry. "Are you all right Mary?" "I am so happy Henry and I love you so much." With that I began to cry. We embraced and held each other for a long time. The porch light was blinking and so we kissed goodnight. "I'll see you tomorrow Mary. I love you." "Good night Henry. I'll dream of you tonight."

As I walked back to my dormitory it was if I was floating. The emotions I felt were overwhelming and I experienced true euphoria for the first time in my life. I vowed that night that I would marry this girl and care for her for the rest of my life. I prayed to God that night, thanking Him for Blessing me with her and asking Him to watch over both of us as we went through life together.

I wrote Old Man a brief letter the next morning. I told him that I now knew that I was truly in love with Mary Blyth. I tried to describe her to him and how I felt, but mere words were not adequate. Somehow I knew he would understand.

In the following days I spent as much time as possible with Mary. We grew closer and more in love, day by day. "Mary, I want to marry you." "Henry, I will marry you. I'll love you until we die. I want to care for you and honor and respect you. I want to rest in your loving arms and give myself completely over to you. I want to share in your life and in the lives of our children. You fulfill me Henry. I will marry you."

We decided to tell our parents during the holidays. We anticipated their wanting us to finish school first and we agreed that we would be obedient to this possibility. We couldn't conceive waiting that long but would honor our parents and respect their wishes. It would not alter our deep love and commitment for each other.

CHAPTER FOUR

It was hard to believe that I had been in school for over three months. Classes were going well and I was sure that my final grades would be very good. Finals would be coming up shortly and then Christmas vacation would begin. We would return to school to begin the second semester in mid-January. I could hardly wait to go to Ocean Springs for Christmas and meet Mary's family. I felt as if I'd known them for years and would really get along well with them. Mary had told them how we felt about one another. However, her Father was concerned and I knew that he and I would have several private discussions. Mary was their only child and they were understandably concerned about our intentions in general and my character in particular.

After church Sunday, Mary and I ate lunch in a café downtown and then walked back to campus. It was a beautiful day and not as cold as it had been. We dreamed of our future as we strolled along. We could never have foreseen an event that would change our lives dramatically.

I walked into my dorm after dropping Mary off. A large group was gathered in the downstairs reading room. They were all intently listening to the radio. The date was December 7, 1941 on a Sunday afternoon. Johnny looked up to see me entering the room. "Henry, the Japanese have attacked Pearl Harbor!" "What do you mean?" I asked, puzzled and confused. "Henry, Japanese planes have bombed Pearl Harbor and sunk some of our ships. This is war Henry." My mind was racing, trying to comprehend this. "Where is Pearl Harbor exactly?" I asked. "It is in Hawaii and the attack just happened. They caught us sleeping Henry and killed a bunch of our people and may have destroyed our whole Pacific fleet." "Good Lord Johnny, what does it mean? Will they attack our mainland? Where did they come from? Isn't it thousands of miles to Japan? How did they get planes on top of us like that?" It still had not fully sunk in. "I am going to call home." Everyone then got up and headed for the telephone. The phone lines were jammed with calls all that day and night. Some people were in a sheer panic. Others were wandering around dazed and overcome by the enormity of the event. I felt a great urgency to contact my family. I was fearful for my country. Old Man's letter of October 1 took on a fresh meaning as I recalled it.

It was after midnight before I got through to Mom and Dad. "This is Henry. Did you hear what happened? What do you make of it Mom?" "It is so good to hear your voice Henry. We were worried about you after the news. Here is your Dad." "Hello Son. This is an awful thing that has happened to us. We will surely declare war on the Japanese. I heard the President will speak to the nation tomorrow so be listening." "Dad, I think I should come home." "There is no need for that right now Henry. Your schoolwork is important and there is nothing you could do here now. Don't you have finals soon? We will make a decision after President Roosevelt acts, and I believe he will act quickly." We visited for about fifteen minutes. It was reassuring to talk to my parents and to receive comfort from them. I love them both dearly. I closed by requesting that they contact Old Man to let him know that, for now, I would stay in school. "Pray for our Nation Henry," "I will Mom, goodbye. I love you."

President Roosevelt spoke to the Nation the next day and I sincerely believe that every person in America, able to do so, listened and hung on his every word. He referred to December 7, 1941 as "a date which will live in infamy." His brief speech acknowledged the fact that the attack was unprovoked and would not go unchallenged. He stated that the Empire of Japan had practiced deception and lies. It was obvious to him that while Japan feigned peace they were making plans for this deliberate attack. He advised that Japan had opened multiple fronts in the Pacific region and that they had become aggressors by virtue of premeditated invasions. He said that many ships were severely damaged and many lives were lost. He added that American ships traversing the high seas between Hawaii and San Francisco had been torpedoed. He assured the American people that this act would not go unanswered and that with God's help and our righteous might we would ultimately prevail. He closed with a request that the Congress declare us in a state of war with the Japanese Empire. Congress met in Joint session that very afternoon and, by resolution, declared that the United States of America and the Imperial Government of Japan were at war as of December 7, 1941. Great Britain immediately joined us in declaring war on Japan.

Three days later, On December 11, 1941, Germany and Italy declared war on the United States. Thus the lines of battle were drawn. Our enemies were now identified and our isolationist policy was no longer possible. God be with us was my prayer.

Mary was distraught. We talked at length, trying to decide our future. It was futile, for no one could act with any degree of certainty in such perilous and uncertain times. I acted on impulse and suggested that we marry right away. She and I looked at each other for a brief time and then agreed that we needed more time to think. I had every intention of volunteering for enlistment and considered that if I served in combat I might never return. She told me that she would wait for me for as long as it took. "I could never love another person Henry." "Mary, we need to let some time go by and think this through clearly. Right now we are reacting based on our fears and emotions. My love for you will never die. Regardless of our decision, I will always love you. Do you understand that?" "What will we do Henry?" "Unless something drastic happens my parents want me to finish this semester." "Good, that will give us more time together. Are you still coming home with me for Christmas?" "Yes, but I think I should only stay until right after, perhaps the day after Christmas, and then go home." Mary understood. It was settled then and now we would watch and wait.

My first experience with college final exams was interesting to say the least. In spite of how well you know the subject and prepared you may be, there seems to be an unwritten rule that one should stay up all night, coffee cup in hand and cram a semester's work into one's brain. A group of four dorm buddies who took classes with me sat in the lounge and quizzed each other at length. This was for the most part a waste of time. Invariably we would lose the moment and drift off into subjects totally unrelated to the task at hand. We discussed the global conflict, girls, bad coffee and occasionally, class work. I left after about an hour and spent the next three nights in solitary study.

Professor Alzwinger gave a three-question algebra exam and allowed three hours to complete it. It was very difficult, but I'll admit that the questions covered most of our class content for the semester. The rest of the exams were not that difficult and I am sure I passed all with ease. I really enjoyed my English class and the test was easy for me; consisting of multiple choice, true or false and essay-type questions. It was the lengthiest exam, some ten pages long. Chemistry was the most challenging and we had a lab experiment to complete as part of the testing. I know I passed. I might choose a field of science as a profession someday. Mary told me that she did well on her tests, also.

With exams behind us I prepared for vacation with Mary and her family. Mary and I arrived late at night at her home, having caught a ride with Johnny and one of his friends who had a car at school. In college if you had a friend with a car that was special indeed. A friend who loaned you his car for a tank of gas was outstanding. We said our goodbyes and they drove away leaving us in the front yard with our luggage. Lights came on in the house and the door burst open to the sounds of joy and laughter. Mary's Mother ran to her and embraced her and lifted her from the ground and twirled in circles. It was quite a sight to see this small woman lift her daughter with such ease. They both were laughing and crying at the same time. "I missed you so much." "Its so good to be home Mom. This is Henry!" Her Mother released Mary and extended her hand, then withdrew it instantly and gave me a bearish hug and told me how thrilled she was that I was able to come. Mary's Dad stood at the door for a minute and then proceeded down the walk. He was a big hulk of a man, standing at least six foot and had an air of authority about him that was immediately noticeable. He kissed Mary on the cheek and then turned his attention to me. "Good evening, Sir, I am Henry Jimson." "So you are, son, and I want you to know that you are welcome in the Blyth home for Christmas. Have you any experience in stringing Christmas lights." "Yes, Sir." "Good, I have a job for you then," he exclaimed. I later found out that the lights were his chore each year and he jumped at the chance for help.

Their home was alive with seasonal decorations. I could tell by the feel of it that love dwelled here. The warm, peaceful feel of the place permeated the air. After placing my belongings in the guest bedroom we went into the kitchen and sat around the table, drank hot apple cider and visited for about an hour. They wanted to hear about school and the exams.

Then the subject turned to me. Mr. Blyth asked me about my family and I shared my life with them. "You must miss your parents and are anxious to see them," Mrs. Blyth said. "Yes, Mam, and I will enjoy celebrating Christmas with you as well," I replied. It was almost two o'clock when Mr. Blyth noted the time. "I think we should call it a night. We've plenty of time to talk more." He glanced at me as he said that and I nodded in agreement. We settled in for the night. No one mentioned the war.

I awoke to the smell of coffee and muffled conversation the next morning. Mary knocked on my door. "Henry, are you awake? The bathroom is empty and I've laid out a towel and washcloth for you." "Thank you. I think I'll get cleaned up."

The living room had a fireplace and it had warmed the room nicely. As I entered everyone was seated and drinking coffee. "Would you like a cup of coffee?" Mrs. Blyth inquired. "Yes, Mam," and I sat down and looked around the room. It was full of beautiful antiques. The sun was shining through the paned windows and cast streams of light across the floor. "What a wonderful house you have." "Thank you Henry. After breakfast I'll show you the rest of it and take you and Mary into town," Mr. Blyth replied. "After you finish the tree first," Mrs. Blyth said. He laughed and agreed, saying how good it would be to have some help for a change. After breakfast we did string the lights and then sat back and watched the ladies decorate. The tree was about seven feet tall, native pine and very full. They placed an angel on top, which I was told was an antique handed down through three generations. The tree lights were turned on and we just sat there in silence taking in the beauty of it. "This is going to be a Blessed Christmas Mother," Mr. Blyth said as he reached for her hand. "I know."

Ocean Springs was very interesting and not quite like any town I had ever seen. The streets were narrow, with enormous live oak trees lining many of them. Spanish moss hung from the trees in abundance, looking like gray beards gently swaying in the breeze. The area was surrounded on three sides by water. On its southern perimeter was a bay, separated from the Gulf of Mexico by barrier islands. The back bay of Biloxi bordered its western perimeter and the Northern portion of the town fronted along Fort Bayou. The area was very old, dating back to French and Spanish exploration and habitation. The principle industry was fishing, crabbing and shrimping. Small shops lined the downtown area. There was a bridge that crossed the bay to Biloxi. I noticed the smells of the plants, processing seafood there. Along the shoreline were wharfs lined with skiffs, sailboats, and commercial fishing boats with outriggers drying nets in the morning sun. There were seafood stores selling the days catch and much activity along the waterfront. We went into a stucco building right on the water, where oysters were being sold. Boats were off-loading large burlap sacks full of oysters when we arrived. Inside were five men on stools shucking oysters with oyster knives. There were mounds of oysters in shells on each mans left side and a bucket half full of water on their right. Some of the men wore heavy cotton gloves. They would reach for an oyster, place it on what appeared to be a lead tool used to retain the shell, run the two-edged knife blade into the rear of the shell, perform a back and forth slicing movement, pop the top portion of the shell off and into a pile of empty shells in front of them against the wall, run the knife under the body of the oyster to separate it from the shell where it was attached, throw the oyster into the bucket and the remaining shell into the pile and then reach for another. This procedure was performed at lightning speed. There was absolutely no wasted motion as they went about their work, shucking an oyster every ten to fifteen seconds, I guessed. Occasionally, a shucked oyster would go into a mouth instead of the bucket. As I stood there one of the men thrust an open shell at me and asked if I'd like to try it. Everyone stopped in unison and all eyes, including Mr. Blyths' were on me. This was obviously a test. "Sure I said as I took the shell and looked at the gray, slimy, live creature it contained." I took one anxious look around, closed my eyes and lifted the shell to my mouth, tilted it and the thing slide inside. Now what was I going to do. My mouth was full of this slimy, watery creature and I couldn't spit it out. So, without biting, I swallowed it. All the shuckers were grinning at me. My tormentor held out another that he had opened while I was suffering the first and said, " Have another." "Thanks," as I took it in and bit it this time. Much to my delight I liked the taste. "Where you from boy?" "Georgia," I responded. "Your ok in my book boy," he said as he returned to his work, laughing and talking about me with the other men. Mr. Blyth bought a quart mason jar of oysters, which he said was for one of his wife's specialties; oyster dressing for stuffing the turkey.

Christmas morning I awoke to the smell of baking. The kitchen was the focal point of activity, the women busy with preparing the food and the men coming in from time to time to taste test it all. Mr. Blyth carved the bird and laid out the dark and white meat in neat rows on separate platters. An elderly couple from next door was invited to the meal. Glasses of sherry were distributed to all and I had my first taste of alcohol. It nearly took the top of my head off as I gasped for air. "Not used to drinking I see," Mr. Blyth commented. He seemed very pleased. That may have been the most sumptuous meal I had ever sat down to and I said so. The rest of the day passed quickly. Presents were presented to all, opened and admired, with an occasional comment about how it was what the recipient had always wanted. The family had given me a very nice, wonderfully crafted and scrolled pocketknife. I had purchased some perfume for Mary and had secretly made a trip to a local florist for flowers that I had ordered the day before and hidden that night in my room. They were placed in a vase as a centerpiece for the table. I was made to feel so at home there that by the time I left I felt like a part of their family. Mary and I took a walk together later that afternoon, leaving her parents in the living room, napping. At about dusk Mrs. Blyth gave Mr. Blyth a cardboard box, brim full of food left over from the Christmas meal. He motioned for me to follow and without a word; we got into the car and drove to another section of town. The old house was of wood siding construction and in need of paint. The yard had no grass in it. As we walked to the front door several children peered through the torn, screen door. "Mamma, somebody here!" A middle-aged woman appeared and opened the door exclaiming, "Mr. Blyth, what ya'll doing here?" "The wife and I thought you would like some Christmas food. We had so much we couldn't eat it all. I hope you can use it. It would be a shame to throw it all away." As he handed her the box of food I noticed that he also placed an envelope in her hand. "Praise the Lord Mr. Blyth, you and Mrs. Blyth are angels come to us." She took the box and smelled deeply and said, "This sure is kind of you, Sir. God Bless you and yours." "Merry Christmas to you, and also to this young man with you." From inside a reply came from the mouths of several small children. "Thank you."

On the way back I told Mr. Blyth how kind it was to help people in obvious need. He said they had been helping the family for several years. Her husband had died in a boating tragedy. He had been caught in a violent storm that had come up suddenly out of the North. Before he could reach shore the boat sunk. The boaters searched all the next day before giving up. His body washed ashore two days later. The local people were deeply affected by the loss. Everyone knew the family and responded with an outpouring of love and assistance. The deceased husband left a wife and six children. She was uneducated and supported her family by doing washing and ironing in the community.

Mr. Blyth pulled over on the street next to the house. "Henry, how do you feel about Mary?" I wondered when we would have this talk. I was very nervous about saying the right thing. I felt that he and his wife liked me and I so wanted to be accepted. "Mr. Blyth, I love her with all my heart." "She feels the same way about you Henry." "You are both very young you know," as he looked intently at me. "I know that, Sir, but I've had a lot of time to think about the future. Mary fulfills me and makes me feel so special. I can't imagine my life without her in it." I paused and then continued, "I want you to know that when the time is right, I will ask you for her hand in marriage and I hope you will say yes." He smiled and looked away. We both sat silent for several minutes. My heart was pounding in my chest and I think he could almost hear it. "Are you going to enlist?" It had surprised me that, until now, there had been no mention of the war; a subject of nearly every conversation before arriving at the Blyths' home. "I have to go home and talk it over with my parents first. I also have a friend that I trust who will give me advice." "I want you to know that we here will support you in whatever decision you make. Mary is our only daughter and we will look after her until this is all over. If you need anything from us all you need do is ask." "Thank you, Sir." He pulled into the driveway and we went inside. Mary looked at me and instantly knew that we had talked. "What have you two been up to?" she quizzed. "Oh nothing," I responded and gave her a wink and a knowing smile.

We spent the next few days together until it was time to leave. Thursday, Mary drove me to the train station where I got a ticket to go home. We sat on the wooden bench and looked out the window at the tracks. Seagulls were on the boarding ramp scavenging for scraps and fighting for territory.

A worker was pulling a cart loaded with luggage and packages for the train. We sat there holding hands, not knowing what to say. "Write me, Henry." "You know I will." "Let me know the minute you decide what you are going to do." "I will. I love you." I kissed her.

The train was running about ten minutes late, but it seemed to arrive too soon for us. I got my ticket out and walked to the train with Mary holding on to my arm tightly. "Be careful now, get some sleep if you can, and eat in the diner tonight. Here are some snacks Mom fixed for you," as she handed me a paper bag. "All aboard." There were men in uniform boarding and several civilians as well. Mary held me even tighter and her eyes welled up. "I love you." The train began to slowly pull away from the station with Mary waving on the boarding platform and me doing the same from the train. Great billows of smoke rose from the engine and the clanking of the wheels against the rails announced my leaving. Mary stood there alone on the walkway. I felt as if I might die at that moment. Leaving her was so hard.

Dad was waiting at the station when I arrived. He saw me as I left the train and got out of the pickup to meet me. He had brought the dogs and they began baying as if on a trail when they saw me. Their tails wagged so hard that even their bodies were wagging along in rhythm. "Welcome home, Son, you are a sight for sore eyes. You have put on a little weight haven't you?" He grabbed me in his burly arms and almost crushed me. "Hey Dad, easy I might break!" He gave me a punch in the arm and took my luggage as we walked to the truck. "How was your trip?" "Fine, we made good time. It beats riding on a bus all to pieces. I was even able to sleep on the seat and woke up this morning not knowing where I was." He laughed as he threw the suitcase in the back of the truck and then admonished the dogs to get away from it. He said the dogs had been restless all day. "I believe somehow they knew you were coming, Henry. They were both by the truck when I walked out to leave the house." As we rode along to my home I couldn't help but notice how little had changed in Mark Hill. As we rounded the courthouse I saw the old men sitting on the benches, talking about Pearl Harbor no doubt. "Dad, what is the talk on the street about the war?" "We will talk about that later," he replied. "How did your finals go?" "I think I passed everything but I won't know for sure for a couple of weeks. They should send a copy of my semester grades here." We pulled into the driveway and drove to the house.

Mother came down the porch steps on a dead run and grabbed me as I got out of the truck. "Henry!" She held me tightly, stroking the back of my head furiously and kissing me constantly on both cheeks. She held me for several minutes and then pulled back and chastised me for not writing often enough. "Get down you worthless dogs. Come in the house. We have your bedroom ready and supper is almost ready." The first thing I noticed when I stepped into the living room was the Christmas tree. Usually it comes down the day after Christmas in spite of Dad's protests. Mom would say that it makes such a mess and it is coming down. Dad would reluctantly remove it out back and burn it in what always seemed a sacrificial manner. "The tree is really pretty, Mom. I missed not helping with the decorations this year." It was the first Christmas I had ever spent away from home. She had left the tree up just for me and we celebrated that night with presents and another full banquet. I slept soundly that night in my bed. There is no substitute for ones own bed and pillow. As usual, at about six o'clock the next morning, Dad stuck his head in the door and advised strongly that I should be getting up. I did as I was told, and quickly.

It was Saturday and Dad did not have to go in to work, so we spent most of the morning at the breakfast table visiting and catching up on college. When the subject turned to Mary and I started telling them about her, they both leaned forward and hung on my every word. I suppose I talked about her and our plans for at least twenty minutes, non-stop. When I finally finished Mom looked at Dad and remarked, "I think our Son is in love, Father." "Seems that way," he replied.

Then the conversation turned to the war and Mom excused herself, saying that she had some ironing to do. I learned that she would not discuss the war and it upset her terribly when others did in her presence. "Henry, you know Mr. Spencer at the draft board. I saw him in town last week and he asked about you. He wanted to know how school was going and whether or not we had talked about your plans. He said you might consider applying for a deferment if you wanted to stay in school. He said that it depended on whether your course of study was defense related and he couldn't make any promises but it is something to consider." I had not even thought about a deferment. "I think I would like to finish my freshman year and then volunteer rather than be drafted. I believe I'd like to join the Army and request duty as an Army medic. I like the idea of helping people more than I like the idea of killing them." "You know Henry that in combat as a medic you will see a lot of killing and may even have to kill to survive. But that is a decision that only you can make. Pray about it please Son." "I have been and will keep on until I know, Dad." "Have you stayed in touch with Old Man?" "Yes, Sir, we've written each other several times." "You need to talk to him about it also. I think he may have some experience in war matters. I don't know if he has, but he could have served. Have you ever talked with him about that?" "No, Sir, he will not discuss his past with anyone. Even the people at the home out there have tried, but can't find out anything about him. I've often wondered what he is hiding. Perhaps he was in trouble at one time or ran away from some thing in his past. He just showed up and no one even knows his name." "Well it won't hurt to ask will it?"

The next day was Sunday and we all went to church. Everyone was so glad to see me. It was good to be back in familiar surroundings and to see friends again that I grew up with. I asked about some of the guys that had graduated with me. They were usually in church, but noticeably absent today. Some were still away at school, while a few had left Mark Hill to find work. Many had already enlisted or had been drafted.

Reverend Hill had not changed a bit. His sermon ran long as usual and people fidgeted in their seats in protest. Some of the men would hold their arms high in the air and pull a sleeve back to expose a wristwatch, and then point at it as their wives punched them in the ribs. This had absolutely no effect on the preacher as he continued on and on. After the service several of my classmates and I remained to catch up on what we had been doing. When I told them I had met a girl, they were all astonished. Bobbie Jean, a classmate of mine quipped, "Henry Jimson, I had a crush on you all through high school and you never paid the least bit of attention to me, or to any girl for that matter." I pretended not to hear her and quickly changed the subject. "Are you going to join up, Henry?" one of the boys asked. "Yes I am, but I am not sure when yet." My friend said he was joining next month and couldn't wait to get in combat. I thought to myself that he might not feel so strongly about going into combat when it actually happened. Personally I was very fearful at the prospect, while at the same time, feeling duty bound to do something for my country We all wished each other well and went our own ways. Later that afternoon I went to visit with Old Man.

I stopped to talk to the attendant on the front desk. She advised me that the old man was doing fine, just lonely. She said he had been doing a lot of reading lately and that they had put a radio in his room because he wanted one to keep up with the news. "I just don't see why he cares about the war. He don't have to worry about doing no fighting at his age, does he?" she asked in an incredulous tone. I looked in his room and he wasn't there. I then went to the library and there he was, near a window, for more light apparently, deeply engrossed in a newspaper article as I approached. I had never noticed that he read without glasses. "Do you find anything of interest in that paper, Old Man?" He did not look up or even acknowledge my presence. He continued to read. I sat on a nearby couch and waited patiently. I was sure he heard me. After several minutes he raised his head and looked in my direction. It was as if I had only been away a day or two. "Henry, do you want to get in this thing. Our enemy Japan is to our West and Germany to our East. Italy is no big threat because I don't believe they have the stomach for it. But Adolf Hitler would have us all dead right now. What do you think?" He got out of his chair, laid the paper down on a nearby table and began walking toward the door. I followed him back to his room without comment.

As was his usual manner, he pulled his chair up near to the one I always sat in, took his seat while motioning for me to do the same. As I dropped into the seat he drew near and fixed those eyes upon me and repeated, "What do you think Henry?" Everything in the room was exactly the same as I remembered it, except for the radio. Old Man was the same as he was when I had left for school. The conversations now were being continued as though there had only been a short interlude. "I think that you look great to me and I am so glad to see you again, Old Man." He nodded as if in agreement. "I want you to come to visit me at least twice a week until you decide what you are going to do," he responded. He knew. How could he know me so well I wondered, as we continued to look in each other's eyes? He leaned back and smiled. "It is not an easy decision is it, Henry? Important ones that could change the outcome of your very life never are." After a brief pause, I said, "I want to enlist rather than be drafted. I want to be an Army medic and save lives rather than take them. I want to finish my freshman year but don't think I'll be able. I want to serve my country. I want retribution for the awful thing that Japan has done to us. I fervently wish for a quick resolution to this global conflict and a return to peace. I want to live my life with Mary in the certain knowledge that I can do so free from the fear of tyranny. I don't want to die, but I will do so if necessary to help protect our country. I trust President Roosevelt and believe that God is with him and that our cause is a just one. That is what I think for now." "But Henry, what about Mary?" "We've decided to get married, but not now. I feel it would be unfair of me to marry her and then go to war. That would be selfish and insensitive to her needs." "Do I hear your head thoughts now to the exclusion of your feelings, Henry?" "A little of both," I responded. "Henry, I am so glad to see you and to have our little talks. Go home now and think some more about these things. I'll be seeing you Wednesday, right?" "Yes, Sir," and with that I left him standing and looking out his window.

I gave the future considerable thought over the next few days. I also prayed to God for guidance. I called Mary and we talked at length about our lives together when this was over. My parents both encouraged me to do what I felt was right. Mother had very little else to say except that she couldn't stand to think of me going overseas into a situation where I might be harmed. Old Man was supportive but he insisted that in the end only I could know what I must do. On my last visit with him he shocked me with an observation. "Henry, medics are often the unsung heroes in combat. In the heat of battle they answer a call that defies logic. Much like a doctor is bound by his oath to preserve life so it is with the medic. You may be called upon to do the impossible, that is, to abandon your strongest instinct to survive and sacrifice your life to save another. That life may be a comrade or an enemy. War is an insanity fought by desperate men in a surreal setting. Men use it to impose their wills on their fellow men, calling them enemy to justify it all. There is almost always, in the final analysis, right versus wrong at play, but those lines become blurred by the horror of it all." "How do you know so much about war, Old Man?"

He looked away and out the window. His appearance seemed to change in an instant, suddenly becoming agitated. He jumped from his chair and began to pace from wall to wall and back again. He glanced nervously at the doorway, walked over to it, looked out into the hall and then shut the door. He walked to his dresser and started to open a drawer but stopped and looked up into the mirror. He then shook his head as if disagreeing with himself. His shoulders dropped as he stared at himself in the mirror. Finally he spoke to me again. "Remember to surround yourself with the quiet ones, the ones who will stand to the front, side and back of you when it gets rough. They will stand firm. They may save your life Henry." He shouted the last sentence at me and then reclined on his bed with his arm covering his eyes. "I am very tired Henry." I left him there as the sun was setting in the West and the room was growing dark. "Will you be all right? Do you need anything?" He did not respond and so I bid him goodbye and left. I am afraid that I opened a dark, foreboding memory within him. We saw each other several more times, but spoke of war no more.

Time to return to school was near and so I said my goodbyes to everyone, including a quality visit with Old Man. He told me how proud of me he was and encouraged me to remember all the things we had talked about over the past couple of weeks. His countenance was once again upbeat and positive and I was relieved. He told me a strange thing when we last parted. "Henry, if anything happens to me talk to the administrator. I will give him some instructions concerning my possessions and he will know what to do. Don't forget it whatever you do. It is very important to me." I told him I would not forget. When I got home I told Mother about what he said and asked her to notify me if anything happened to him.

It was very hard to leave all my memories of this short time in Mark Hill and go back to school. The day before I left the semester report came in the mail. I had made straight A's in all subjects, much to my delight. Dad was beaming but admonished me to continue to study hard and not become distracted. I knew what he meant by that. Once again the bus pulled away from the station and I was on my way.

Mary was waiting for me as I stepped off the bus. I grabbed her up in my arms and twirled her around in circles until we both were dizzy. We embraced and kissed, oblivious to the people all around us, staring. Some were smiling. We walked all the way back to campus, talking and laughing about our home visits and the joy of being with our families. Second semester was a blur. The time melted away with class work, tests, friends, Mary and my growing love and interdependence on her. We became much closer over the next few months and loved to be together.

Johnny had also decided to finish out the year before enlisting and so we continued to room together. One evening he asked me if I'd like to go to a dance his fraternity was having and bring Mary. She later told me that it would be fun and so I agreed. "Henry, would you like me to get you some whiskey for the party?" "No, thank you!" I told him about my encounter at Mary's house with the sherry. He found that very amusing and kidded me about being so sheltered and naïve. "Well, will you ride with me to get mine?" he asked. "Where can you get alcohol Johnny? I thought this whole area was bone dry." "My buddy is lending me his car and I'll get him some too. After dark we will take a ride." I was at first hesitant to agree to such an obviously risky venture, but curiosity got the better of me. Johnny was very secretive about the whole business. After nightfall, at about eleven o'clock I found myself in the car with Johnny about forty-five minutes away from the campus on a dark, narrow two-lane dirt road. He slowed in the middle of a curve and turned off the road onto what was little more than a wooded trail and continued to drive. Several hundred yards deep into the woods we came to a clearing and stopped. Johnny turned his lights off and then on and re-peated the process again. Then he drove to the far edge of the clearing and got out of the car. I looked around trying to see but it was dark and very still. Nothing and no one was in sight of the headlights. In the meantime Johnny had walked over to a large stump, placed money on it and secured it with a rock he found next to the stump. He walked back quietly and got into the car, turned around and we left by the same route. "What in the world is go-ing on?" I asked. I was totally perplexed by it all. "Well Henry, you have just witnessed what very few people on campus know about." I could see that he was very pleased with himself and was enjoying watching me trying to figure it out. "What time do you have Henry?" "It is fifteen minutes until twelve midnight, why?" "At twelve fifteen we will go back." That is all he would tell me. At the stated time we pulled back across the clearing to the stump. I could see something on top but couldn't make out what it was in the dark-ness. Once again Johnny got out of the car, walked quickly to the stump and picked up what appeared to be two objects and was back in the car and pull-ing away in a flash. He deposited two quart jars on the seat between us. I picked one up to inspect it. I could now see two clear mason jars, each con-taining an equally clear liquid. "What is this Johnny? Where did they come from?" "Compliments of old John," he acknowledged with a big grin and a laugh. "You have in your hand the best white lightning made by man." I had heard of this stuff made by moon shiners at home, but had never seen it before. My next question was probably the most foolish I had ever asked. "What does it taste like?" "Well sir, you just unscrew that lid and take you a little snort," he replied. That sounded like a dare and so I did just that. I opened the jar and tilted it, lips on the rim and took in what I estimated later to be no more than a double spoonful. Simultaneous with that act Johnny hit the brakes and pulled over to the side of the road and watched me intently. I had white lightning in my mouth. Never, ever, had I experienced such a rush. First the smell, comparable to a mixture of turpentine and gasoline invaded my nostrils. Next, followed an instant, intense heat starting at the tip of my head and rapidly flowing into my mouth. Simultaneously my eyes teared up, as if some object had dropped on me with extreme force, crushing me. My ears developed a ringing and my forehead broke into beads of sweat. I felt sheer panic, sitting there in a rigid state, the branding iron heat scorching my mouth and gums. My teeth began to ache. I could feel my face turning crimson red. Only mere seconds had passed when I heard Johnny exclaim, "Swallow it!" Then through the fog of pain, I realized that I had not swallowed it. I did so involuntarily without thinking. First the throat and then the chest was seared as white lightning flowed down into my stomach. Immediate rebellion occurred. I rose up off the seat, my hands lifting me up in a vain attempt to escape the torrent of pain within me. My mouth flew open and I screamed, but no sound issued forth, only a squeak and a gasp. Oddly enough, my next sensation was intense warmth like a down comforter feels when one settles into a cold bed on a winter night. Slowly the warmth overtook me, beginning at my feet and moving upwards through my body. The tension began to ease and I suddenly felt relief and strangely enough, a sense of well being. The next swallow went down smoothly, my insides having become numbed by the first, I suppose. "Ain't that fine stuff, Henry?" I closed my eyes as Johnny put the car in gear and pulled away from the side of the road. "Henry, that's fine sippin' whisky, don't you think?" It was several minutes before I regained my composure in order to respond. "That was unusually fine, Johnny. I think I'll go straight to bed when we get back." I suddenly felt as though I was in a revolving room and couldn't distinguish up or down. "I've heard that white lightning will strip paint off of things."

I felt really bad the next morning and my mouth was dry as cotton. The top of my head pounded and light was very painful. I told Mary about our adventure and my first experience with white lightning. She was not amused. "How do you feel now, Henry?" "Awful, my stomach is all upset," I responded sheepishly. "Good," she stated curtly. That was my last experience with alcoholic drinks of any kind.

The fraternity party was that night. I borrowed a tie from Johnny and dressed in my best long sleeve shirt and pants. I polished my shoes and then spent an inordinate amount of time in the bathroom shaving and combing and brushing, trying to look as proper as I possibly could. Johnny told me that the party would be very informal but the tie was a good touch. There would be a band playing and there would be plenty of drinking and fun. "There will be no alcohol for me Johnny. I've learned my lesson!"

I arrived at Mary's dorm at exactly seven o'clock to pick her up. I sat in a chair in the hall to wait after announcing my arrival to the floor monitor. "Nice tie, Henry," she observed. "Thanks," I replied nervously. Ten or fifteen minutes past and I began to wonder if she knew I was here. Finally she appeared. I watched her slowly walking down the stairs from the second floor. Several of her friends were standing on the landing above to see my reaction. She was stunningly beautiful. Her hair shimmered in the light and touched her shoulders, pushed to one side so that you could see the side of her face. She had a gold necklace pulled close to her neck and matching gold earrings. The black satin dress was cut straight, knee length and accented her every move. She smiled at me as she flowed down the last few steps, walked slowly to me and curtsied in front of me with her hand extended outward. I took her hand and bowed and kissed her hand at the same time. The girls on the upper landing all applauded and cheered as if we were royalty. "Mary Blyth, you are gorgeous!" "And you, sir, are very handsome," she responded.

As we walked to the front door of the fraternity house we could hear the music coming from inside. I loved music, especially the big bands. I knew a lot of the songs that were regularly played on the radio. The band sounded really good. There was a boy at the door who welcomed us and told us where we could check our coats. We thanked him and stepped inside. Johnny spotted us right away and came out of the adjoining room where people were dancing to greet us in the hallway. "Mary and Henry, I am so glad that you could come. This band is first class. There is a piano, sax, clarinet and drums. They are a local group who travel around the area to perform. They really swing!"

"How many people came tonight Johnny?" "Oh I guess there are thirty or more right now; more will come as the night goes on and some will leave. You know how that is. There would be more here but fifteen of the brothers have left school to sign up," he said. He sounded upset about them leaving but quickly continued. "Now the restrooms are down the hall and you can put your coats over there," pointing to a doorway. "Come on in and you can sit with me." He led us into the dance area that was lined around three sides with tables and chairs. The room was darkened because all the lights had been replaced with red bulbs. Smoke hung in the air and the room was very warm even though windows were opened for ventilation. The room was very noisy and we had to talk loudly to be heard. I leaned over to Johnny and asked if there were refreshments. He grinned and stated, "I have a quart jar out back." Mary looked up and scowled at me. "Absolutely not. After that experience that I won't soon forget, I've learned my lesson. How about soft drinks?" Mary said she would like anything cold and I followed Johnny, weaving through the dancers, to a table with cold drinks, glasses and ice buckets on it. I returned with two glasses of soda and sat down to listen to the band. "They are really good, Henry. What is that they are playing?" "I believe that is 'In The Mood'." "Yes, that's it," she replied. I noted several other couples sitting at tables with drinks in front of them. There was much laughter in the room that rivaled the band sounds. Everyone seemed to be having a great time. Some of the fellows were very boisterous and I think they were a little tipsy. In one corner near the band platform were a group of girls, standing in a tight circle with a drink in one hand and a cigarette in the other, all talking at the same time. When the band finished the piece everyone applauded. The piano player seemed to be the leader for he stood and acknowledged the crowd and then pointed to the edge of the bandstand to a lone female sitting there. She rose and walked to the front where a stand microphone was positioned. She looked at the piano player and nodded with a smile and he began to play an introduction. She turned back to inquire, "Who knows this one?" and began to sing 'More Than You Know '." She had a throaty, low ranging voice and could really sing. Several of the couples stopped dancing to listen to her. Mary leaned over to me. "I love that song, let's dance." "Mary I am embarrassed to say that I don't know how." She stood and took my arm and tugged and said, "I'll give you a quick lesson." We walked over to a corner of the room; I took my right arm and placed it on her waist. Then she took my left hand and held it out slightly and told me to take a step back, slide to my right side, step forward and then slide to the left, and then repeat. I am not a stupid person and can follow instructions with relative ease. But it seemed that my feet were totally out of touch with my brain. As I stood there stiff and erect my feet refused to move in the direction indicated. "Now Henry, the first thing you must do is relax. You are holding me, and not a sack of potatoes. Don't look at your feet. They won't abandon you. Look into my eyes instead. Now stand still and listen to the music." I did as she instructed and soon all I had in my head was the music and Mary. "Now, I am going to step forward with my right foot and you step back with your left." I almost fell over in the attempt. "Hold me loose Henry and step back, sideways, front, sideways." After several goose step attempts I began to feel the flow of it. Before long I was actually moving in time with the music. "Excellent Henry, now hold me close and close your eyes." She followed me effortlessly and we were soon gliding across the floor. She rested her head on my shoulder and pushed her cheek gently against mine. "How do you like dancing?" she whispered softly. "I love it." The song was over and I stood back to look at her. "Let's do that again." She smiled and held my hand tightly as we waited for the next song. We continued to dance until the band stopped for a break. I did not want to leave the floor. Holding Mary and moving to the music with her made time stand still for me. "Perhaps heaven will be like this, Mary." I leaned over and whispered in her ear. "I love you more tonight than I ever have before." I felt at one with her as we stood there on the floor looking into each other's eyes and holding each other's hands. "Hey, the band quit." It was Johnny reminding us where we were and bringing us back to the present. We were the only couple on the dance floor. It was the best night of my life and we had each other. It seemed that no one else was in the room as we held each other close that night and moved in unison together, so much in love with one another.

The next day Mary and I met for lunch at the cafeteria. I asked her how school was going. "Good, I guess. I haven't been studying like I should. How about you?" she asked. "I am having the same problem. I have a suggestion. I want us to spend as much time together as we can between now and when school is out. Perhaps we could study together. What do you think?" She thought it was a good idea and so we began studying at the library three nights a week. I got back into good study habits and got to see Mary often. My grades continued to hold up and all my tests were being passed without any trouble. It was important to me to finish the year with top grades, so that when I came back to school, I could pick up where I left off without falling behind.

I met with my counselor about leaving school. He told me that because of the war, exceptions were going to be made for students. If I left, through enlistment or by being drafted, then I could be re-admitted into the same program of study without loss of credits. He also told me that my scholarship could be placed on hold and preserved, pending my return to the college. I knew that others in the same position would be as relieved as I was.

I called my parents with the good news and told Dad that, depending on the timing, I may want to work in Mark Hill during the summer and spend as much time with them as possible. I wanted very much to do the same with Old Man. Dad said he would look around for work and let me know. I wanted to bring Mary to Mark Hill to meet everyone and to spend some time together at my home. She thought that a wonderful idea and upon asking her parents, they wholeheartedly agreed. With all that settled, time passed quickly. Before it seemed possible we were taking our end of school year exams and preparing to leave campus for the summer.

CHAPTER FIVE

I saw the truck as I stepped off the bus. Dad was leaning against the fender shading his eyes from the noonday sun with one hand and waving with the other. He quickly came over and grabbed me up in a big bear hug, sat me back down and bent over to get my bags. "Good to see you, Son. How was the trip?" "It was long and hot. I had a three-hour layover before changing buses. I met a couple of boys who were on their way to an induction center and we talked about the war a lot," I replied. "I found you a job at the mill. You know how hard ginning is on all the machinery so we can use you as a helper with our mechanics. The cotton is in bloom now and will soon be bolling. We will start ginning and baling around late August and in the meantime you can work with maintenance on the machinery. That should keep you busy for awhile," he said with a laugh. Working in the mill was hot, dusty and noisy, but I was pleased to have the job and the little extra money that came with it. "I know that will be new to you, but Mr. Johnson will put you with Mose. He will supervise your work until you get the hang of it. You remember Johnson and Mose don't you?" "Yes, Sir, I do. Is Mr. Johnson still hard to work for?" "You bet he is, but you can learn a lot from the man. He's been around cotton all his life and can run the mill as good as anyone, including me." "When do I start?" "A week from tomorrow," Dad replied, as we pulled away from the depot to go home.

Mother was on the porch rocking in her chair as we came to a stop. The hounds were howling and running in circles, greeting their long lost friend as he returned. As I got out of the truck they jumped me and felled me to the ground. They were all tongues, licking me about the face and continuously jumping over me, back and forth with tails wagging. Mom and Dad were laughing all the while. "I do declare Henry, I believe they missed you as much as we have," Mom said with a laugh. She stood up with arms open to receive me and we held each other for a minute or two. There is nothing so comforting as a loving hug from Mother. "Now go get cleaned up. Supper is almost ready." We all walked into the house together and I went back to my room, deposited my things on the bed and then did as I was told. I was home and it felt so good.

After supper we sat on the porch. Daylight faded into darkness and the night sounds were very noticeable. Frogs in the pond out back were tuning up for their evening performance. Crickets were chirping and the breeze rustled the leaves. It was like nature's symphony. These were sounds that I really missed and which one could not hear with the constant activity on campus. We talked of school for a while and then the conversation turned to Mary. "Henry, Mary's parents called yesterday to let us know that they were going to visit relatives in North Carolina. Mrs. Blyth acknowledged your plans to have Mary come visit here. We discussed it at length and decided it would be fine so long as it was no imposition on us." "That's great Mother," I replied. "Did she say when?" "I told her that you would call to make plans, but they want to make the trip next month and agreed to spend the night with us before going on. She was a very pleasant person and we got along wonderfully. They seem to be very nice people, Henry." "They both were so good to me during Christmas and I felt like one of their family when I left. Will we have room for them?" I asked, thinking that the house was small compared to what they were used to. "I'll fix up your Grandfathers room and we will get an extra bed in there for Mary for the one night and then she can stay in his room for the rest of her stay with us," she said with excitement in her voice. I could hardly wait for them to arrive. I knew our families would really enjoy each other and Mary would be taken in as one of our own.

The conversation turned to the war with Dad asking if I had made a firm decision to enlist. "I think I'll go down to the draft board tomorrow and talk with Mr. Spencer about signing up and the timing of it." Dad thought that was a good idea. Mother did not say a word. "I want to talk some more with Mary and with Old Man before I make a firm decision, but I'm leaning toward the end of the summer," I said. Mother got up from her rocker. "I'm tired and think I'll go to bed." Dad and I followed her in. I slept soundly that night.

Mr. Spencer was next door at the drug store having coffee with a gathering of business people getting ready for the day, so I went over and had a seat at his table. Coffee and donuts before store openings was a regular event in Mark Hill. Usually the same men would gather at a table and the conversation would always run to current events and town gossip. The discussion as I took my seat was centered on the coming cotton harvest. "Well it is the best crop I've seen in years. All my neighbors will also have bumper harvests if the weather doesn't do us in." "That's what I think too. Henry, has your Dad got the gin ready for us? We need a good Christmas you know." "I hear that the government is going to buy all the country can produce, what with the war and everything." "I just hope we can get in the fields before the rains come. I hear there may be some bad weather coming. All the signs point to it you know, humidity being what it is, and the winds being out of the South and regular." "Wouldn't surprise me if we got a hurricane this year." And so the conversation droned on with each man expressing his own opinion and, for the most part, all being in general agreement. Except for old Mr. Thomas that is. Mr. Thomas never ever agreed with anyone. If you took black he would immediately take white and vice versa. Most times the group would just let him go with his contrary views but once in a while when he came from way out in left field with some cockeyed theory or opinion a free-for-all generally commenced. Such a heated argument arose over whether we should be in Europe. Just as one of the gentlemen jumped to his feet the waitress came up and said "Now boys, you know that at your age you could just stroke out and fall dead and then we would have to haul you out the door and call the undertaker so settle down and I'll bring you a free cup." Calm was instantly restored. "Well thank you darling. I take mine black," was Mr. Thomas' reply. Everyone got a big laugh out of that.

The waitress was one of my classmates and gave me a big hug. We were good friends and I was glad to see her again. "Henry, I didn't see you come in. It sure is good to have you home. You look great. What are you going to do this summer?" she asked. "Well that depends on what Mr. Spencer here tells me, Sarah." She laughed and said that I might not like what he says. "How is school going, Henry?" "Fine Mr. Spencer. In fact, that is part of what I'd like to talk to you about if you have the time," I answered. "Let's finish our coffee and we will go back to the office and you can catch me up on everything."

We finished, said our goodbyes to the men at the table, and went to the office to discuss my future. As you entered the office the size jumped out at you. It was about twelve feet wide and twenty feet long, had a wooden rail across the room within six feet of the door with a swing gate to enter an area containing a desk, chairs and several file cabinets. Paperwork covered the top of the desk in a disorganized pile. Mr. Spencer worked the office alone. "Excuse the clutter, Henry. It has been pretty hectic here since Pearl."

"Have there been any drafts here yet," I asked. "Yes there have and so far the Board has acted on all of them. Are you going to wait for your draft notice?" "No, Sir, I intend to volunteer as an Army medic if possible. That is why I wanted to talk to you. How long do you think I have?" "Well Henry, you just don't know. I look for the numbers to increase as we get this war cranked up. I could give you about a week's notice before the next draft happens, which may be near the end of the summer. That is what my superiors in Atlanta are telling me right now." "I'd like to work at the mill this summer and earn some extra money to help out before I leave and cover my expenses until I join." Mr. Spencer leaned back in his chair and gazed at the ceiling for a few minutes. He had a worried look on his face as he rose to go to a file cabinet and pulled a document out. "Henry, we've lost three boys already, you know," glancing at the paper as he spoke. "This is the toughest thing I've ever had to do."

"I am going to call Atlanta and find out when and where you can enlist. I'll also find out the details for your induction. There is an induction center in Atlanta. You will have time to plan your enlistment and be ready if another draft is announced for this office." "Thank you, Sir. I'll be in touch. Call me if anything develops, will you?" "Henry, I've always thought the world of your family. Your Dad and Mom are salt of the earth people and they raised a fine Son. Good luck at the mill." "Thank you, Sir."

That night I called Mary to find out exactly when they would arrive and to give her directions to the house. They planned on coming through here around the second week in June. Her parents would come back through Mark Hill, stay a day or two and then return home in time for the Fourth of July holiday. "Henry, how are things going there? Have you talked to the draft board? What about work this summer? Have you seen Old Man yet? I can't wait to see you again. It seems like time is standing still."

I rode my old bicycle to the nursing home. It was early, about 6:00 am, and the morning was wet with the humidity of summer. The heat would be unbearable today. About five minutes into my ride I was sweating and puffing along, thinking how out of shape I was from just sitting in a class-room for nine months. Working at the mill would take care of that. A few trucks passed me and we exchanged waves. Most folks in the county know our family and are very friendly towards us.

As I pulled up to the front steps I wondered how Old Man was doing and pondered his age that his looks surely belied. One of the attendants saw me as I entered and spoke out loudly, "Mr. Henry, you home from that schooling, boy? You looking mighty fit." She laughed and her shoulders shook with real joy, which was obvious to me as I greeted her and asked about Old Man. "Lord Mr. Henry, he ain't changed a smidgen, except that he sure goes on about you all the time just like you was his own child. That old man loves you boy." "Yes, Mam" I replied as I moved down the hallway to his room.

There he was looking out the window with his back to the door, rocking slowly with tilted head, as if pondering something. I stood there for several minutes in silence and watched him as he slowly rocked back and forth. His head never moved and then suddenly he sensed my presence.

"I know you are there." "But do you know who is here?" "I got eyes in the back of my head you know". He rose from his thoughts and turned to me and continued, "but mostly I recognized your voice." He was smiling from ear to ear. "I think we will have a hurricane this summer. What do you think?" It was always this way with him. No matter how long we were apart it was if the next sentence from him was a continuation of our last, distant conversation. "You look well, Sir," I noted as I moved to my usual chair and he turned his to face me and sat. "They take good care of me here. Now, about the hurricane, what do you think?"

For the next several minutes we spoke of hurricanes. Now, I don't have a clue about whether a hurricane is coming or not, unless it is near the coast. Then you can see signs. A red morning sky with fitful, gusting winds foretells stormy conditions. Seagulls onshore are also telling. Sometimes a hurricane is useful to break a drought, but a direct hit can cause tremendous damage and even loss of life. I had rather not put up with them.

We had a bad one when I was little and I still remember it like it was yesterday. Dad and Grandpa had noticed the signs and gotten the cattle in and boarded the windows on the house. They went to town to gas up the truck and get provisions and we filled the tub with water from the well. They said we could be without electricity and stranded for days

The winds had been gusty all day and toward evening the trees were swaying violently and limbs were breaking off and crashing to the ground. About evening the sky got pitch black as the wind steadily increased in intensity and howled constantly. We had moved to the interior of our house and huddled together with only a coal oil lamp for light. It was eerie there in the yellow, flickering light of the lamp. I was scared and felt helpless as the storm continued to strengthen. When it is dark, of course you can't see what is happening outside in a hurricane, so your imagination takes hold. The howling, wailing wind seemed to take on life and sounded like some ferocious animal in the heat of a battle. About an hour into the storm the house began to shake and quiver. The walls were moving in and out several inches due to the violent winds and water was blowing into the rooms in sheets, coming in around the windowsills. I believed the roof would collapse and we would all likely die.

Mother was holding me so tight I had trouble breathing. In her attempt to comfort a crying, frightened child, she kept saying over and over again that it would be over soon. We heard a tremendous crash in the rear of the house, near the kitchen and my ears popped from the sudden change in air pressure. Dad said that tornadoes often accompanied these storms.

Then the wind suddenly quit and the quiet was noticeable to all of us. We cautiously ventured to the front of the house and saw that the front door was gone. Dad, Grandpa and I went onto the porch and we could see stars in the sky. Mother would have no part of going out. Dad speculated that we were in the eye of the storm. We couldn't see much in the dark, but there did not seem to be any trees where they should have been. The barn was still there. Debris littered the front porch and yard. I heard a whimpering sound and it was a dog under our porch. I coaxed him to come out but he would not budge. Grandpa noted that the worst was yet to come and he was right. In about thirty minutes the winds again gained strength and now were coming from the opposite direction. We had retreated to our room for safety and the storm once again began to rage outside.

By the time it ended we were all exhausted from the fear and anxiety and the stress of having experienced such a thing. Mother and I fell asleep, as the winds seemed to be subsiding. When I awoke it was daylight and the sun was shining. That was incredible to me. We went outside and I couldn't believe my eyes. Hugh oak trees were pushed over and limbs and debris made walking around almost impossible. The tin roof on the barn was gone. All the boards on the windows were still there but glass panes were somehow broken anyway. There was not a shingle left on the roof. The kitchen was entirely gone as if some giant had lifted it and carried it away.

We later sat on the front porch on the floor as there were no chairs left and we pondered what could have happened to us. Several days later I suddenly felt totally exhausted and used up. The whole family noticed it. It must have been a delayed reaction to the stress. We found the pot bellied stove down in the creek some 200 yards from the house. Kitchen utensils were strewn helter-skelter over the creek bank and also in it. The water in the creek was out of it banks and anywhere there was a low place there was standing water. The fences were all intact much to our surprise. I wondered about the birds and wild animals, and then I say birds flying overhead. How can that be in the midst of the chaos? Mosquitoes suddenly appeared in swarms and it was almost unbearable.

Except for the extensive damage, you would never have known there had been a hurricane in Mark Hill, Georgia. Later, after we fully recovered, we would spend time with neighbors recounting our experiences and agreeing that we never wanted another hurricane to hit us.

"Old Man, have you ever been in a hurricane?" "Yes, I was in the one you just related and also in one other," he replied. He sat there silently musing the events I suppose. In time I asked about the other. "Henry did you know that in the Atlantic Ocean hurricanes can cause waves in the proximity of one hundred feet high. Did you know that if a ship, say a freighter, were caught in such a storm, that it could be broken in half on the crest of such a wave or swamped in its trough?" He fixed me in his stare, rocking more vigorously now and frowning slightly as he continued. "On the open sea in a hurricane, there is no escape from the peril of it. Many men get violently ill and suffer from vertigo. Others try to go above decks to escape but there is no escape and some are washed overboard. I've seen men cry out to God for mercy. The ship actually groans under the strain. The will to survive is sorely tested in such times. Your lifetime of experiences flashes before you and you often lose hope in those desperate times. Others reach deep within themselves and bravely shut out the danger in order to survive on their wits alone. The prospect of imminent death is paralyzing for most, however."

We sat there together in silence. I could feel his experience within me. I noticed that my palms were wet and that I felt dizzy, as my mind digested his words. My old acquaintance fear gripped me, as if I too were in peril, sitting there in Old Man's room. "But that was another time and another place, and now I have you to confide in, Henry. But I've had enough of these memories. I hear you are going to work at the cotton gin?" "Yes Sir, I start next week and will be working in maintenance under Mr. Johnson. I'll probably stay on through the summer and then decide about enlistment, unless Mr. Spencer at the draft board tells me differently." He nodded as if in agreement. "I'd like to see you the next time with all ten of your fingers intact if that is agreeable with you." "Yes, Sir. I suppose I should go now. It is almost noon and I need to check in with the folks."

Mary called that night and we talked for an hour about events since I got home. She wanted to know exactly what Mr. Spencer had said, all the details of my visit with Old Man and what it would be like working at the mill. I related all that had happened and she soaked it in. I could hear the excitement in her voice as she said, "I can't wait to see your parents and Old Man. Will you please prepare them for me. They may think me very different or not good enough for their son." We both laughed out loud at the same time and expressed our love to each other before we hung up and went to bed.

CHAPTER SIX

During ginning season, which will probably begin in early August, the cotton gin works eighteen to twenty-four hours a day until the season is over. I went to work early Monday morning and looked forward to seeing old friends there I had grown up with and knew well.

Monday morning came early and it was still dark when I got up. Mother was already preparing breakfast for us. We arrived at the gin at 6:30 and Dad took me to meet up with Mr. Johnson. I suppose he was in his 70's, stood about 6 feet and had skin like shoe leather. He had been with the gin since the co-op was formed and was general foreman.

He was a man who did not waste much time in conversation. "Good morning, Mr. Johnson," as I reached out to shake his hand. "Morning boy. Got any tools? Suppose not. Go to the tool shed and check out whatever you need. You will be on diesels, motors and belts. Probably be putting a new impeller in a pump and some new gaskets today. You can help Mose. He's in the shack now. If you need me for something I'll be around. Watch yourself around the machines boy. Don't want the boss's son to get busted up on account of my not warning you." With that he walked away at a fast clip. No response was required from me. Just get to work.

Mose was a black man and the descendent of slaves. His kin were brought here from Africa and sold into slavery on the Charleston slave market. Mose was born here in Mark Hill and worked on a cotton plantation. He started when he was six years old picking cotton. There were six children in his family and he was the youngest. Life was hard in those days for blacks in the south. The plantation owner provided a clapboard three-room shack for them and fed them through a commissary. The pickers worked for meager wages that, for the most part, were always used up for food and a place to live. Mose started in the gin about the same time as Mr. Johnson. Mose was illiterate and unschooled but had a batch of common sense. It didn't take people long to realize that Mose was smart and a hard worker. He pretty much did every job in the plant over time and was now the one everyone came to when something tore up or went wrong. The man was a whiz with tools and understood machinery. If you worked with him you generally put in a full day.

I went to the shack and got a tool belt, some wrenches, screwdrivers, tape, hammer and then went looking for Mose. I found him on top of one of the diesel engines. It was running and he was lying on it with a steel rod on its surface and his ear pressed against the other end, listening intently. Directly he noticed me and shouted for me to turn the engine off. He climbed down and walked over to me. "Henry Jimson, boy you gonna work with ole Mose?" "Yes, Sir, I am." He studied me for a few seconds and asked, "What's wrong, Mr. Henry. Didn't you take to that book learning?" "Well Mose, what with the war and all, I decided to come home and work for awhile and then go fight for America." He grinned and said, "I wish I could go with you. It's likely easier to shoot at folks than to work here in this old gin." He laughed and then pointed at the diesel. "That old diesel is leaking by and it needs some new rings. You reckon you could give me a hand?" "Whatever you need Mose, I am here to help any way I can." "Good then," he replied, "go get us a tow bar and a two inch open end and a piece of three inch pipe about two feet long and we'll see if we can bust these old nuts loose." "Oh, Henry, and some oil too." We spent the rest of the day breaking the head loose, pulling the old rings and replacing them. Time flew and we both worked hard but could not finish before dark. "You a good helper, Henry Jimson. I'll be seeing you in the morning and we'll finish up with this old girl and crank her up and see if she is in a good mood," he said with a grin. "We got us a pump making a whole lots of racket and spewing water all over so that's what we will be doing tomorrow after we finish this job."

I was sore as a boil the next morning and could barely straighten up to get my clothes on. The days melted away as the work became more intense, getting ready for the cotton to start coming in. My Father told me that the government had already contracted for all of the production for the year. The farmers were all pleased to hear of it. Mose and I stayed busy and got a lot done. You could feel the growing sense of anticipation as the workers readied the mill for what would be a very busy time. The cotton crop this year would be one of the best in memory.

I always looked forward to the weekends and spending time with Old Man. Today as I entered the home I had a sense of this being a special visit. I don't know why. Mary and her family were due in a few days and the thought of her and my dear friend meeting for the first time pleased me. It was more than that however. On my last visit I found him preoccupied and distant. I had never seen him depressed but, to the contrary, considering his surroundings, he always seemed content in his circumstances. My premonitions were correct as it turned out.

"Let's go outside for a walk, Henry," was his greeting to me. It was overcast and the smell of rain was in the air. The wind came in gusts and I could see it was getting darker, even though it was only three in the afternoon. "I think a storm is coming, Henry." "Yes Sir, I can smell it." "No, Henry, I am talking about a universal disturbance. We have madmen loose upon the earth who seek to do us in." For the next thirty minutes Old Man talked and I listened intently. This was one of those life-shaping times I would later learn.

"Henry, you are just a boy. Your age determines that. Your mind is capable enough and in your case, advanced beyond your years. Right now the world around you shapes your attitudes, and your experiences are there to teach you life's lessons. For a period of time, life at the university and here in Mark Hill are your world. Your friends anchor you and your family gives you guidance and wisdom. A Higher Power looks down on you and seeks your devotion and obedience. God given senses round out your constant ability to learn from your experiences. What you do with all these factors will determine what kind of man you shall become. But what of the madmen, Henry?"

He paused and then continued, "Hitler, Mussolini, and Hirohito are among the most evil men to ever walk the earth. Even so, they share a commonality with all evildoers. They have a perverted cause and the apparent means to achieve it. From time to time the megalomaniac will rise up out of the sea of humanity to become a doer of evil. Their personalities, their goals, their leadership and their charisma mesmerize mankind. Man blindly follows as sheep stretch out behind the shepherd. Outwardly they say things that please the people. They promise safety, prosperity, and success for the people. But inwardly they owe allegiance only to themselves. Their goal is to attain ultimate power over people, and not for the good of the people, but for the sake of absolute power only. The people are pawns that they manipulate in order to win what they desire. They don't care about the people. People are expendable and those who oppose them do so at their peril. They are godlike in their use of power. They will lie, kill and steal to prevail. They see nothing wrong with this, as they are self-deluded to justify their actions. The egomaniac must have ultimate power in order to achieve a godlike existence."

Old Man considered his thoughts and then continued, "Many have perished following such men. Throughout history, the evildoers rise and fall and mankind never seems to understand the consequences of following them. Perhaps the problem lies with the state of man himself. I believe that within each of us is the capacity to do ultimate good and also to commit unspeakable evil against our fellow man. And so, within us the battle rages to decide which will prevail, good or evil. What then shall we do, Henry?"

I hesitated to answer Old Man. What shall we do, indeed? The smell of rain was in the air and the clouds on the horizon were now shades of black and billowing upward. The wind blew steadily now and we turned back for the home. Just as we entered the front door the rains began in a torrential downpour. "Let's go to your room and watch this storm from your window," I suggested. Old Man nodded in approval and, from the quizzical look on his face, I knew he was waiting for my response. The storm blew the rain against the side of the building, making enough noise to make it difficult to hear conversation. The sky was black now and visibility from the window was non-existent. "I am going to stay here until this clears, Sir."

We sat in his room in silence, listening to the rain. There is something frightening about the storms that come without much warning, and quickly. The rainstorms along the coastal plains seldom last for very long. On very hot days they are often preceded by heat lightning silently flashing far in the distance. The powerful ones are accompanied by peals of thunder and powerful strikes of what is often referred to as stroke lightning, reverberating in waves and deafening when close by. This storm would be over soon.

I spoke first as he stared out the window, patiently awaiting my response. "The war we are now in is no ordinary event is it? Madmen are indeed on the loose and great armies are being marshaled upon the Continents of Europe and Asia. We must respond to the unprovoked attack on Hawaii by Japan, and our naval forces have been severely diminished. No one wants to go to war and face the uncertain future. How shall we respond and in what measure? Our freedom may be in jeopardy. Is liberty worth the fight? Will the sacrifice of our people be too great? Shouldn't we attempt to preserve our Nation for the good of future generations? Will we prevail or will we fail? These times will require great leadership and much resolve to begin and finish an awesome task. I believe in this country and its people. We will do the right thing and do it well. God is ultimately in control. We have right on our side. With much prayer and a National calling, I believe we must respond for the sake of our Nation. God help us."

We sat in silence, watching the storm pass and light once again breaking through the clouds. A calm came upon the scene outside and also upon us as we sat in the quiet room. "I must go now Old Man," as I rose and patted him on the back. He was smiling and nodded his goodbye to me.

The following Monday morning at the mill Mose and I worked until noon and stopped for lunch. We went outside behind a storage shed and sat on the ground with our lunch sacks and mason jars. "What you got in your sack, Mr. Henry?" "Mose, I wonder what you got in your sack? Also, don't call me Mister if you please. I reserve that term for men of standing and I am your helper if memory serves me." "Well Sir, I have me a leg and wing from a fine chicken, fried up by my wife. I also got some cornbread with butter on it and some cookies. And, Mr. Henry, in case you haven't noticed, I happen to be a black man and you are white, the last time I looked."

"Now Mister Mose, I've noticed you are black. You are black as pitch. And I know what some would think if you did not call us white men, 'Mister'. But when we are alone, we are equal, except that you know how to run this mill and I don't. So I'll make a deal with you. If you won't call me Mister,

I'll return the favor and just call you Mose. I have two ham sandwiches on homemade bread with mustard. I also have some boiled eggs and a jelly sandwich. I'll swap you a ham sandwich for a chicken leg" Mose broke loose with a belly laugh and grinned from ear to ear. "Now Henry, you are all right by me. But I got to also have one of them fine boiled eggs to make it a good deal!" "Done," I replied and we divided up our bargains and ate.

After lunch we both stretched out with hats covering our eyes and rested. The warm sun dulled our senses and we both fell asleep. Some thirty minutes later Mose exclaimed, "Henry, you and I need to earn our keep and it don't include sleeping on the job. What did you give me all that food for and make me sleepy in the noonday sun." After work we left together and decided to walk home. Mose lived closer to the mill but in the same direction as my house, and it was a nice day for walking together.

"Mose, you are a good man and I know you won't think badly of me for asking this. I've often wondered what it would be like if I were a black man. What is it like Mose?" I could tell by his countenance, which changed immediately, that he was not entirely comfortable with the subject. He stopped walking and suggested we sit under a nearby tree in the shade.

He then looked into my eyes with a steady gaze, drew a deep breath and said, "Well, Sir, it is like the night and the day. They are very different but go together. Just as sure as the day fades, the night comes. The night becomes the day and the other way around.

"Now Henry, I am going to answer you as best I can, but you can't really understand what being a colored person is like. I know that shoe won't fit you. You also need to know that some are apples and others are oranges. There is no one answer to being black, because we are people just like whites and everyone lives different. I'll tell you what it is like for Mose to be black.

"There were six of us children and I was the youngest. Momma took care of us as best she could. She took in wash, picked cotton, cleaned houses for white folks and whatever else came along she could do to make a living. Somehow she managed to raise us proper.

"I never knew my Daddy. He was never around and never spoken of. I suppose he didn't take to a wife and children and I never learned where he was or if he was even alive. I wanted to know but I just couldn't find out much about him. So my oldest brother was my Daddy.

"All but two of my brothers and sisters are living, but don't live here in Mark Hill. One drowned in the creek when she was three and the other died with consumption they said. We were dirt poor, but we got by. I got in the fields when I was six, picking cotton and toting water. Everybody tried to get jobs to help Momma but it was hard to find work. We would hunt and fish and had a garden. We got by.

"When I got older your Daddy took notice of me and kind of took me under his wing. Your Momma would bring us food she would cook from time to time and was real good to us. We loved both of them then and still do. Not many whites would have done that for blacks.

"There was no schooling, although two of my brothers learned to read and write. They tried to teach me when I got older but it was too hard for me. Besides I liked working with my hands and being outside every chance I got." Mose stopped talking for a little bit to gather his thoughts, I guess. He leaned back against the tree and closed his eyes. Several minutes passed before he continued.

"Now Henry, those were easy times. But you know there were hard times, and they were fearful. One of the black families we knew got crossways with a white man who claimed that they were disrespectful and troublemakers who didn't know their place. The white man beat up the oldest boy real bad and he later died. Then the Klan had one of those cross-burning meetings up on the hill west of town. The blacks all over the area were scared to death. Momma kept us home for several weeks until it blew over. I was mad about my friend being killed and scared of what could happen to my family and me.

"Us children would wear hand-me-downs. We had Sunday clothes and we took real good care of them. Momma believed in church and loved the Lord. Us kids liked going to church and listening to the singing and praising. We would get out in the aisle and dance and carry on something fierce. Every now and then the Preacher would lay hands on somebody with a problem and they would fall to the floor. People say they were slain in the Spirit and maybe so. They seemed to be all right afterwards and sometimes even better.

"Friends would get together on Saturday nights from time to time. When I got to be old enough, I'd sneak some white lightning and get stupefied. I took to girls early on and spooked several right regular." Mose grinned and stopped again. "But I didn't have a hankering to marry or settle down, understand. Them girls did though, but I was crafty as a fox about that.

"Henry, don't ever believe that your color is of no account. If you're black then there are places you can't go. You are not allowed in a movie or a cafe or a hotel or a train or bus station, unless there is a separate colored section for you. If you ride a bus you have to sit in the back. If you're walking down the street and a white comes toward you, get out of the way real quick. Don't look at any white women in the eye or speak to them unless they say something to you first. If they ask you to do something for them, you do it quick. Don't never argue with a white and always speak to them as 'Yes Sir', or 'No Mam'.

"You can't vote, Henry. Well, if you answered the questions the Clerk asked, you could, but then you had to pay the Poll Tax, and no black had enough money to do that. Sometimes when you go to the Courthouse you find out that you are not a person. The only place at a courthouse you are a real person is at the colored water fountain outside in the back or in the jail upstairs.

"Now Henry, I could go on for some time to come and it would get dark and I still couldn't tell you all things about being a black man. I'm proud to be black, but it's not an easy row to hoe is it? I want you to know that I'm happy and satisfied with my place. But I'll say that all that talk in the Constitution about men being equal and freedom and liberty seems to be for the white man only. I guess that's just the way it is. But I'm still a happy man. And I am black as pitch," as he finished with a grin. "Thank you Mose for sharing with me. I don't know if I could bear up under your load."

When we reached his house we said our "goodbye's" and "see you tomorrows". As I walked away Mose ran up to me and said, "Mister Henry, I know this don't need to be said, but I'd be grateful if you would forget everything I said to you today so that I don't have trouble come after me." "I understand, Mose. I'm your friend and you can trust me. I don't remember what you told me today. My memory fails me every now and then you know." I shook his hand and waved as I walked away. I thought it a privilege to know such a man.

Mother and Dad were sitting on the front porch as I walked up the driveway. "Well boy, you must have worked late. I've been home for almost an hour. Your Mother and I ate while it was hot." "I'm sorry about being late. Mose and I walked home together and we had a long conversation that made me late," I explained. "What did you talk about? Something happen at work?" "No, Sir, it was personal and I promised Mose I would not share it with anyone. You understand don't you?" They glanced at each other, nodded as if approving my response and I went in to cleanup for supper.

The week at work passed quickly and Mose and I completed most of the repairs and maintenance needed for the coming season. Thursday was here before we knew it and it was time to go home.

Mary called just before bedtime to tell me that they drove to Atlanta and decided to spend the night there to break up the trip. They would be here in the late afternoon tomorrow she went on to say. "I am so excited to get there and meet your parents Henry. Let's plan on looking around Mark Hill for the first few days." I laughed and told her we could do that in less than an hour. "But I do want to bring you down to the drug store to meet some of my friends. I also want you to see the cotton gin where I am working. And I very much want you to meet and spend some time with Old Man. Would you like to do that?" "Yes, and what I'd also like is to see you and to be with you and to talk to your Father and Mother to get to know them, and I also want to spend time with your Mother alone to talk about you." "I am not sure I like that, but then, who am I to stand in the way of a woman's plans?" We both laughed. "Good night, my love." "See you tomorrow." I went to bed later, but had trouble going to sleep.

The next day was Friday and Mr. Johnson let me off early so I could go home. He wanted to know what was more important than work, grinning all the while. Word had gotten around about Mary and my Dad must have mentioned that the Blyths' were coming today. I turned into the driveway on the bicycle and saw their car. Everyone was on the porch, watching as I pedaled toward the house. Mr. and Mrs. Blyth were in rocking chairs and Mary was sitting on the steps. Mother waved and Mary jumped up and ran down to meet me.

"Henry, I didn't know you could ride a bike!" She laughed as she threw her hands into the air to grab me. What happened next was humiliating. "Oh yes I am an expert with bikes," and then thought it would be fun to act as if I had lost control. I turned the handlebars rapidly from side to side and sped up. I did not notice the deep rut that the front wheel fell into;

causing the bike to violently pitch to the side while my body continued moving rapidly over the handlebars. In my minds eye everything seemed to slow as I catapulted over the handlebars, stretched out like a diver about to enter water. The dirt driveway seemed to come up suddenly to meet me. I hit with a thud, slid a few feet and rolled a few times while Mary looked on in shock. When one falls unexpectedly I think the instant response is to jump up and look around to see if anyone saw the fall. It is usually a time of surprise and embarrassment, as it was for me. So I did just that very thing, giving no thought that I might have broken a bone or torn a ligament or worse. "Oh my gosh, Henry, are you ok?" "Why sure I am," as I hastily checked. "You don't think that was an accident do you? I was just kidding around to make you think I didn't know how to ride my bike," looking back over my shoulder to see the bike on the ground with the front wheel severely bent and several spokes torn loose from the wheel. She mused, grabbed me and kissed my cheek and said, "Of course not sweetheart. You thoroughly convinced me. Tearing up the front wheel was a good touch too." I could feel the red flushing in my face as I picked up the bike and pulled it to the side of the porch as the spectators watched. "I think I fell," I announced and the tension broke and laughter commenced. I greeted Mr. and Mrs. Blyth and as he shook my hand he noted with a smile that I had made a grand entrance. "It is so good to see you again, son. Thanks to you and your family for your hospitality," as he glanced at Mother. Mrs. Blyth gave me a hug and we spoke of their trip and safe arrival. Mary stood at my side, holding on to my hand tightly and smiling at me constantly. We were so glad to see each other and couldn't wait to be alone. I could see that in her smile. After supper we sat on the porch and watched the sunset.

CHAPTER SEVEN

Just as dawn broke, I was up getting ready for the day. After dressing I looked down the hall and saw Mary slipping out of the room where she and her parents slept last night. "I heard you and decided to get up also," she said. Then she wrapped her arms around my waist and kissed me. We stood there in the hall embracing one another for some time and then, without a word, went outside just as the sun was clearing the horizon. It was still cool and the overnight dew had not yet burned off. "This is going to be a really pretty day for us to make the rounds," I observed. "Where are you taking me today? Will we go downtown? I'd like to see the drugstore because I know from experience that's where friends gather in the summertime. I am really curious as to what they will tell me about you. I'd also like to go to the cotton gin and meet this Mose that I've heard so much about. And of course, Old Man is way up on my list." Mother called out from the house. "Henry, you and Mary come on up for breakfast." We all gathered at the table, asked the blessing and ate a wonderful breakfast. Mr. and Mrs. Blyth were especially impressed with Mother's homemade biscuits and cane syrup. When finished we all talked about topics of the day and then the Blyths' prepared to continue on their journey. "Mary, we will be back through on Wednesday. You have a great time, mind your manners, and help Mrs. Jimson!" "Yes, Mother, and you know I will, and now it is time for you to go," she said with a little exasperation in her voice. Her Mother laughed and kissed Mary and then Mary kissed her Father and they left.

"I'm going to show Mary around metropolitan Mark Hill. We'll probably grab a bite in town and will see you about supper time," as they walked out the door.

"Are we going to double on the bicycle?" "Oh gosh, that's right. Can I borrow the truck?"

Henry's Dad handed him some money and told him to put some gas in the truck and to have a good day. Then he walked up to Mary hugged her. "That's the best hug I've had in ages," she said with a big smile. "Why thank you darling. You are very huggable." We parted with laughter all around.

I pulled in to the local gas station and my friend David ran out and immediately began to clean the windshield. "Hi there Henry. Who's the good looking girl?" "This is Mary Blyth from the gulf coast of Mississippi." "Well it is a true pleasure to make your acquaintance, Mary. Have you known Henry long?" "She has, and you can check the oil and give me two dollars worth and don't start with me David. She is taken!" "Why Henry Jimson, this young man is just being friendly. Aren't you David?" "If you ever get tired of Henry…" He finished pumping the gas with a smile. Henry broke and stated rather sarcastically, "See you David," and pulled away in a cloud of dust. "Why Henry Jimson, I do believe you are jealous," she coyly noted.

As we entered the drug store, everyone turned and stared at us. Mr. Thomas, the town's most argumentative character, asked if that was the Jimson boy and his group of antagonists stated it was and that he knew it was. A disagreement over poor eyesight ensued.

Sarah, the waitress, ran up to Mary and extended her hand. "You must be Mary. We've heard so much about you. If you have the time, I'll tell you all about Henry," she said with a smile. "Henry. At the back table are some of our high school buddies." Three couples were sitting in the shadows as we approached. They all saw us at the same time.

The local football hero, quarterback and leader of the team, suddenly jumped up on the table. In a loud voice he stated, "Ladies and Gentlemen, I present to you the distinguished, handsome gadabout town, Henry Jimson and girlfriend." At that point, as I pushed him off the table and on to the floor, all the girls jumped up as one, and proceeded to squeal in delight as they surrounded Mary and introduced themselves. We sat there for most of an hour reliving our school experiences, who dated whom and who married who and other girl talk. Mary became one of them almost instantly and had a grand time. The guys kidded Henry about everything he ever did. They recounted Henry's claim to fame at the fair and how he was published. Every now and then Mary would chime in with: "Henry, I can't believe that!" and laugh. They allowed as how Mark Hill ground to a standstill when Henry left for college. The owner came over and offered free sodas to all. Mr. Thomas shouted out from across the room, "I'll take mine black!"

These were my friends dating back to grade school. We were raised together and knew each other intimately; both the good and the bad. It was as if I had not been away at all, within minutes of our meeting. Mary felt the admiration we shared for one another and told me so later. When you are raised in a small town, you become like family. You applaud the achievements and feel remorse when one from among you fails. All births were celebrated and all deaths grieved. The parents were parents to all the children. Every Mother knew what every other child was doing most of the time. They were as sentinels at watch posts to protect us as we grew up, to correct us and even spank us when we did wrong and treated us as one of their own. The result was unity; a knitting of the community in a healthy sort of way. In a nutshell, our families had respect for one another.

We said our goodbyes and left. On the sidewalk outside we met Mr. Spencer. "It is a pleasure to meet you young lady. You have a good lad here in Henry." "Please forgive me if I rush away. I have pressing business at the office. Henry, could I speak to you for a minute?" We walked a short distance from Mary as she looked in the window of the local mercantile store. "I'll be right back Mary." "Henry, I've just been advised by a friend in Atlanta that the next draft list will be coming here in two weeks time. You know what that means." "Yes Sir, and thank you so much for the advanced notice. I intend to go to Atlanta next week." He explained the volunteer procedure, gave me the address of the recruitment center and where induction would take place. "Does two weeks seem enough time to join?" "Yes, and I'll be praying that all well be well with you and your family." With that he turned and walked away. He seemed to me to have aged considerably.

Mary knew instantly as I walked back to her. "I know," she whispered. "When?" "Within two weeks." "Oh Henry, I am not prepared for this," as she turned her back to me. But then she turned back to me with tears in her eyes. "I'll be strong Henry. Do not worry about me. You do understand what I am trying to say, don't you?" "Yes," as I thanked God for giving me this strong woman. I knew she would stand beside me no matter the trials. We smiled knowingly, held hands tightly and left.

We drove next to the cotton gin. Mary was very anxious to meet Mose. As we turned in and pulled up to the office, Mose came around the corner. Because it was Saturday there were only a few men on the job and Mose was checking all the machinery. "Mose, come here. I have someone who really wants to meet you." "Now Mr. Henry, why would anybody want to meet ole Mose?" "Well Mose, this is Mary. You remember that I told you about her?" "Well how do you do, Miss Mary? I do indeed remember, as you are all that Mr. Henry speaks of in his spare time. I do declare that this boy is smitten with you and rightfully so, if you don't mind me saying." Mary said she had also heard much about him from Henry and was pleased to meet him, as she extended her hand. Mose smiled and stepped back away from her. Mary felt the embarrassment and quickly withdrew her hand.

Mose asked her if she would like to look around the mill. "Well I'd be pleased to. Henry could you go get me a soft drink of some kind. I am very thirsty and Mose will take me around while you are doing that." Henry sensed Mary wanted to talk to Mose and so, got in the truck to drive away. "I'll be back in about ten minutes." "Take your time," she replied with a smile.

Mary was very direct. "Mose, does Henry ever talk about the war? We saw Mr. Spencer in town and he told Henry it was time to join the Army before he is drafted." They walked over to the porch in front of the office and she sat in the rocker there and Mose sat below her on the step. "Miss Mary, I been dreading this day. Not because I am worried about him going to war but for selfish reasons. Mr. Henry is special. I consider him my friend and a person I can talk to about things I'd never share with others. We are bonded, white and black in a strange way and I hate him going away." "I know that feeling Mose. He and I are also bonded and I love him with all my heart. I am very fearful for him, but I won't let him know that. I don't want him to see me that way. I want to be strong for him and give him every reason to come back to me. I hate this war and the way it's caus-ing grief in our country. I know people where I live who are in constant worry and anguish. I know some who have already lost their boys and men. My heart breaks for them." "Yes, Mam."

They sat in silence for several minutes. Mary continued, "I am going to write to him as often as I can. I am also going to write you once in awhile to share any news I may have. I'll send those letters to Mr. Jimson to deliver to you." "I'd like that very much." This is a good man, Mary thought to herself as she got up and started down the steps. She reached over and touched Mose' shoulder as she passed. He smiled and nodded to her.

"Now Mose, when Henry gets back and asks what we did, you tell him a little white lie for me. Tell him you showed me all around the mill and that I asked a lot of good questions and was really interested in it all, and especially what he does, all right?" "I'll tell Mr. Henry just what you say and will know why," Mose replied with a knowing smile. It was then that Henry drove up, jumped out of the truck and ran over to the two of them and thrust a soft drink into Mary's' hand. "What did you do while I was gone?" Mose broke out in a big grin and proceeded to tell the story as Mary had requested. "Well that is wonderful, Mose. I thought Mary would be bored to death about the mill and my work." "No, Sir, Mr. Henry. She was really interested, especially about you!" It turned out to be a good day for Henry, for Mary and for Mose.

That evening at supper they shared the events of the day around the table. Afterwards, Henry and his Dad went out in the yard and stood there in front of the house in silence. The women cleared the table, washed the dishes, dried them and put them away. They then went to the porch and sat and rocked. Henry and his Dad walked slowly down the drive to the main road ahead. "Pretty evening" Dad observed. "Yes Sir," I replied. They walked on in silence until reaching the main road. We looked up and down the road, noting the absence of cars and the quiet of the evening. "It sure is still. I think a rainstorm is coming. Calm before the storm you know." "Yes, Sir, I know."

Mary and Mrs. Jimson watched the men in the distance. The men talked and gestured for several minutes, looking intently at each other. It appeared to be a serious conversation. Suddenly Father reached out to Son and they embraced each other. "I declare", exclaimed Mrs. Jimson. "It has been a long time, too long, since I saw those two show any affection toward each other." They continued to hold on to each other for some time. Mary glanced over to see tears in Mrs. Jimson's eyes. She looked away and pretended not to notice. Mary pondered the future. Surely they all were doing the same that evening.

The next morning Henry called the county home. He requested that Old Man be told that he was coming to visit and had someone who wanted to meet him. The attendant asked, "Who you got with you Mr. Henry? I bet it is that girl I been hearing about. Has she been keeping you busy Mr. Henry?" She laughed and said she would get Old Man ready for a special visit.

Mary and I walked quickly up the steps and into the front doors. I fully expected Old Man to be there or at least in the hall, but he was not. "Well Mr. Henry, who is this pretty thing you brought with you today? Welcome to our home, young lady." The attendant was one of my favorite people out here. She always smiled, often when there was little to smile about considering the surroundings. "Why it is truly a pleasure to meet you," Mary replied. "May I know your name?" "Yes, Mam, my name is Mary." "Well, I do declare. My name is also Mary, Mary Blyth. I think Mary is a beautiful name, don't you?" The attendant smiled broadly and replied, "I sure do!" We all laughed at the jesting and then Mary and I were escorted to the back porch.

As we stepped down onto the porch we saw a solitary figure sitting in a rocking chair with his back to us. He heard us and rose and turned around. I was absolutely flabbergasted. This man did in no way appear to be Old Man. This man was clean-shaven and his black hair was neatly combed and parted. The piercing blue eyes were the same and seemed to sparkle as he approached us. He wore a pinstriped suit, buttoned and with a vest. The tie was neatly knotted with a gold pin placed directly below, accenting the bright blue of the tie. His shoes were dress black and shined so as to reflect the sun. As he approached us his gaze was fixed on Mary. It was if I were not there. He stopped in front of her and extended his hand, eyes fixed on her face. She reached for his hand and he took it, bowed slightly at the waist, continuing to look into her eyes and gently kissed the top of her hand. Mary was blushing. He then released her hand and stepped back. "I find myself honored to be in your presence my dear. Henry has spoken of you often, but did not prepare me concerning your beauty. No wonder

Henry gets starry eyed when he speaks of you." He continued, "Where are my manners. It is with great pleasure that I receive you here in these less than elegant surroundings. Allow me to introduce myself. I am called "Old Man", which I prefer and count as a compliment. Please be comfortable with my preference and the indulgences of an old man." He smiled at Mary and then nodded in my direction as if to barely acknowledge my presence and then motioned toward two additional rocking chairs. "Would you do me the honor of your company here for awhile?" "Why thank you, kind Sir. Perhaps we could discuss a matter of mutual importance. Tell me, what do you think of the prospect of Henry and I marrying?" Old Man was in his element now. Here was a young lady who was direct and forthright. She won the old man over with that simple inquiry.

"I will tell you what I know and then I'll tell you what I feel," he replied. His gaze intensified, as was his manner. "I know that marriage is a challenging state. If entered into at all, it must be upon a solid foundation. That foundation has as it cornerstone, love and respect. Above all, God must be always at its center.

"It is much akin to oxen pulling a load; that is to say, marriage requires much effort together. I would also note that it should never be about physical attraction only, but must require much devotion and understanding, each to the other. It should be a grand adventure entered into willingly and eagerly. But, it is not at all easy." He paused as if gathering his thoughts. Mary noted the Bible verses that admonish about being unequally yoked. "What do you say about that?" He replied, "The Bible also says that one should leave Father and Mother and become cleaved to one another. What it does not say in regard to marriage is that we are fallible human beings, fraught with imperfections. Therefore, we must acknowledge that our union will often be tested by circumstances that we stubbornly cling to and by circumstances not necessarily of our own doing. It may appear to be a comfortable state, and it often is. But there will be times of testing, strife and sorrow as well. This requires strength to face adversities together. This requires a forgiving spirit and a willingness to sacrifice. And where do you think that commonality of strength comes from. From two people who love the Lord, their God, with all their heart, soul and mind and each other mutually in the same manner." Now it was Mary's turn to ponder. The three sat in silence for several minutes.

"Now I'll tell you what I feel. I feel that you love each other intensely. I can see it in your eyes. I feel that I know you intimately because of what Henry has related to me on many occasions. I know Henry to be, among other things, extremely intelligent, a possessor of wisdom beyond his years, determined in his objectives and good company as well." He smiled and looked at Henry for the first time. "Henry is not just an acquaintance. He is my friend. No greater love than to have a friend who will give you all and ask nothing in return. And beyond that, I feel that your children will be beautiful as well." Once more he smiled.

Mary blurted out without thinking, "I love you, Old Man!" "And I you, my dear." "Now will you tell me what you think of our getting married before Henry leaves?" "I will not," he responded. "That is a decision that only the two of you can make and it will require your mutual love, tempered with wisdom."

Mary was about to ask a question for which she feared the reply. "Old Man, what do you think of Henry going to war? I don't mean what you think of war. I want to know how you feel about Henry going." There was much in her heart that she did not ask him. She was looking for reassurance from this old man as to Henry's safe return. This was the subject of speculation that she couldn't face. Perhaps he could.

At this point he got up from his seat and slowly walked to the edge of the porch with his back to them. He was looking at the oak tree where Henry had found his courage years ago. "I know of your fears Mary. Mine are the same. Do you see that oak tree there in the distance? Get Henry later to tell you of his experiences there. It will reveal much about fears." This was a cryptic reply. She looked at Henry and he smiled and nodded in agreement. Somehow there was comfort in Henry's smile.

Upon leaving, Henry silently embraced Old Man for several minutes, patted him on the shoulder and put his head in the old man's shoulder. Then Mary embraced Henry briefly and then the old man. She kissed him and they left. Afterwards in his room, Old Man cried alone. Later that night at home, Henry and Mary embraced and cried in each other's arms.

Wednesday was upon them suddenly. The Blyths' drove up the driveway. They spent the night. The next morning they all talked. Henry and Mary walked alone for some time, talking about small things. He related his experience at the oak tree to her and she smiled. Then Henry told Mary how much he loved her and that he would be fine. She was looking into his eyes in a manner Henry had not experienced before. It was more than a look. She searched his soul through his eyes. Their eyes explored each other for several minutes as they stood there outside and alone. Time was standing still. They each lost themselves in their searching gazes. Finally, Mary reached out and touched his face and then held Henry and told him how much she loved him. She told him," I'll write often darling. I know you will too when you are able." Henry replied," We will get married as soon as I get back. I love you so much." They held each other for some time and then kissed softly.

Mary left that afternoon with her parents. Henry ran behind the car to the main road. The dogs did not follow. He waved as the car disappeared in the distance. He stood there alone for a long time. He felt a longing and emptiness as the car disappeared in the distance. Mr. and Mrs. Jimson sat on the porch in silence, watching Henry standing alone at the main road. Darkness came upon them all that night.

The next day Henry and his Father drove to Atlanta so that Henry could join the Army. After a time with the recruiter and a brief indoctrination, Henry took the required Oath along with four other men there for the same purpose. The recruiter read from a paper. He instructed, "Repeat after me, the following Oath," and began to read, "I, (state your name), do solemnly swear or affirm (as the case may be) that I will support the constitution of the United States. I, (state your name), do solemnly swear or affirm (as the case may be) to bear true allegiance to the United States of America, and to serve them honestly and faithfully, against all their enemies or opposers whatsoever, and to observe and obey the orders of the President of the United States of America, and the orders of the officers appointed over me."

At the end of the day Henry was advised that orders would be forthcoming in the US Mail. Henry had related his desire to be a medic. The recruiter assured him that every consideration would be given in placing him, depending on a battery of aptitude tests to be given at a later date. Father and Son spent the night in Atlanta and returned to Mark Hill the next day.

The orders arrived and Henry hurriedly opened them. Basic training would take place at Fort Jackson, South Carolina and he was to report to the post reception center the first Tuesday in August 1942. In the mailing were vouchers for a bus ticket, meals and also instructions for what possessions to bring.

He went to the county home to tell Old Man. His reaction surprised Henry. "Well, Henry, your adventure begins. I sincerely hope and pray that all will be well with you. Please be always aware of your surroundings. Pay attention carefully to what you are taught. Don't ever hesitate to follow your instincts. Your friends will be important to you. For many you will become a comrade. Don't be afraid to care about them. Seek out the quiet ones. Try not to become detached in whatever situation you find yourself. Be obedient to orders and be diligent in carrying them out. Become automatic as a soldier, never doubting yourself."

"Yes, Sir," I responded. I sat quietly, trying to take in all that he had just advised. "I'll try to remember all of what you have told me today and also what I have learned from you these many years." "We will correspond when it is possible. I'll reply to your letters in kind. Remember who you are and what you have come to mean to me. I value you greatly Henry." We left his room and walked to the front of the home. He stood quite formally, extended his hand and said, "Now Henry, God speed, until we meet again." "Thank you, Sir." With that he turned and disappeared down the hall. It was very hard to say goodbye to Old Man.

Mary and I talked by telephone every day until my time to leave arrived. We never again talked during those calls of my going to war. We did talk about our future on every occasion. We planned for and dreamed of it. We laughed and we cried. We remembered all our times together. We shared our love, hopes and dreams. Our conversations were always long and full of emotion. The Sunday night before I was to leave was especially poignant. Near the end of our last call I said, "Mary, I'll write you as often as I can. I'll do my best to let you into my heart to see that I am and will always be yours. No matter what happens to me, I want you to know that." "Please don't worry about me," she said. "You are my love. I will have you in my thoughts daily. I'll pray for you. I'll be sure to stay in touch with your parents and to share any news of you. I wish you God speed and His protection." I recalled Old Man saying a similar thing to me during our last meeting. "I love you above all else, Mary." "And I do love you with all my heart, Henry." We said goodbye to each other.

Monday morning after breakfast with my parents, I went to the plant to say goodbye to Mose. "Mose, I got my orders and will be leaving Tuesday to go to Fort Jackson in South Carolina." "I've never been to South Carolina, Henry. What do you think it will be like?"

"Well," I replied, "I understand that it's a big post and near Columbus. I believe the bus is chartered and will take me to a drop-off point there and after that I don't have a clue!" Mose smiled at me. He said he would miss me and that we would see each other again when I got back. I paid my respects to Mr. Johnson and he allowed as how I should be careful and follow orders while in the Army. I assured him that I would, all the while thinking of the advice Old Man had given me.

My next stop was to the diner where my high school friends hung out. Several were there and they all knew that I had enlisted and wished me well. Many of our friends had joined already and we had heard very little of them. We all knew that a few of our classmates had been killed in action, and a third was missing. Our conversation did not include those friends. It was best left unspoken, but I took note of the long periods of silence between talks. "I'll miss you all. I believe I'll go see Mr. Spencer now." "Good Luck Henry," they all exclaimed as I left.

I saw through the window that Mr. Spencer was in his office and so I went in to tell him that I got my orders. "Hello, Mr. Spencer. How are you today?" He looked up from the papers on his desk and came around to shake my hand. "Henry, I am so glad to see you again. I heard that you had enlisted. Have you received any paperwork from the Army?" "Why yes, Sir," I replied. "I have my orders to report to Fort Jackson and I leave tomorrow." He was pleased that I was able to enlist rather than be drafted. "Do you still want to be an Army medic? I have heard that there is a shortage already and don't believe you will have any problem being placed there." "They told me I'd be tested and depending on favorable results, that I could expect that," I replied. He saw no reason that I wouldn't, stating that my education would work in my favor.

Mr. Spencer looked drawn and much older than I remembered. I asked how he was doing. He said that his job had taken its toll on him. "The paperwork is not that bad but the draft notices are always hard to receive and to announce to the boys and their parents, you know. There are times when I must appear to be the 'angel of death' to them." He did not show any emotion when he said that to me. I did not either, and quickly changed the subject. "Well, Sir, I just wanted to tell you how much I appreciate all your help and your friendship. I must go now Mr. Spencer." "Goodbye, Henry. Keep your head down and God speed to you." There was that phrase again. "Thank you, Sir."

That night after supper Dad, Mom and I sat on the front porch until bedtime. No one mentioned my leaving in the morning. We talked about things in the past and how fortunate we were to be a close, loving family. Mother expressed her deep gratitude that my Father was a hard working man and a good provider. He talked of all the happy times during my coming up. They were both proud of me and noted that I was the first in the family to go to college. "Son, what they put in your head no one can take away from you," Mother said, as she has often done before. Father thanked me for being a good son who was a hard worker and a good student. I thanked him. It was a good time filled with pleasant memories. We remembered when Grandfather was still in his right mind and what a thrill it was when he reminisced about his rearing by his parents and his memories of how people lived during his day. He would always talk about sparing the rod and spoiling the child as if the experience of such a custom was personal to him. He found that to be quite amusing. Mother talked of the home and child rearing and dresses and church and friends and likes and dislikes she experienced as a child and young woman. It was a good time to remember and reflect on the past.

CHAPTER EIGHT

We all went to the bus station the next morning. The bus pulled up and the door opened and we stepped down from the platform for me to board. I placed my suitcase overhead and came back for our goodbyes. Mother gave me a sack lunch and Dad placed money in my hand. He had opened a checking account in my name for college, but the cash was appreciated "Now you write and tell us what you are doing. Call when you can. We will miss you, Son." He then turned and walked to the truck. Mother's eyes welled up as she grabbed me by the waist with one hand and placed my head on her shoulder with the other. She held me tightly for several minutes and then kissed my cheek. "I love you, Henry." "I love you too Mom." With that Dad started the truck and Mother got in and they drove away. The bus driver asked if I was ready to go to Fort Jackson, South Carolina. "No Sir, not really." "Well then, let's go anyway," he said as he pulled the door shut and pulled away.

Along the way we picked up more recruits so that by the time we arrived at the post, the bus was full. We pulled up to the front gate and the military guard waved us through with a very precise, structured hand wave. We drove past many wooden barracks, offices and the commissary, and then stopped in front of a large building. There were uniformed men there waiting for us. One of them stepped up into the bus and told us to stand up, retrieve our belongings and get off the bus. His tone was stern and his directions were to the point.

As we off loaded from the bus, the soldiers began to shout at us. "Form a line on me, now!" He was standing to the side of the bus and had left room for all of us to form into a single line. "Put your belongings by your side, straighten your line and look to the front." A single soldier came out of the building we were facing as the bus pulled away. "Today you people will no longer do what you want to do. You will do what the Army wants you to do. Pay attention because I only say this once. The next thirteen weeks will either make men out of you boys or will bust you. The Army intends to make you into fighting machines. Now, let's start getting you ready. Starting on the left end I want you to pick up your gear and proceed into the building behind me. Turn to the left and put your gear on the wall. Remember where it is. You will be given further orders after that. Do you understand me?" We mumbled or nodded. "What was that? I can't hear you animals. I'll say it once more. Do you understand me?" We all shouted, "Yes, Sir!" He shouted, "I am not a 'Sir'. You will not call any noncommissioned personnel 'Sir'. You say to me, 'Yes, sergeant!' "Yes, sergeant!" "Move, move, move," he shouted and we did so quickly.

As we dropped our gear we saw other men in six lines. We proceeded to a desk where we signed papers, which I learned later had to do with pay, next of kin, life insurance and basic personal information. After that we moved to the next line were others were waiting to go into makeshift enclosures for physicals. We were instructed to get in line, four to a line and be quiet. When I entered the cubicle there was a doctor conducting an examination on the person in front of me. He finished and motioned to me to step up. He asked for my name and date of birth. He checked my pulse, heart rate and blood pressure and then examined my eyes, ears and throat. He asked me if I had any communicable diseases now or in the past and then read a list of medical conditions for me to respond to with a yes or no. Next I was measured and weighed. He then tapped my chest and back while listening with a stethoscope. "Drop your pants and drawers and bend over." His examination was brief and uncomfortable. "Put your pants back on and go to the next station ahead."

At the next station I saw a barber who had just finished with the man ahead of me. "Sit down here. How do you want your hair cut?" He smiled and then proceeded to take clippers and completely cut off all my hair. He then shaved my head. He said, "That looks fine. You can leave through there," pointing to the rear of the cubicle.

Outside I saw men in line passing a window and receiving Army gear. We were given a clipboard with a questionnaire on it asking for clothing sizes. I filled it out and handed it to the man in the window. "Go to the next window." By the time I got to the window behind three others ahead of me, I was presented with a duffle bag full of articles. "You people go through your duffle bags now and retrieve your Army issue skivvies, your fatigues, socks and combat boots, belt and hat and put them on in the booths to your left. Place your civilian clothes in your suitcases." At that point our sergeant told us to retrieve our belongings and go outside and line up in front of the building as before. "When you are told, you will board the trucks waiting for you and will be taken to barracks." "Yes, sergeant," and we then did as we were told.

When we arrived at the barracks, which were two story wooden structures, we dismounted the trucks with our gear and were organized into groups in front of each building. Once again we stood in lines about six deep and facing away from the barracks. Then several military men appeared in front of us. One of them announced, "My name is Captain Lewis. I am in charge of your company. You people will divide up into fifty to the barracks. Each barracks will be answerable to a drill sergeant. A platoon leader will be appointed from among you later. If you obey orders and work hard, you will survive your basic training. If you screw up, well, you do not want to. If you need to speak to me during the course of your training you must go through your drill sergeant first. Good luck to you all."

As he turned to leave he commanded the drill sergeants to organize the troops. Salutes were exchanged with "Yes, Sir," from each of them. Each sergeant had a list of names in his hand. "I'll call the names of you who will be in the first barracks. When you hear your name acknowledge with 'here' and reform in front of the first barracks. With that he began to call names out. This continued until the four barracks had approximately fifty men in front of them, with a drill sergeant assigned to each.

"Fall out with your gear, enter your barracks, position yourselves two to the bunks upstairs and downstairs and wait for further instruction." With that, we entered the barracks and selected bunks until all were stationed as directed. The drill sergeant entered and approached the first bunk. Each bunk had sheets, a pillow and blanket folded on them. "Stand at ease and gather in close and watch me." He proceeded to make the bunk, instructing as to detail as he went. When he finished he took a quarter from his pocket and threw it on the blanket. It bounced. "Did you all see the quarter bounce? That is what I want to see at inspections." He then directed our attention to a footlocker near the front entrance. "Each of you has a footlocker for Army issue and a wall locker for civvies. You will place your belongings in your footlocker exactly as this one is. All items shall be folded and arranged exactly like this one. Do you understand me?" "Yes sergeant," we all shouted. "You will now have twenty minutes to make your bunks and arrange your footlockers. Any personal effects that are not in this footlocker and in the wall locker will be stored in rooms in the rear of the building. Now get to it." With that he left and we began furiously trying to make the bunks and arrange items in the footlockers as directed. "My name is Henry Jimson," I said to the boy next to me. "Hi, my name is Archibald Wilkins. All my friends all me Archie, thank goodness. Can't believe my parents hung that one on me," he stated with a big grin. We were both bent over pulling things from the duffle bag and placing them into our footlockers. "Do you want the up or down," he asked, nodding toward the double decker bunk. He stood up and pulled a coin from his pocket and flipped it. "Call it." I called heads and so it was. "I'll take the upper." "Good," he replied. "I tend to roll out of bed once in awhile." With that out of the way we both began on opposite sides to make our bunks. Neither one of our coins bounced, much to our chagrin. We pulled at the corners and tucked the sides tightly and folded the top down and placed the pillow at the head just as the sergeant came in and yelled, "Stop now!" He then started walking down the aisle looking left and right at the footlockers. He stopped in front of several and dumped the contents on the floor. "Do over!" Then he came back down the aisle looking at the bunks. He pulled about half of the mattresses to the floor, including mine. "Do over," he yelled. "What is wrong with you people that you can't follow simple instructions." He came to me and told me to pick up the mattress, strip it and watch. He then proceeded to remake my bunk. I watched closely. When he finished he took out the quarter and bounced it. "Why is it that I can make this bunk military style and you can't," he asked. He was standing about six inches from my face and glaring into my eyes. I tried not to look away, fearing the worst as a consequence. "Now I am going to have to waste my time standing here watching you screw up again. I don't like that one bit. What are you waiting for? Make the bunk."

I pulled the sheets off and began by tucking the two sheets tightly on all sides with a military fold at the foot as he had done. The blanket was done likewise and stretched from both sides. I folded the top of the blanket, pounded the pillow and placed it at the head as near to the center of the bed as I could. I was much quicker this time with the sergeant glaring at me all the while. I stepped back and he came forward and dropped the quarter on the bed once more. It bounced. "What is your name boy?" "Henry Jimson, sergeant." "Well Jimson, you should have done it right the first time. You will learn that do overs are a waste of my time and I don't like that. You understand?" "Yes, sergeant."

By that time the rest of the lockers and bunks had been redone. He told the rest to look at my bed on the way outside. With that he went upstairs. We could hear mattresses hitting the floor and the sergeant yelling. He came back downstairs and to the entrance. "In thirty minutes you will be called outside." With that, he left.

All four barracks emptied on command. "Now listen up. I want to know if we have anybody here with college experience. If you do, take one step to the front." Several of us stepped forward. "Good that I have some educated people with my group. Because you are so qualified you people will have the honor of doing KP for the first week. Now we are going to run to the mess hall. Line up six abreast and follow me." With that said, he took off at a dead run and we followed, trying to keep up. When we arrived, he asked for the college graduates to come to the head of the line. We then marched single file into the mess hall and sat at tables. Food was placed in front of us on metal trays. Knives and forks and a glass of milk followed. "Now you have thirty minutes to eat and then form up outside in front of your barracks to be dismissed. Those who so kindly volunteered for KP will report to the cook and do what he tells you until he releases you to return to the barracks. Eat!"

We scrubbed the tables after clearing them. Some mopped the floors. Others scraped food into big cans and put trays into oversized stainless steel sinks. Hot water had been previously drawn and it was soapy. The trays were washed while plates and utensils were done in other sinks. Then all washed items were rinsed and dried and placed in designated cabinets and drawers. At the same time all the cooking gear including large pots and pans, baking sheets and other items used to prepare the meals were scrubbed with steel wool, washed and hand dried. Next all the garbage was taken outside into outside cans. The kitchen cans were hosed out and returned to the kitchen. It took just over two hours to get the mess hall ready for the next meal.

The cook told us to return to our barracks and he said sarcastically that he looked forward to working with us tomorrow night. I later learned that other 'lucky' individuals took care of breakfast and lunch. It was all very efficient and tiring. We were all sweaty and dirty. Those at the barracks had already showered and cleaned up when we arrived. Some were lying on their bunks while others were writing letters. When we came in they all shouted in unison, "The kitchen brigade from Podunk U," and laughed at us. We were the brunt of many jokes that night. We cleaned up in the showers, which were in a large common area with about ten showerheads along the walls. It was a place where modesty was in short supply.

Promptly at ten o'clock we heard taps being played by a bugler somewhere on post. There were men all around me but I felt alone. "Good night Archie." "Good night." After that we heard "lights out" and we went to sleep, exhausted.

It seemed that I had just dropped off to sleep when the lights came on in our barracks. The drill sergeant stood at the door and shouted, "Get your bodies out of those bunks right now and get your fatigues on. You have exactly twenty minutes to fall out in front and stand at attention." With that he spun around and left. Everyone scrambled to get dressed. I searched through my footlocker for my fatigues, still groggy from sleep. Somehow I got my uniform and boots on and ran for the bathroom only to stand dancing in pain in the line trying to keep from urinating before I reached the urinal. You could hear the sergeant outside yelling, "Let's go! Move it, move it!"

As the last man cleared the door and fell in, we were instructed to climb into big trucks waiting there for us. The same thing was happening at all four barracks and it appeared to be bedlam. I sat down just as the truck began to pull away. "Where are we going?" someone asked. "I don't have a clue, but we're sure in a hurry," I replied. Laughter filled the truck. We drove for about ten minutes and the trucks stopped. Drill sergeants began to yell at the trucks. "Get out and fall in. Let's go, ladies. We are going to have some fun this morning," our sergeant said, sarcastically. "Follow me. Stop! This is not a Sunday stroll. You men form up ten to a line facing me." When we finished he said, "Now extend your left arm out to get a uniform distance from each other. Look to your right and get your line straight. Then on command you look to the front. When you do that, drop your arm and stand at attention. Do not move. Do it now!" When we were distanced and aligned, we received the command, "Ready, Front." He continued," Now you will maintain your line and distance and begin to move forward, left foot first and march until you are told to halt." The next order was, "Forward March!"

We moved out and onto a large tract about the size of a football field. "Halt!" We were still in formation, more or less, and the sergeant walked down each row, shaking his head. "That short stroll was just awful. You are out of line, out of step and your distance stinks. But tomorrow we will correct this little problem."

By this time more men had arrived and were similarly grouped. It was still dark and dawn was not yet breaking, but shading to gray so that we could see. Up front was a platform visible to all. On it was an Instructor. Drill sergeants were standing to the left of us, walking up and down the lines and watching us. The Instructor shouted, "We are going to have a little workout this morning to get your blood flowing gentlemen. Right now I want you to remove your hats, shirts and undershirts. Spread out about five feet from the man on either side and place your clothes next to your right side. Then face me and I'll demonstrate the first exercise. This is a jumping jack." He did several and then instructed us to do the same in unison with him. "Start." We all started doing jumping jacks. It seemed simple enough. But as I jumped, spread my feet and raised my arms and returned to position to repeat the exercise it became obvious to me that this required a great deal of coordination. Others were having the same problem getting the rhythm right, or they jumped without spreading or raised their arms with feet together. Very few were in sync. "How did you goof-balls ever learn to walk? First, arms go up and feet go out and you jump, all in one motion. Then you jump while arms come down and feet come in. Do this with me. Do it again with me. Again." The drill sergeants were yelling, "Do what he does and with him you idiots!" We finally got it and soon all were jumping together. "Well this is not so bad," I thought to myself. But after about five minutes I began to tire. The Instructor seemed very relaxed and at ease with this exercise. Finally, he stopped and we gladly did the same. "Now that you are warmed up, lets do a few more and little tougher exercises."

The next hour was the most exhausting, difficult physical exertion I had ever experienced. We did sit-ups, push-ups, squats, running in place, bends to touch our toes, bends from side to side, lying on our backs with feet held slightly off the ground and elevated and other exercises I couldn't recall later. All the while the drill sergeants were running up and down our lines yelling at us and criticizing us and humiliating us to the point that we became disoriented. When we finally stopped I was so tired my legs were shaking uncontrollably and I was sweating profusely. I felt nauseated and dizzy.

"Put your clothes back on now, form up and proceed to the trucks." I could barely get up into the truck and many had to be given a hand up. From there the trucks took us back to the post and to the mess hall. As we formed in a single line to go in, I noticed a chin bar about seven feet in the air placed at the head of the line. There was a recruit doing chin ups in front. Each man had to do the chin ups before he could go in. When I reached the front the sergeant said to me, "Jump up, grab the bar and give me ten." I jumped up, grabbed the bar and could only muster seven. "Back of the line! Do ten or don't eat." I ran to the back and waited while the men in front of me chinned. Some were successful, but many were not. The back of the line was growing in numbers. I reached the bar again and this time with all the effort I could muster I barely got the ten in. I ran in and ate. Afterwards I returned to the barracks and fell into my bunk and lay there. Archie called up, "How you doing Henry?" "I don't really know. I'm tired and can barely move."

It seemed minutes later that we were ordered back outside. "Now boys, we are going to learn to perform close-order drills. You will learn how to form up, dress right and come to attention. You will learn how to march together. You will learn how to move about as a formation. Now doesn't that sound easy?"

"Fall in! Dress right. Ready, front." He continued, "What is wrong boys? Those commands were simple enough. Why are you just standing there with your mouths hanging open?" For the next two hours or more we watched demonstrations on marching commands and then repeating them. It was like Keystone Cops. It's amazing to me that one can think he is coordinated until he has to be so in marching formations. It's very difficult to march in formation and seems impossible to perform. I thought I understood which was right and left, but not so much anymore. Confusion reigned among us that day.

We broke for lunch and had to repeat the chin-up drill as before. Then back to marching for another extended period. Near the end of the drills we were beginning, as a unit, to get the hang of it. The drill sergeant was relentless in shaping us up. He wanted us to be prompt and move smartly in each maneuver. Time passed quickly as we continued and we were finally dismissed to return to our barracks. It was almost suppertime and I couldn't believe it.

Back to the mess hall we went, to repeat chin-ups and eat. Then I had to pull KP again, and each day that week as well. I decided that pulling KP was not a good thing!

Upon returning to the barracks, I lay down for about thirty minutes. The sergeant came in and told us to write to our parents and tell them what a good time we are having. "You have one hour until lights out." With that, he left and I got pen and paper and three envelopes and began to write to my parents, Old Man and Mary.

In my letter to my parents I told them about my trip here to the post and all the details of the past two days I could recall.

Dear Mom and Dad

I'm fine and getting plenty to eat. The barracks are comfortable enough. Our drill sergeant is rough and very loud. He expects us to follow orders and do our very best. We have been introduced to physical exercise and it's very difficult. I'm doing KP this week.

I have one good friend now. His name is Archie and sleeps on the bunk below me. There are many, many rules to follow. We've not been told what we will be doing over the next thirteen weeks but I'm sure everything is designed to make us into soldiers or else, send us home.

I'll write to you as often as I can. Please pray that I'll learn all

that I'm taught and required to do.
I love you.
Henry

I wrote the same letter to Old Man except that I ended it with "Write me back when you can."

In my letter to Mary I told her that the Army was very different than civilian life and that I was learning how to listen and take orders. I told her about KP, knowing she would be amused.

"Mary, I miss you so much and thought of you all day today. I love you with all my heart and want you to pray for me. Every-thing here is going to work out fine. It's hard, but at the end of my training I'll be better for having gone through it.
I'll close now and will dream of you tonight. Love you."

I showered and went to bed. Five o'clock came quickly again. I was so sore I could barely move. Muscles that I did not know were there hurt me. When I walked, I could only do so with knees straight, much like the Ger-man goosestep. Several days past before I felt able to move without con-stant pain. The same daily routine repeated time and time again over the next week. My life now consisted of exercise, chin-ups, eating, close order drills, marching, KP and finally to bed, exhausted.

Saturdays consisted of a repeat of Monday through Friday. The days were the same routine and the pressure only increased. We did receive a break on Sundays when a Chaplin spoke to us. He talked to us in an am-phitheater. I guess the whole company was present. Archie wanted to know what religion I was. "I go to the Methodist Church where I'm from." He replied, "I'm a Presbyterian." We had become good friends in our misery. I do believe that misery loves company. I jokingly inquired, "What's the deal with 'falling from Grace'?" He responded in kind, "Are you one of the 'Elect'?" We both shrugged and considered the matter and searched for an answer to the questions. "Let me know if you figure it out," I said, to which he smiled and laughed quietly.

I liked the Chaplin. He had a pleasant smile and was soft spoken. We leaned in to hear him as he spoke into a microphone and through a loudspeaker. He never indicated his religious affiliation and his talk was pretty much generic.

"Men, my name is Chaplin Walden. It is my pleasure to address you this morning. I suppose for many of you that this is your first time away from your homes. That must be very hard for you. Your lives have been interrupted by the course of human history. We, as a nation, find ourselves in a worldwide conflict. I am acutely aware of the forces of good and evil in our world. There is hidden from our view a constant battle raging all around us as I speak. That battle is two-fold; both for our very souls and also for our freedoms we enjoy in this great country we call the United States of America. It is our history as a nation of freedom loving individuals to respond to the call when our liberties are threatened, whether from within or outside of our borders. Often times we are called to arms to maintain our freedoms. As a great people, we do so willingly and without hesitation. And so, we are all called here in this time of worldwide conflict to train to be effective soldiers, prepared for war, so that we might live in peace.

Don't think that this task will be easy. Many of you will be tested beyond your understanding. I implore you to do your very best for God and the United States of America. But I also beg of you to not rely solely on your own resources in this battle. There is One who is a great Comforter on whom you can confidently rely. There is a true saying that may sustain you, and that is 'All things work together for good for those who love God'. I don't know if you can fully grasp this now, but in the heat of battle it will be a source of strength for many of you. Finally, I encourage each of you to find wisdom in His Word. Take your Bibles with you and read them often. For those of you who may not believe in God, I would remind you of another saying, 'There are no atheists in foxholes!' Now may the Peace of God be with you and may He watch over you and protect you and bring you safely home." With that, he dismissed us. We spent the rest of the day cleaning the barracks and policing the area outside.

Monday we did close order drills after physical exercise. Then we had an outside class on basic first aid procedures. We were in a group of about twenty that day and had one Instructor. He had first aid field packs with him and gave each of us one for demonstration purposes. He gave a brief lecture on battlefield conditions and what we could expect with regard to wounds and injuries. He covered several conditions including cuts, sprains, open wounds, simple and compound fractures, bleeding, head wounds, shock, bullet and shrapnel injuries and many other situations as well. We then examined the contents of the packs. Among the items were tape and gauze, bandages, antiseptics, vials and needles for administering morphine, tourniquets, and ointments for burns and eye injuries.

The instructor then demonstrated several procedures, utilizing the pack contents. He had each of us apply bandages and tourniquets on one another as he observed. He showed us how to make splints with our gear and how to recognize shock and treat the condition.

He concluded with instruction on how to care for ourselves if wounded. He observed that Field medics would be assigned to platoons, but that we should be familiar with basic first aid and be prepared to assist others if needed. This was the first time no one yelled at us and I found the class to be very interesting.

We went back on base afterwards and entered a large building where a projector and screen had been set up. It appeared to me that the whole company was there. We were advised that the film was The Great War footage and its purpose was to expose us to battlefield scenes where soldiers had suffered various types of wounds or died. "If any of you get sick and need to throw up, then go outside and come back in when you finish."

Archie and I were sitting next to each other when the room darkened. "How bad can it be?" Archie inquired. I thought about it and stated, "Well it probably shows some blood and some pretty rough conditions, but I can't imagine it would make you throw up," I responded. The first scene was a long, winding trench, about eight feet in height with soldiers lined up against the wall. The soldiers had pie shaped helmets and they were kneeling down with their rifles and fixed bayonets in what appeared to be mostly mud and rainwater. There was an obvious battle ongoing. The noise of howitzers firing and machine gun fire was deafening and the explosions were very violent, with earth and debris flying everywhere. On occasion, a shell would hit just outside the trenches and throw great volumes of debris into them. It was a somber and sobering scene to watch. You could see fear in most of their eyes.

Suddenly a shell exploded in the trench and threw men into the air, while others fell into the mud and water, bleeding and screaming. Blood flew from the bodies of the men nearest the blast and onto those who were nearby. Other soldiers were running full tilt, away from the scene. Some in their state of panic climbed to the top of the trench, only to be shot, and fell back into the trench and died or were dead already. Some fell back into the trench with open wounds, most of which appeared fatal. Some of the men were screaming, while others just stood there with a dazed look on their faces. After a time a medic ran forward to retrieve bodies and with assistance from the survivors moved them to lines or piles being formed of the dead and dying. Most of the corpses were mangled by the blast and concussion that followed. Their faces were pale. Many of the dead men lying there had eyes open and stared without expression into space. It was a violent, extremely graphic view of the finality of combat for these soldiers. Many of the survivors had the appearance of dead men walking as well.

Archie and I were instantly on our feet as were many more in the theater. I had not realized that I was standing. We ran for the rear entrance and outside. I was in dry heaves and very sick. Archie was vomiting violently. "I don't understand. Why did we have to see that?" Instructors at the back door were yelling at us to hurry up and go back inside. The film lasted about fifteen minutes and was the most gory and frightening thing I had ever witnessed. I couldn't watch the whole thing and hung my head between my legs to avoid a second wave of nausea.

As the lights came up many in the room were obviously shaken and no one was talking. We just sat there with very little expression and tried to digest the horror we had just witnessed. The Instructor began to speak. "The first time I saw this film I threw up too. I know you are wondering why we show it to you. Because, the day may come when you will be there. Not necessarily in that surrounding but death and dying will be there with you. What will you do? You will be soldiers! You will react and try to save yourself or others who are wounded and in pain. You will reach way down inside and force yourself to be soldiers. Some will die. You may die. But your training may also save you and those around you. Each of you will have to learn to face your own personal demons and find it within yourselves to be brave. Listen to what we teach you. It is vitally important. Now rise and fall out outside in ranks and you will be taken to the mess hall. Eat if you can."

That night back at the barracks and lying in our bunks, we talked about the day. "Archie, what do you think about all this?" "Man, I don't know. I enlisted to go fight for my country but I guess I didn't think it through. It never crossed my mind that I could get killed." I had a hard time going to sleep that night.

As the days passed I noticed that we were being transformed. It was a subtle change. Our exercise periods were going smoothly now. Our close order drills and marching were becoming routine and executed with more precision. Our time in the barracks was taking on an order and assignments were carried out without complaint. We shared duties there. Aside from our personal spaces we were expected to clean the latrines, mop and wax the floors, police the outside grounds and pass unannounced inspections.

One thing I personally noticed had to do with the chin bar. We were standing in line one day, waiting for our turn at the bar when I heard laughter and cheering from the men up front. As I got closer it became obvious that a contest was taking place. "Up to fifteen now! Who wants to go for eighteen?" The next man jumped to the bar and counted off twenty, quickly and with some effort. He dropped down to cheers and pats on the back. Several followed with the usual ten and went in to eat, accompanied by boos and jeers. "Hear comes Jimson, the college boy. What you going to do Jimson, scrub the bar with steel wool?" They remembered my lapse in good judgment, and resulting KP at the beginning of my training. I was surprised to note that many in my barracks knew my name. We were beginning to act as a unit and friendships were developing among us. I taunted the men by stating, "Now you guys know I am soft and educated. What can I possibly do on the bar?" I thought as I jumped up and grabbed the bar that I might have overloaded my wagon. Surprisingly, I quickly did twenty. The next three were harder. By then they were chanting, "Go, go, go," and shouting my name over and over. At twenty-five I struggled and barely got my chin over the bar and dropped to the ground with everyone breaking line and gathering around me. "You are okay in my book Jimson," one shouted. That day I made many more friends and attitudes about me changed.

"Attention. What are you people doing? Get back in line. You in front; step away from the bar." With that our sergeant moved back and smartly saluted as a Lieutenant approached from the side and to the bar. He had on a uniform that fit him perfectly. The pants were starched and creased. His boots glistened in the sun. His eyes were cold and penetrating. He smiled and approached me, saying, "How many did you do?" Twenty-five, I think, Sir," He answered. "Not bad." With that he jumped to the bar. We were all watching intently as he dropped one of his hands to his wrist so that now only one hand held the bar. He began to chin. It was a fluid motion with no hesitation from the bar to full extension and then back up again. We stood there amazed as he past thirty, paused and then did ten more with no apparent effort. He dropped and without saying a word or looking back, he went into the mess hall. We all stood there, mouths agape, and shook our heads in disbelief. The sergeant noted that we had just seen a combat paratrooper who was working out on his on time to stay in shape. "Twenty minutes left to eat," as he walked away.

CHAPTER NINE

I noticed that our everyday routines were changing. Now there seemed to be more time spent on instruction. The days still began at five o'clock in the morning and ended at ten o'clock at night. We were still in the Army seven days a week. We were still trainees with much to learn.

Today we marched in formation to an outside area with bleachers. There was a lectern set up in front of us. In the background was an old house that looked out of place there in a wooded area. A few personnel were busy at the house, moving what appeared to be equipment into the house. We broke ranks and sat on the bleachers and an Instructor appeared at the lectern. He had an object in his hand that appeared to be a gas mask of some sort. Archie was sitting next to me and a new friend named Bill sat to my left. "What do you guys think we'll do today?" I asked. Bill was from Selma, Alabama and had a drawl. "Well Henry, I don't rightly know whats been goin on any day. I been sort of lost ever since I got to this place. They don't spend no time explaining much at all and I just follow the crowd. I reckon we be learnin how to kill people or somethin like that. But, I just ain't sure." He sort of drifted off into his space after that statement with a rather blank look on his face. Archie said, "I think we are going to get gassed today and I hope they teach us how not to die." He looked at Bill as he said that and Bill looked at me and I just shrugged my shoulders and wondered.

The instructor stood facing us and held the object high into the air. "Now what I have here is a standard Army issue gas mask. You will notice it is in a canvas bag that has a carrying strap for attaching onto your web belt. Now when I remove the mask you will see that it has straps and eyepieces. It also has a place to screw on a canister that will isolate you from any gas in your area. Now I need a volunteer. You on the front row, you just volunteered. Come up here." One of the soldiers went and stood next to the Instructor. "Now stand sideways to the group and I'll demonstrate how to use this gas mask. First, undo your belt and put the bag on it on your left side." He did so. "Now remove the mask and the canister from it's pack and hand them to me. Now you all watch as I assemble the canister to the mask." He took the canister, placed it in the receptacle on the front of the mask and screwed it in tightly. He then held the gas mask in the front, stretched the straps back and slipped his chin in first, then pulled the mask over the top of his head and pulled the straps tight. He then took a deep breath and while covering the canister with his hand, he blew inside the mask and then took in a deep breath. He rechecked the straps and then slowly turned in a circle to show us all sides of the mask. Then he loosened the straps, removed the mask and canister from the mask and handed it back to the 'volunteer'. "Now I want you to put this back in the pack and close it and secure it." After he finished the Instructor continued, "When you are in combat you may and probably will encounter gas. It will surely be poison and will kill you or severely damage you or neutralize you if breathed in. If at anytime you see or smell gas you are to immediately yell at the top of your lungs, 'gas' and then put your masks on.

He turned to the volunteer and yelled, "Gas! Get your mask out! Put in on. Hurry! Any delay could result in your death." He opened the pack pulled out the mask and dropped it to the ground. Then he picked it up and tried to put in on his head. But he had forgotten to insert the canister and pull the straps out. He dropped the canister and bent over to pick it up. "Stop! You are now a battlefield casualty. You have been gassed to death." He stood there looking at the Instructor with a look of bewilderment, tinged with fear. Bill leaned over to us and whispered, "I feel sorry for that fella!"

The Instructor continued, "My demonstration looked easy, didn't it? It was simple and straightforward, wasn't it? The difference was the need to move quickly to save your own life. You will feel panic in a combat situation. You must overcome that. Now, put your gear back in your pack. This time I want you to go slowly and complete the procedure." You people up there. No talking. You watch this carefully." This time he methodically went through all the steps and successfully got the mask on. "Take it off, as I demonstrated and place it back in the pack." As soon as he buckled the retaining strap on the pack, the instructor yelled, "Gas!" and the volunteer responded. He completed the task. The Instructor, noticing the volunteer struggling, told him to breathe. "You can safely breathe with the mask on, you know. Good, now take your seat," as he finished with the volunteer.

"Now we will go row by row. First row move out to the house over there and form a single line." We were each given a mask and we practiced several times as the Instructor watched. He corrected some and helped others until we all got it right. "Now this group on command will enter the house through the front door and once inside, stand in place until you are directed to leave by the back door. Do not remove your masks until told to do so. Do you understand? At some point there will be gas in the house. It is not pleasant to be in. Do not panic. Get the feel for being in gas. Move out."

We entered the house and stood as directed. Without any warning we heard several popping sounds and then saw a white cloud fill the room we were in. In just a few minutes we couldn't see because of the thick smoke. I sensed a burning sensation on my exposed skin. At first I held my breath, but then took shallow breaths to see if I smelled anything. My instinct was to run, but I stood still for several minutes until we heard the command, "Exit the rear door." Once outside and when told to do so, we removed the mask, disassembled it and stored it into the pack and deposited it on a table. We then returned to our seats to watch the next group. At one point we heard someone in the house coughing uncontrollably and the Instructor, with his mask on, ran into the building and pulled the soldier out and took off his mask and poured a bucket of water over his head. "Your mask was not on properly." He had the guy put his mask on again and pull the straps tightly and clear the mask this time. "Get in line with the next group and go in again." After all had completed the exercise, we returned to base. That day was over.

That night I wrote to Old Man, my parents and Mary. I related the events of the past few weeks. I gave them details on those things that impressed me or that seemed more important. I did not talk of the film we viewed or of the talk of killing and dying, but rather, tried to put everyone at ease. We have a place to post our letters and also have a mail call each day. I received three letters after several weeks of training.

Dear Son,

We all miss you and hope you are fitting in to the military way. Everything here is going fine. I hear that we will have a good cotton crop this year and the military is buying all that the gin can produce. Your Dad says to tell you that Mose asks about you a lot. Mr. Spencer sends his regards.

I hope you are getting enough to eat. Do you need anything that we can send you? Let me know.

Mary has called twice to see if we've heard anything. You are staying in touch with her, right?

Take care of yourself and write when you can. We miss you and pray for you.

Love,

Mother

Dearest Henry,

It seems like you have been gone forever. I think about you day and night. I pray that you are doing well and adjusting to military life.

Will you be able to come home after your training? I hope so! I miss you so much. I often hear your laugh when going to classes or at the Grill. Do you remember when we first met and you knocked me down? I believe I called you an oaf. That was before I really got to know you.

I love your parents and your friends that I met. I especially liked Old Man. I think he liked me as well. I think he is a very special person. I know how much he means to you.

Please be careful while there. I've heard how hard it is. You are a strong person, Henry, and God will watch over you. I'll dream of you tonight and I live for the day when I can hold you in my arms and kiss you.

    Write soon.

    Love,

        Mary

Henry,

    Have you learned close-order drill and marching yet? Do you have two left feet? What about KP? Tell me about your barracks and your drill sergeant. What is your biggest challenge so far? Have you found the quiet one yet?

    Mary is very special. You need to write her often. I believe she will wait for you Henry. Do you miss not being at school and your studies? I know that at this point where you will go is unknown. After Basic Training you will receive specialized, advanced training. I know you want to be a medic.

    Think Henry, and remember not to be a victim of fear. Learn well everything they teach you.

    Have they issued your rifle to you yet? When they do, I want a lot of detail about your training with it.

    I weary of writing now, so I will close. Write me soon.

    Old Man

It was so good to hear from everyone. I told Archie about the letters. He had gotten a letter from his family too. "I miss my family, Henry." Henry replied, "I don't know much about your family Archie. Do you mind telling me?" Archie was quietly thinking about how he would answer that. "Well Henry, I don't talk about it much. But I feel you will keep this just between us." "You can count on me not to discuss your private life. But let me say that if you don't want to talk, you don't have to. We can talk about something else. I don't mean to pry." I could sense he was uncomfortable.

He nodded and began to talk. "My Dad died two years ago. We were very close. He was my best friend. He loved me and my Mother and Sister and cared about us. We used to go to football games together. He was a big-time Packers fan. He could name all the players and their positions.

"He would take me fishing on the lake in winter and we would cut holes in the ice. He had his own shelter on the ice and it would get so thick you could drive out on it to the hut. We spent some good times in the hut, out of the cold, trying to catch the big one. Cancer killed him Henry." Tears were welling up in his eyes. "I am so sorry, Archie." He rubbed his eyes and then continued, "My Mom took it real hard. They had been high school sweethearts and married as soon as they graduated. My Sister is younger than me by seven years. She is still young enough not to fully realize the loss, but there are times when she asks about him and wants Mom to tell stories about him." He paused and looked away. "Where do you live Archie?" "I live in a little place named Algoma, Wisconsin. It's about forty miles East of Green Bay. My Mom works in a local office as a secretary. Dad had a pension at the plant where he worked and so they get by, I guess. Someday I'll go to college and get a degree to be a doctor and then I can take care of her." I could tell by his tone that he would someday do just that. We talked on and got to know each other better. The lights went out at ten o'clock. I lay on my back and thought about all the events of the day. I was homesick and missed Mary. I prayed for all my people and prayed for Archie and his family that night.

Those of us in our barracks noticed that one of the men was peculiar. He slept on the floor at night. For the first few nights no one noticed this odd behavior because we were all pre-occupied with our own problems. After a week however, his top bunkmate asked him about it. I believe the guys name was Jonas. "Jonas, why are you sleeping on the floor? Why don't you get in your bunk?" He said, "I can't sleep there." "Why not?" Jonas looked at the floor nervously, and then gazed out the window near his bunk. He was clearly agitated and started to walk away. "Wait a minute Jonas, I really want to know what's going on with you." He turned and returned to his inquisitor and said, "I can't make that bunk like they said. I ain't got no quarter anyway. I don't like it here and I want to leave." Then he shouted, "I'm going to talk to somebody right now about getting out of here!" With that, he left the barracks. Jonas did not return that night. We later learned that he went to the captain's office and lost it because he could not see him. He became violent, was apprehended and was taken to the Post Hospital. There he was sedated and kept for several weeks for evaluation by medical staff. We heard that he had to be restrained after he tried to kill himself. He later underwent mental fitness evaluation. A military board review was convened and he was discharged Under Section eight, being deemed mentally unfit for service in the military. None of us thought he was crazy. Archie said that maybe he was crazy like a fox.

One morning after PT, the drill sergeant told us we were going on a "little stroll," to use his words. We were issued field packs with attached butt pack. The packs had some equipment in them, but not the complete, standard issue. I think the added equipment was for additional weight. We also got a canteen and a hinged container to drink and eat with and a storage pack to attach to the belt.

We were instructed to line up three abreast and maintain cadence and distance, and moved out in company formation into the South Carolina woods along dirt roads and paths. At first I enjoyed the exercise and the woods were nice and cool that time of year. But as time passed I began to tire, as we had been marching for well over an hour. Finally the drill sergeant ordered us to halt and told us to sit down in shade and drink water. One of the guys asked about smoking. "Smoke 'em if you got 'em," the sergeant replied.

So we rested and Archie, Bill and I sat under a large pine tree near the road. "Where you think we goin to?" Bill asked. "I don't know but I hope we're about to get turned around. I'm getting tired of this pack and it's hot," I replied. I think the sergeant overheard the conversation and walked over to us. "You girls getting tired? You just need something to do to get your mind off this stroll we're on. I think you need to learn how to dig foxholes." We had fold up shovels on the back of our packs. Everyone got up and followed the sergeant to a clearing where he took the shovel from my pack and unfolded it. "Gather around us and watch now," he yelled out to the rest. "Now girls, this is known as an Army issue entrenching tool. You use it to dig a hole that you can climb in to keep from getting killed. There are several different types of holes. These three will demonstrate them for you."

Archie, Bill and I each prepared to dig holes. I was instructed to dig a rectangular hole, roughly three feet deep and wide enough and long enough to lie in a prone position within it. Archie was to dig a cylindrical hole about three feet in diameter and about four feet deep. Bill had to dig his about five to six feet deep and wide enough to accommodate two men, with a ledge in half of the bottom for one man to stand on and fire a weapon. "You are in combat and you are told the enemy is advancing in the distance. They will be on you in about thirty minutes. There is covering fire. This hole is to lie prone in to avoid shrapnel and fire. The single foxhole is for cover and returning fire. The deep foxhole is for two to cover and return fire and defend a perimeter. You have thirty minutes. Dig!"

Thirty minutes is not long, especially for Bill. We dug furiously and watched each other's progress to keep up. It was hot, extremely tiring and frustrating work. The soil was somewhat sandy but tough to dig in. Archie and I finished ahead of Bill. We watched him as he continued to throw dirt out of his hole. He muttered, "Man, this here ain't no picnic." The sergeant looked at me and said, "You just going to stand there Jimson while your friend works his rear end off? Get in that hole and help him!" Together we finished and jumped up out of the foxhole and admired our handiwork. Then each man in our company was instructed to climb into each foxhole and assume a combat position. Everyone lined up and one by one did as instructed. It was almost like a game, but the sergeant never changed expression. As soon as everyone had a turn, the sergeant said, "You people may think this is Mickey Mouse stuff. You remember this day when you hunker down in your own foxhole and hope to God it saves you."

We fell in and marched back to the post. "Sound Off," "One-two," "Cadence Count," "Three-four." "One, Two, Three, Four. One, Two! Three-Four!" We called out that cadence all the way back. Once in the barracks, field packs hit the floor and we hit our bunks, exhausted. Bill came over to our bunk after chow and before lights out. "Hey Jimson, I sure thank you for helping me out there, down in my hole, you know. Man I was so beat I don't think that there shovel had many more throws in it. Anyways, as my Pappy says to me, 'Boy you was about muled out'." Archie and I laughed and we started shooting the bull. "Tell me about yourself Bill." "What you wanna know?" "It doesn't matter. Just about you're coming up, your family, what you did and where you lived. You know. I'm just curious." Archie chimed in. "You got a funny way of talking, if you know what I mean. Does everyone from Selma talk that way?"

Bill thought about that. He looked puzzled and a little distressed. "What you mean by, I talk funny? I don't think I talk funny, just natural like," he said with a big grin and a slap of his knee. "You the one who talks funny, Archie. I think you been raised up North, right? No offense," he quickly added. Before Archie could answer Bill continued, "Well looka here, I was reared in Selma, Alabama. My Ma and Pa come up poor and we never had much in the way of money and all. But I'm telling you now, we was always happy. After a spell you come to like eating possum, sweet taters, cornbread, collards and all. Makes me hungry to think on it you know!"

"What kind of schooling did you get before coming here, Bill?" "Sixth grade. I tried seven twice and didn't see much use in trying again. I ain't much on books and stuff but I got plenty of walkin around sense." He thought about that for a few seconds and then continued, " I can work circles around most folks. Why my Maw use to say I was like an ole mule because 'you had to pull my head off to get me started and my tail off to get me stopped.' I got me five brothers, me being counted with em, and one sister. Everybody but me stayed right there in Selma and still do you know. I was workin at ole John's filling station, pumpin gas, changing oil, doin windshields, and different thangs when they told me to get myself into this here Army and go fight and all. So I did." He pondered on what he had just said and went on. "Now they ain't much goin on in Selma ya know. We had to make our own stuff up to have fun. My buddy Jeff had an old twelve cylinder Packard that sounds like a freight train when he winds it out. Boy that thang would get on down the road. He wore tires out all the time. Anyway, we could get eight of us in thar at one time and we would go out at night and fill up balloons with water, and find cars parked in the hot summer with their windows down and kinda ease up on em and thar would be a boy and a girl in thar neckin and we would lob that ole water balloon in thar and the yelling would commence, and we would high tail it, because they wasn't particularly fond of getting wet and all," he said with a laugh and a grin. "Man, that was some fun. Oh, and one night on a dare, we turned off all the red lights in town from the throw switch on the pole and got em all off at the same time. We quit doin that though because we heard the cops were stakin out looking for us and all, but we never got caught. My Pa woulda worn my bottom out if he found out, and I'm proud he didn't."

By this time all the people on the first floor had gathered around to listen to Bill tell his stories. Everyone was laughing and having a great time. Bill looked around and said, "Why looka here. I done got me a crowd rounded up. Ya'll like my stories?" Everyone said they did and that Bill was one of the good guys. Bill responded, "Well I'm gonna tell you what I think.

You guys is all right and I count you all as my buddies. This Army thang is workin out just fine by me. I'm plum tuckered out now and think I'll go to bed. Goodnight and don't let the bedbugs bite," he said with his by now, familiar grin. He left and we all packed it in for the night. Bill was a pleasant break from the tension of the day.

After the routine of the morning was completed, we were taken to an outside instruction class on the use of a compass, navigating over different terrains and map reading. A short course had been laid out in an open area with ten or so stations. After about an hour of instruction on nomenclature, demonstrations, and practice the instructor broke us up into groups of four. Within each group one man was given a compass and another a list containing compass headings and distances between stations. The remaining two found the stations on the map to verify the headings. We began at a start point and proceeded to station one, and so on, until the course was completed and all groups had participated. "Do any of you have any questions or need help in understanding what we have covered?" A couple of hands went up and they received further explanation of the procedure. "It is one thing to navigate with compass bearings, distances and a topographical map out here in the open with birds singing and the sun shining. But you will find that in combat it may not be so easy. This will become more familiar to you with practice. The maps will be used in the field to locate your position, find landmarks and traverse from point to point without getting lost. A lost soldier could be a dead soldier and those types are of little use to the Army," he stated with a cold stare. "Some of you are probably thinking that this is pretty easy. When you are in unfamiliar terrain and it is dark you will learn that it is not so easy after all. That is what we will do tonight right after chow."

For the rest of the day, we marched in formation and practiced drill maneuvers. Upon returning to the barracks we talked about the instruction we had received. Archie told me that he had a lot of experience in the woods. "You may not believe this, Henry, but you can get turned around real quick in deep woods. My Dad and I got lost one day hunting. We headed out in the direction we thought would take us back to the road and after about an hour we wound up in almost the exact same spot near the stream where we started. I learned later that you tend to go in a circle if you are lost." Dark was coming and I asked Dad if we were lost. He nodded and said that we were losing daylight. He walked over to the stream and noted the direction of the flow. He said we should follow the stream in the direction of its flow and eventually we would get out. Thankfully we had some food and water and a flashlight with us. We walked through heavy brush, went around big boulders, sloshed through mud and proceeded along the stream until almost midnight. The night sounds of woods are spooky and your imagination runs wild. You think of bears, cougars, bobcats and mountain lions and try not to. Finally, we saw lights in the distance and came out of the woods and into a town near ours. We found a filling station, with sleeping quarters in the rear. We knocked on the door and when it opened, Dad said, "We got lost in the woods this afternoon and we just got out. I'll pay you if you will take us to our truck back there on the road where we left it." The man was waking up and stretched and said, "Now Wilkins, how could you get lost in those woods? You've been around here forever. Let me get dressed and I'll get you to the truck. Come on in where it's warm." Dad knew this man and they had worked together at one time. "You not going to tell anyone about this are you?" Dad asked sheepishly. "Now Wilkins, why would I do that? It'll stay strictly between us." It was obvious to us that he couldn't wait to spread the word on how a good woodsman and his son got lost in the woods.

Bill had been listening. He walked up to us and chimed in, "Folks that know me say they could blindfold me and put me in one of them airplanes and fly me off to some place I ain't never been and drop me off, and it could be a hunert or two hunert miles away, and I could git back home, no sweat! And, they would be right! I ain't ever been lost in my whole life!"

Henry noted, "Well, I never had any experience in woods. Where I'm from is mostly farmland and for the most part, flat as a board. I guess if I were in Atlanta I could get lost, but I could stop and ask someone on the street for directions." "Shoot," Bill replied, "you could walk from end to end in Selma and almost see where you started from." Everybody really liked Bill. He had a way with words.

That night we loaded on trucks and drove for about twenty minutes into the woods. As we got out we saw what appeared to be a small shack with an overhead light on a pole.

We were broken up into pairs and given our written instructions, compasses and maps. "Now, listen up. Follow your instructions. Your stations will be marked. There are six of them. One of you handles the compass and instruction sheet and the other, the map. It is nine o'clock now. You have two hours to finish the course, which begins and ends on this spot. You will be quiet and speak in a whisper at all times. If you miss a station reverse your direction, back to the last station and redo. There will be observers watching you. Any questions?" There were none and so it began. Teams left the shack location in five-minute intervals on the first compass bearing and counting distance by stride. It was very dark.

I was paired with a person I didn't know. He asked which I wanted to do. I chose the map and he agreed. As we proceeded to the first station several hundred yards away, we double checked the information on the sheet and each looked at the compass with the flashlight several times to verify our direction. The distances from station to station varied and we really had to pay attention to the number of strides we were making. Without the flashlight we would have been in total darkness. Our surroundings were meaningless because we were isolated within our immediate position by the darkness. One tends to lose balance and often stumble in this environment. We were forced to maintain contact with each other at times by a hand on the shoulder. We were successful in completing the course in one hour and forty minutes. Several of the groups went over the time limit and got to pull KP and clean grease traps at the mess hall the next night. Everyone did manage to complete the course.

I talked to Archie and Bill about how they managed. Archie said that he felt lost at first, but then, got used to being in the woods and had little trouble with the pacing and finding the stations. Bill said, "I didn't have nothing to do with them instructions. My buddy did all that figgerin. I weren't much better with that compass, but I got the hang of it pretty quick. We did good to the fifth station but we wuz havin trouble tryin to make out the last part. So I said, 'come on' and I struck out and by golly, there we wuz back at the shack. Shoot, we didn' need that stuff. It wuz easy like, ya know! They told us we did good at about an hour."

The next day as we were policing our area and my mind was wandering, I noticed something remarkable. We had been in training for almost four weeks now and I was bulking up. Not only that, but I felt stronger and better than I had in years. My appetite had increased to the point that I stayed hungry most of the time. I also noticed a much greater interest in the training we were receiving and found myself concentrating on details and feeling more and more confident in my abilities. I confided in Archie and he agreed with me. He was also experiencing some of the same attitudes as mine.

After chow, we were issued mock wooden rifles and received instruction on how to handle our "weapons". We were ordered into formation and watched as the Instructor demonstrated each basic move with the rifle. After each, we repeated the move and continued until we all had done each one correctly. Over the next few days we handled our mock rifles with increasing dexterity until the movements became rote. We learned, among other things, how to execute present arms, order arms, port arms, parade rest with arms, inspection of arms, right and left shoulder arms, etc., over and over again until our arms and shoulders ached.

Over the next few weeks we practiced several more disciplines. We learned to negotiate an obstacle course. It involved climbing, lifting, running, crawling and assisting each other in strenuous tasks. The drill sergeant was always nearby, screaming at us and forcing us to do more than we thought humanly possible.

Of particular note was our instruction in hand-to-hand combat. We were divided into teams of twos, padded, helmeted and presented with poles with padded ends and set upon each other to knock our opponent down, out or senseless. Some were more aggressive than others. They seemed to take great pleasure in inflicting pain and dominating their perceived enemy. We were taught how to defend ourselves and to counterattack and incapacitate an enemy with basic maneuvers. I did not care for this class because I fell in the non-aggressive category and I paid dearly for it. Not only was I beaten senseless by my opponent, but had to endure the Instructors insults and my fellow trainees jeers or, in rare cases, encouragements. This training only reinforced my conviction to become a combat medic.

At mail call I got a letter from Old Man.

Henry,

The Brits are in North Africa now under Montgomery and are engaging Rommel's forces in the desert areas. I also hear that Hitler decided to occupy Russia in May and has his hands full. He is not the first to try to conquer Russia. The winter is usually harsh over there and it is reported that this winter is especially demanding on an invading land force. The battle for Stalingrad has been going on since August and it is not going well for the Germans. The Russians are experienced fighters and know how to handle invaders. They usually retreat and burn everything and kill all the livestock, so as to leave nothing behind for Hitler's forces. I see nothing but defeat, death and starvation for them.

Of course the Pacific is raging with many battles between the Imperial Japanese fleet and our surviving naval forces, greatly diminished by the Pearl Harbor attack. Much territory has been lost and many of the islands as well, through Japanese occupation. The Philippines fell as well. McArthur was not happy about that. He vowed to return. I also hear that the battle of Midway may have been a turning point. The battle for Guadalcanal was particularly difficult.

We have a presence in North Africa now and the battle continues. I hear a lot about General Patton and his rift with Montgomery. I hope he makes wise decisions with his forces. There is very little room for making tactical mistakes in war, especially now that we are trying to trap the German forces and keep them from retreating, intact, to Italy, where they may regroup and give us more trouble.

Are you still interested in the Medical Corps? If so, I would advise letting your company commander know so. Be sure to go through your drill sergeant. Don't ever go around him. He holds the "keys to heaven or hell" where you are concerned. Does he know your name? Be tactful, but when an opportune time presents itself, try to engage in conversation with him. Do you know the recruit who was appointed as your platoon leader? Let him know who you are. Some would frown on my advice. I think it could work to your advantage.

Have you been given your rifle yet? Write me soon and answer my questions.

Old Man

As coincidence would have it, the following Monday we were issued our M-1 Garand rifles and turned in our now familiar mock wooden ones. It is no exaggeration to say that this weapon was impressive. I have experience shooting squirrels with a 22. But that was a BB gun compared to this. When I first picked mine up from supply I was forewarned that I had better look at the serial number and memorize it. I'd be asked for it many times in the coming weeks. We were lined up to receive our rifles and then went to an introductory class on the weapon.

Archie said, "I have a 30 caliber rifle at home I hunt elk and deer with. I also have a double-barrel 12-gauge shotgun. But this thing is beautiful. It is heavier than mine and I am not sure about the caliber. I can't wait to fire it."

Bill looked his over, flipping it and sighting down the muzzle. He raised it to a firing position and looked down the beaded sight. He never touched the trigger or tried to operate it. He was obviously in awe of the rifle. "Man howdy, this here is one fine gun." The drill sergeant was nearby and heard Bill. He ran up to him and got nose to nose with him. He shouted, "Soldier, that is not a gun. Guns are on battleships. What you have in your hands is a rifle. If I ever hear anybody say 'gun' again, you will regret it!" Bill fell back and shouted back, "Yes, Sir, I mean Yes, sergeant." "Boy, you done called me 'Sir'. Now you drop down and give me thirty!" Bill instinctively thrust the rifle into the sergeant's hand and fell to the ground and did thirty pushups faster than you could say it. The sergeant was shocked at having been handed the rifle and watched in amazement as Bill rose and held his hand out to retrieve the weapon. "You a piece of work boy," as he pushed the rifle into Bill's chest. "Yes, sergeant."

From there we went to an introductory class on the M-1. We learned it was a powerful and extremely accurate rifle and that its ammunition was 30/06 caliber. It had a web sling. It was loaded with an eight round, top loaded clip and firing was single shot and fast. The sights on the rifle were excellent.

We were then taught basic handling of the M-1 in close order drills and while marching. The drilling and marching with weapon was incorporated into our routine. We became so connected to the rifle that it became a part of us and of every movement. A few days later our drill sergeant demonstrated how to field strip and reassemble the weapon to the class. He repeated the process several times as we watched intently. Then we were divided into small groups with our rifles to practice what we had learned. We proceeded in steps with the instructor guiding us through each one.

First we were to make absolutely sure that the rifle was not loaded by pulling back on the charging handle to eject the clip if present and any possible round in the chamber. Next, push down on the follower while holding the bolt and then allowing the operating rod to move forward. At that moment one of the trainees let out a scream and a litany of profanity, some words of which I had never heard before. "My thumb!" which he held up for all to see, was turning blue and beginning to swell. The sergeant calmly walked over to the unfortunate soul and grabbed his hand with the injured thumb. "Man that hurts. It's throbbing now," the trainee murmured, as he let out another string of profanity.

"Now boys, what we have here is your basic 'M-1' thumb. It happens to those idiots like this one here who fail to hold the bolt when the follower is pushed down. If you don't do that then the operating rod will do what it is supposed to. It will fly forward with a fair amount of force and mash your thumb. We instructors like to call this (waving the trainees injured thumb around for all to see), your basic training 'M-1 thumb'. I don't recommend it!" With that he laughed and released the hand. We, nor the injured man, saw any humor in what just happened. However, none of us made the same mistake from that day on.

"You people are going to take care of that Army issue rifle. If you don't care for it, then it will not take care of you. While it is in your possession you will not let it out of your sight. Let me repeat that. Never let your weapon out of your sight when you have it. It should be within easy reach at all times. Tonight you are going to sleep with it in your bunks. I want it to become a part of you for the next several weeks.

Tomorrow you will be taught how to clean the rifle in the field. A dirty rifle can malfunction and you could die as a result of your negligence. When it is not in your possession it will be either locked in racks in your barracks or turned in to supply. You will notice that the weapon has a serial number. Each one has a unique number. You will memorize that number and be prepared to give it whenever asked. Failure to do so will result in punishment. Do you understand me?" "Yes sergeant." One of the men raised his hand and the sergeant nodded at him. " Sergeant, can I ask a question?" "What?" "When will we get to shoot?" "Soldier, you will get to shoot when I say you are ready to shoot! In the meantime I am not willing to put my life on the line by handing you a loaded rifle." There was a murmur of laughter and an immediate reprimand.

The next day we had a class on cleaning the M-1 rifle. We learned to break it down, clean and reassemble it. Then we did it blindfolded until it became second nature to us. This exercise was repeated twice a day. Archie said, "I wonder why we repeat everything we learn?" "Well the Instructors here use a classic teaching method. The Instructor does and you watch. Then you do and he watches. Then you do." Henry continued, "Now compare that with learning in class at the university. You find out pretty quick that the professor is not going to do that. You better take good notes and listen. I had an Algebra teacher who had chalk in one hand and eraser in the other. As he wrote, he erased. If he didn't he would fill up the blackboard in no time. I don't think he really cared if you got it or not. But I think that here they really care, because we are being taught about how to survive. That puts a whole different slant on things, don't you think?" "Yes," Archie said, pondering the matter, and then observed, "You sure think a lot Henry." Bill grinned and said, "That thar Henry, he's got lots of smarts, ain't he."

That night Henry wrote the family, and asked his Dad if he would show Mose the letter also. Then in a letter to Mary he told her of his activities but spent most of his time telling her how much he loved and missed being with her. He told her he missed her laugh and her smile and even her sweet smell. He said things in that letter that made him blush. By this time she would be back in school and asked her to tell him all about that. He particularly wanted to know what she was taking and if she had made any new friends and what dorm she was in. "Tell me about what you are thinking and feeling every day," he added.

Then Henry turned his attention to Old Man.

Old Man,

I miss our times together. Thank you for the update on the war. We are pretty much isolated here and confined to the post. We get very little news from the outside. I'm trying to read between the lines on your observations concerning our battles in the Pacific, Europe and Africa. I realize that no one can predict outcomes in the war and certainly not of individual operations. There are so many variables. I wouldn't want a general's responsibility in planning and executing; especially where not only is the security of our Nation at stake but also the lives of our men. That must, at times, be an overwhelming responsibility. I'd like to know what you think of the war, and in particular, how long it might last and its outcome. I value your insight. I must tell you that based on our many, meaningful conversations, that I sense that you have personal experience with war. Am I correct?

I guess that preparation for combat is where military training becomes vital. It's interesting to me that what we learn here is a microcosm of what every soldier must learn. At every level of training and within every rank, men must be taught how to reach an objective and complete it. I guess it's about fighting and surviving in the final analysis.

I still want to be a medic. I've been wondering if reaching my goal is a matter of luck, education and intelligence or rather, how I make my wishes known to the proper parties. You have, once again, given me guidance. I'll do as you suggest, starting with a request to my drill sergeant. There must be some sort of qualifying exam to determine if one might be accepted. I'll request to see the company commander. His name is Captain Lewis. I haven't been able to get a good read on any of the drill sergeants, our sergeant or the company commander. The drill sergeants in general and our sergeant are tough nuts and have zero tolerance for screwups. I believe that their intention is to be authority figures and unapproachable so as not to become overly involved with the trainees. Now the Chaplin is a different story. I could tell after hearing him talk to us on Sundays that he is always accessible, with the drill sergeant's permission of course.

My drill sergeant doesn't even know my name. At least I don't think so. He did use it one day because it was sewn on my fatigues, but he doesn't really know me. In any event, he has never singled me out or carried on a conversation with me. In fact, I haven't seen him do that with anyone, except for those who foul up. Those that get his attention live to regret it. I'll look for the chance to let him know who I am.

The drill sergeant in charge of us singled out our platoon leader from among the trainees for that duty. At first I thought it was an honor. But I think he would be the first to tell you that it is not. He catches flack from both sides. If he does his job, then the men don't like him. If he doesn't do so, then the sergeant lights into him. He's told others that he is trying to figure out how to get replaced because the job is driving him crazy. I hope he doesn't notice me. He may decide to suggest that I replace him.

We were recently issued our rifles. They are M-1 Garand rifles that fire a 30/06 caliber shell. They are rather heavy at first, but carrying them and even sleeping with them has somehow made them seem lighter. We've been instructed how to field strip, clean, drill and march with them. I know the serial number by heart. The sergeant is not ready to turn us loose to fire them. I am anxious to do so.

Got to go now. Write soon.
Henry

The following week we received classroom instruction on various types of ordnances and what they could do. In the film we had previously watched we had seen what incoming rounds from the big guns could do to a body. We watched a training film where machine guns were setup and fired. I believe they fire 50 caliber rounds and can literally eat up a target. The film also illustrated other weaponry in use by the Germans, Italians and Japanese. The German ground troops used a Mauser K98 bolt-action rifle with some exceptions. It's not as good as our M-1 but could still kill you.

A frightening weapon used by the Germans was the 'bouncing betty'. When tripped it would send up a cylinder into the air about 4 feet where it would explode, throwing steel balls in all directions. It was deadly.

We also saw mortars, bazookas, anti-tank guns, sub-machine and machine guns exhibited and demonstrated in the film. Combatants are well equipped to kill men in various ways with these weapons.

After much anxious waiting, the day finally arrived when we were taken to a firing range to test our skills with the M-1 rifle. We were instructed without ammunition at first and learned to fire from standing, knelling and prone positions. The firing line had stations, one for each man with an Instructor to coach him in firing the weapon. It was there that I learned I suffered a handicap never before noticed. I could easily close my right eye by winking while sighting, but couldn't do so with my left eye. I tried sighting with the rifle on my left shoulder. It was very awkward and totally ineffective. The Instructor had seen this before and told me to leave both eyes open. The result was a double image target. When I told him that, he advised me to shoot the left image.

Next we were given an eight round clip and loaded it. "Now your weapon is hot. Keep the barrel downrange at all times. Assume the prone position. When you are told you may commence firing at the bulls-eye target in the distance, the one directly in front of you when it is raised. Keep the rifle tight against your shoulder. It will kick but you should hold the rifle as steady as possible. Fire at roughly five-second intervals, but not before you have your target sighted. When you have fired eight rounds the empty clip will eject itself. Retract the bolt and check the chamber. Do you understand?" "Yes, sergeant." He stood up and slightly to my rear and raised his hand. When all had done so, an Instructor in a tower to our rear, with a bullhorn said, "Ready on the right. Ready on the left. Commence firing." The targets were lifted. I took aim at the left image and pulled the trigger. The rifle fired with a loud discharge and the butt jammed against my shoulder. I continued to hold the weapon tightly and repeated firing until my rifle had fired all the rounds. The instructor said, "Retract the bolt. Be sure the weapon has no round in the chamber. You can now rise to a knelling position. Remember to keep the rifle aimed downrange when you move." He helped me get into a proper kneeling position and support my rifle with my elbow on my knee and wrap the web around my lower arm for stability. He handed me another clip and I loaded it and readied to fire. "Ready on the right. Ready on the left. Commence firing." The target reappeared and I fired my rounds again. " Check your chamber and stand at rest with your weapon pointed toward the target. Your scores will be given to me shortly. Within minutes the scoring sheets were distributed to each station. The sergeant looked at my scores and said," Son you scored 14 out of 16 inside the target with 11 in the bulls-eye from prone and 12 out of 16 inside the target with 8 in the bulls-eye from kneeling position." "Is that good sergeant?" "For a man who can't wink his left eye that's not bad. Now fall in and board the trucks."

When we got back to the barracks we couldn't wait to compare notes. I scored slightly better than Archie, but he was very pleased with his score and his Instructor seemed satisfied as well. "How'd you do Bill?" I inquired. "I guess ok. I missed that dadburned bulls-eye once on each of them tries." "You mean you put 14 rounds in the bulls-eye?" "Yea, if they hadn't made me wait so long between shots, I coulda hit it ever time. I guess that's just the Army way though. I do better when I'm shooten them movin turkeys in the woods, you know." Everyone listening nearby shook their heads in amazement.

The next day we formed up and marched about three miles off base to a remote area and sat on bleachers. In front of us was a large open field. In the foreground were eight concrete enclosures, roughly six feet high and eight feet square. Each contained a narrow entry point to the rear of the enclosure and what appeared to be a pit inside. Archie whispered to me, "I think we're about to throw some hand grenades." He was correct. We received about thirty minutes of lecture time during which a hand grenade was exhibited and its elements explained. We then divided up with drill sergeants, one on one and we were given dummy grenades to practice with. We were taught how to throw from different positions, basically from prone to kneeling and prone to standing.

Throwing a hand grenade in the manner taught was very awkward to me. You faced your target, armed your grenade, extended your non-throwing arm out and up from your shoulders and placed your throwing arm cocked and just to the rear of your cheek. Then, with a forward thrust, you threw the grenade, in a stiff armed fashion, upward and outward in a lofting trajectory. We were told that it was more important to strive for distance, as accuracy was not that critical. We learned that the kill range of a fragmented hand grenade was very impressive. Next we took our positions and threw several dummy grenades to get the feel of it. Once the Instructor was satisfied we advance to the concrete bunkers. When inside the enclosure we learned the purpose of the pit. It was there to jump into for cover in the event the grenade did not clear the wall or was accidentally dropped. It was at that point that the deadly seriousness of handling a live grenade hit me. The Instructor expected me to be nervous and so, told me to relax and think about what I had been taught. With one more dummy grenade he gave me step-by-step commands, from prone to standing position. I parroted arming, preparing to throw and then threw the grenade over the wall. He watched me and then over the wall at the trajectory of the grenade until it landed. "Good," he stated and then he placed me in prone position and handed me the live grenade. Once in my hand, I gripped it in a death grip, being careful to hold the body of the grenade around its arm, but not to cover the top or the ring pin.

"When you stand, look over the wall briefly to identify your target. In combat be quick because you will be exposed to the enemy. Now, stand. Identify the target. Arm the grenade." I pulled the pin and assumed the throwing position. "Throw and duck!" I did so and in short order there was a loud explosion. We stood together and looked out to see debris all around my target and dust settling. "How far did I throw it sergeant?" " About thirty yards. You did that well, Jimson. Now we will do it again." I repeated the procedure with two more fragmentation hand grenades. With my ability evident, I was dismissed and returned to the bleachers to watch the others.

There seemed to be a system to redo at the dummy grenade stations. If for any reason the instructor was not satisfied you waited and then went back for a repeat until you got it right.

I watched as Bill took his turn in the bunker. He completed the first live grenade task as instructed. He seemed to be talking to the Instructor as he was handed another live grenade. He went through the procedure, except that this time he threw it like a football. Everyone watched with amazement. The grenade traveled upward and outward in a high lofted arc and landed some seventy yards into the field and exploded. "Wow!" was the response from the bleachers. The Instructor was clearly agitated. After a nose-to-nose chewing out, Bill ran back to the bleachers, as ordered.

We later learned that he was put on pots and pans for a month for the stunt.

The next phase of our training involved the use of our rifles in simulated combat conditions. Everyone took a turn at firing at pop up silhouettes placed at varying distances and random positions in front of us. We took prone positions and fired at the targets. The area had trees, mounds and brush and the targets were well concealed. The drill took place with an Instructor and consisted of firing an eight round clip, reloading and continuing to fire until completed. When a target was hit, it would drop and another would appear at another location and distance. You were scored on whether you identified the target, how quickly you engaged it and number of shots required to hit it. I think there were sixteen targets in all, but I was not sure.

We took our stations and received instruction on what to do. We were being graded on time and accuracy. Then to demonstrate, several pop ups, which had the appearance of the upper torso of a man, came up and descended so that we could see how they worked and appeared. They did not stay up very long. The first one was very near and I fired and it descended. I did not see the next at all. From then on, I saw and hit every target. I had become accustomed to instinctively shooting at the left image. There were spotters with binoculars that watched each trainee's results. Archie and I both received a "Sharpshooter" designation and Bill an "Expert" which was the highest level.

I wrote Mary that night to catch her up on our life at Fort Jackson.

Mary,

You won't believe what I've done here. We've been worked into excellent shape through extremely difficult physical regimens. We drill and march and then we do some more. We practice everything over and over until it becomes automatic. We've been exposed to gas, thrown live grenades, marched for long distances, watched very graphic wartime movies, learned how to navigate at night with maps and compass, and now have a rifle with which we've become very familiar. It is my constant companion, but not nearly as comforting as you. I am a pretty good shot with the rifle and my scores show it.

We gain confidence every day and behave more like soldiers and less like civilians. The transformation is remarkable and I notice it in all my fellow trainees. I guess that is the purpose of basic training. You are dragged, kicking and fighting into manhood I seems. But inside, I have not changed. My love for you since we've been apart has only grown. I think of you often, but mostly in the quiet of night, lying in my bunk. I live for the day we are once more together, and married. I hope you still like me. Do you?

We have barracks to sleep in and mess halls to eat in. However, we don't sleep that much. The food is ok. They serve liver on oc-

casion and I put a lot of ketchup on it to hide the vile taste. I eat it because I'm always hungry.

KP is no fun but we all have to pull it. Army pots are immense and you literally climb halfway inside to scrub them. We police the grounds around the barracks and clean inside. We also clean the floors and the latrines until they shine and glisten. The object is to pass unannounced inspections. The sergeant abhors what he calls, 'do-overs'. That has become a part of our lives as well.

It is amazing how organized my belongings are, with Army issue stored neatly in my footlocker and civvies in my standing locker. We haven't worn our civilian clothes since arriving. I'm not sure what civilian shoes would feel like anymore. We always wear combat boots. We have khakis and dress uniforms, but have not worn them yet either. I hear that when we graduate there will be a parade with what is called, 'passing in review', and we must be very sharp that day. I can't wait for that to happen.

Tomorrow I'm going to ask for permission to see the captain in charge of our company. Old Man advised me to do this. I want to tell the captain that I want to be a medic and whether it is possible to get it worked out before basic is over.

Well, it's time now for lights out, and I'll close with hugs and kisses.

I love you,
Henry

We had a short break before going to the mess hall, so I went to our drill sergeant's office. I knocked on the door and I heard a voice say, "Enter". I walked in and stepped up to the sergeant. He was sitting at his desk and looking at some paperwork. He glanced up and said, "What do you want, Jimson?" "Sergeant, I would like permission to see the captain." "And why would you want to do that?" He was looking at me with suspicion now. I remained at attention and replied, "When I finish my basic training I want to go to advanced training to be a combat medic. I'd like to find out from the captain how to go about that," I answered. The sergeant tilted back in his chair and was looking at me inquisitively now. "You are one of the trainees that went to college. You got a full year behind you?" "I did finish my freshman year. I want you to know sergeant that it's not because I don't want to be an infantryman. It's because I'd like to help men who are wounded or need medical care and perhaps even work with doctors in a field hospital." "I've noticed you, Jimson. You have a good attitude and catch on quickly. I did notice that you were one of the ones watching the combat film that had to go out and puke. Right? So how does that square with you being able to handle blood and guts in combat?" "The fact of the matter is, I've never seen anything like that before and it shocked me. But I'm sure that the purpose of the film was to show how terrifying war can be and to prepare us in advance for what will be coming for us as well."

He nodded and smiled and then said, "You go back to duty now. I'll speak to the captain and tell you what he says." "Thank you, sergeant," and I turned to leave. "Jimson, do you know what is next for you people? You are going to experience a little reality. See you after chow." He was right about the reality part.

Our platoon leader instructed us to get our helmets because we were going to need them. Our helmets came in two pieces. The outer, steel shell and a hard inner lining with adjustable straps for a good fit. There was also a chinstrap. We also secured our rifles from the racks and fell in outside.

The drill sergeant addressed us while in formation. "You are now going to be exposed to live fire in a controlled setting. But it will feel very real. 'Attention! Inspection arms!"

We came to attention and brought our rifles to inspection position. The sergeant went down each row, taking each weapon, inspecting it, and returning it. We then released the bolt and returned the weapon to our side. "When we are finished today, you will field strip and clean your weapons back to the condition in which I've just seen them. You will then reassemble them and fall in at attention and wait for further orders. Understood?" "Yes, sergeant!"

"Fall out and get in the trucks." We scrambled into the trucks, left the main post and bounced along for about thirty minutes on rough, dirt roads. Dust was swirling up and into the back of our truck. No one complained. "Anyone have an idea where we're going?" I replied, "We're going to experience a little reality." Everyone looked at me as if I had lost my mind.

Upon arriving we disembarked and fell in. An Instructor then arrived and addressed us. "Men, you are at the live fire combat training course. The purpose of this exercise is to teach you how to react when being fired upon by the enemy. That means that there will be live, fifty caliber shells passing over your heads and being fired by machine guns. The course will be fifty yards long and divided into lanes. You will stay in your lane at all times. You will crawl and not walk or run. You will not, under any circumstances, stand up until instructed to do so. At times you will have to move from your belly to your back to negotiate the course. You will know when that is necessary. There are barbed wire strands immediately above you for the full length of the course. When you get to the end of your lane, you will remain on the ground until the 'all clear' is sounded. If for any reason, panic or otherwise, you are compelled to rise up above the barbed wire and try to run, in that event, we will notify your next of kin. Have I made myself perfectly clear? Are there any questions?" He paused, looked up and down the ranks and then said, "All right, realign yourselves in ten lines and then follow me. Keep your spaces!"

We went behind the Instructor into a clearing. Everything was there as he described it. Our sergeants were following us to the rear. When we halted we were told to watch a demonstration. One of the Instructors moved about half way down the lines and away so that everyone could see. He fell to the ground on his chest, held his rifle in both hands in front of him and began to crawl. He used his elbows and his knees to push and pull his body forward. He did not raise his head or body any higher than a foot while moving. He then pulled his rifle in to his body and rolled over and placed the rifle on his chest. Then he used his shoulders and feet to pull and push with. He kept his head low at all times.

The machine guns where aligned so as to lay a pattern of fire across all lanes. In the distance, dirt had been mounded up to stop the rounds. "Now line up on the lanes, first man on the ground. When he is about ten feet out, then the second man proceed and so on, until all have completed the course. There will be explosions in addition to the live fire overhead. Under no condition will anyone raise up from your crawl position. Do you hear me?" We all responded, "Yes, sergeant!"

When the first two men had entered the course, crawling along on their stomachs, suddenly the machine guns began to fire. The sound was deafening. You could hear the shells whistling as they passed overhead. In a few minutes there were two loud blasts followed by a rain of dirt, mud and water. The staccato sound of the machine guns never let up. You couldn't hear anything else but flying bullets, explosions and your heart pounding in your chest. At the halfway mark, I encountered a swale with about six inches to a foot of water in it. As I went down the swale it became obvious that I'd have to get on my back to get through the water and mud. I finally cleared the obstacle with my rifle on my chest. I tried unsuccessfully to keep the weapon out of the water. By this time I was soaking wet and muddy. I kept repeating to myself as I went up the opposite side, "Don't raise up." Near the top I flipped over and continued to crawl. An explosion near me threw mud and water all over me so that I had to wipe it from my eyes, without lifting my arm. In addition to the reports of the machine guns and blasts and the barbed wire overhead and the confusion of it all, I was becoming exhausted. I glanced up to see the end about ten yards ahead. I finally reached the end and stopped. I lay there, gratefully, until the Instructor told me to get up, go to my left to tables set up there and field strip and clean my weapon. I did so and then waited as more came and finally, the last one finished the course.

We were allowed to drink the water provided after re-assembling our rifles. The sergeant again inspected our rifles, after which, we returned to the trucks and went back to the post and to our barracks to shower and change clothes. As we finished up our sergeant entered and went upstairs for an unannounced inspection, which he performed upstairs and down. When he got to our bunk he stopped. "Jimson, report to the captain immediately after noon chow. Be at his office at 1230 hours promptly." When he left Archie leaned over and whispered, "What have you done?" "Nothing. I asked to see the captain and he obviously agreed to see me." I smiled and Archie frowned.

I walked up the steps for my appointment and knocked on the door. A voice called out, "Enter." I went in and told the orderly I had an appointment with the captain. "Name?" " Private Henry Jimson corporal." He looked in his file basket and pulled a file, stood and instructed me to have a seat. He went into the captain's office and then re-appeared. You can go in now. As I rose to do so, he approached me and whispered, "Knock first and be sure to come to attention and salute the captain, hold the salute until he returns it and then state your name and rank." I nodded and thanked him.

Upon knocking I heard the captain say, "Enter," and I went in and did exactly as the corporal advised. "Private Henry Jimson reporting as ordered Sir." "Stand at ease, private. State your business." "Sir, I am not sure how to go about requesting assignment to the Medical Corps upon completion of my basic training and don't want to miss the opportunity to do so timely." He was reading my file as I spoke and when he finished he looked up. "Sit down Jimson, and let's talk about this." "Yes, Sir," and I sat.

"Tell me why you want this assignment and when you made that decision." "Well, Sir, I guess it was some time after Pearl Harbor. I saw the films depicting the wounded at the time being given medical attention and those who went in the hospital later on. I felt I needed to do something for my country and caring for men like those seemed the right thing to do."

"I see here, looking at your file, that you have a year in a university. How were your grades?" "I am a good student Sir. I carried a very high average." "Four point," he inquired. "Yes Sir." "How are you adjusting here?" "Sir, in the beginning I was overwhelmed with the pace and difficulty of it. I felt lost and homesick. But my family taught me that whatever I did, to do it to the best of my ability and to take pride in my results. I've tried to do so here. It is getting much better. I've come to appreciate the benefit of the discipline and of being pushed to the limit. Lately, I've also come to realize that this is serious training that it is designed to make me an effective soldier. And above all, Sir, I am motivated by love of my country. I want to protect it and my family from this aggression which has forced us into war."

"Good. Is being a Doctor of Medicine in your future?" "Sir, I don't really know right now. I've not ruled it out and it would seem logical if I am assigned to the Medical Corps. But I try to live in the day right now and prepare myself for what lies ahead. Decisions like that can come later, Sir."

He sat there for several minutes. I could hear the clock on the wall ticking as he continued to review my file. Finally, he looked up at me and said, "I am going to arrange for you to be tested, Jimson. I personally have no doubt how you will do, but my recommendation will depend on the outcome. I'll arrange for you to be tested Saturday morning at 0700 hours. Afterwards, you will be advised concerning your advanced training request. This is not exactly standard operating procedure, but I'm going to do this for you. If you have no questions then you are dismissed." I stood and saluted and exclaimed, "Thank you, Sir." That night I wrote everyone about the news and assured all that they would know as soon as I did.

Saturday I took a battery of tests and with the support of a letter from the company commander, I was later advised that my request for assignment had been approved and, that upon completion of basic training, I'd be sent to a new base for advanced training.

Our last field exercise would be a 32 mile forced march with full combat gear. It consisted of 16 miles out, a stay overnight in tents and then 16 miles back to the post.

Rising at 0500 hours, time to get ready for the day, and then, after chow, we were taken to a class on wilderness survival. Archie was right at home with this subject. He had taken many trips with his Dad and others into deep woods in Wisconsin and near the Great Lakes.

We were taught how to set up camp, construct latrines and how to organize the medium tents used for equipment and supplies. The setting up and striking of two man tents was demonstrated. Dos and don'ts on building fires, establishing perimeters and procedures for guarding them were also taught. Simple things on where to pitch tents in inclement weather were covered as well as the use of camp tools. We learned about C-rations and the various foodstuffs they contained and how to treat native water with chlorine tablets for drinking.

After class and noon chow we were issued additional gear for our backpacks and instructed how to arrange the gear in them. Our fully loaded packs and gear weighed on the order of eighty pounds. We all helped each other to adjust the backpacks with the provided strapping so that it would not slip, rub or move on our backs. If it did it would be a serious problem. A caution was given to bring three extra pairs of socks and to lace the combat boots tightly. We were told to change socks as needed and basic first aid procedures for the feet. The sergeant warned us that blisters on the feet would be inexcusable and very painful. There would be no stopping for such a problem and the march would only be interrupted by extreme emergencies.

We divided into platoons and marched as a company. The maneuver began at 1300 hours and we could see that it would be a clear day. That was a good thing. It would not have mattered, however, if we had marched in the pouring rain. It made no difference to the Army. Archie was in the column in front of me and we were able to talk quietly when the sergeant was not near. We marched for about an hour and I calculated that we had gone about three miles. "How you doing Archie?" "I'm fine. Thank goodness it isn't raining, although I am beginning to sweat. That's probably from the weight of all this gear. I think it will get hotter as we go. How about you, Henry?" "You know, when we first got here and started training we were in pretty bad shape. Could you imagine back then, carrying this weight and bearing up under the hot weather and the non-stop distance we are going to travel today? In fact, even though I'm in great condition now, I still have my doubts about today. I can never get over how they can push us to do things I never thought possible. I'll be glad to get wherever we're going." "I'll second that!" After a couple more hours the conversation had ceased because we were beginning to struggle at this point. You could see men in front of us slowing down and then hastily regaining their positions in ranks, only to slow again. Most of us were drinking water from canteens by now. The word passed back to take a salt tablet, so we did. Some of the less fortunate were obviously having trouble with their feet because they were limping and hobbling along. Occasionally the sergeants would admonish those who fell behind to pick up the pace and maintain position.

By 1800 hours we were a sorry sight. The backpacks that were roughly 80 pounds in weight now felt twice that and shoulders were drooping under the burden. Every muscle in my body ached and I had the uneasy fear that the next step I took might be the last one I could take. I thought I might be losing consciousness. My vision was blurring, my mouth was bone dry and instead of the profuse sweating as before, now I was feeling flush. Worst of all, I began to lose my strength and my determination to continue. I was not alone in my condition, as men ahead of me were obviously in a similar state. Mercifully, I heard a command passing down the ranks. "Company, Halt!" As each sergeant relayed the command, a second came. "Fall out!" We broke ranks and walked to the edge of the road. The sergeants were telling us to remove our backpacks, drink water and sit down off the road and rest. That order did not have to be repeated. Most collapsed on the ground, using the backpack as a headrest. Men were moaning and groaning up and down the area. I almost fell asleep as I tried to relax. Bill had been two lines up and he came to where Archie and I had collapsed. "I'm plum tucker'd out. I ain't never in my whole comin up ever toted such a load that far." As he stood there smiling over us I said, "Bill, you need to drink some water and lie down. Your face is beet red. Aren't you tired?" "Henry, that thar was a dumb question. I reckon I ain't never felt this way before. Them Army folks git off on seeing what you made of. I got to say that I'm close to broke! I think I'll rest a bit," as he removed his backpack. If I had not been so exhausted I might have laughed. Archie just shook his head in disbelief.

Most of the men had removed their boots and socks to check for blisters. Those that had them applied iodine and a bandage and then put on clean, dry socks. We were allowed a twenty-minute break and then put to work setting up camp. It took about an hour to complete the camp and then we sat up our two man tents. Archie was an expert at this and I simply assisted him. We were some of the first to put our gear inside and finish.

The camp was organized in groups of platoons. The time to eat came and we all broke out our C rations. There were provisions for three meals. Ham, chicken or turkey were the meats and included were biscuits, crackers, sugar, fruit bars and candy. Also included were powdered coffee and other powdered drinks and to top it off, gum, cigarettes, toilet paper, spoon and matches. After opening the pack I observed, "Man, the Army thinks of everything don't they?" Archie said, "I'm so hungry I could chew on shoe leather so this looks pretty good." I wouldn't have called it pretty good, but it was filling.

At nightfall assignments for perimeter duty were given to designated sentries. Each group would be responsible for standing guard in two-hour shifts until daylight. A password would be relayed to each replacement when they took their positions. During the night, a sergeant would test the men. "Halt, who goes there?" "Sergeant Smith," was a reply. "Password?" If the correct password was given, the individual passed by. If not, then the intruder was challenged. We were taught that morning in combat, if the incorrect password is given or none was given, then the sentry was ordered to shoot the intruder.

We cleaned up and settled in our tents for the night. I listened to some of the men nearby talking and shortly all conversation ceased. Everyone was really tired and went to sleep quickly. I listened to the night sounds. The wind had picked up a bit and trees in the distance were amplifying the wind sound as it blew through the limbs, making a rustling sound. I heard a distant howl, probably of a dog, that sounded mournful and haunting. He continued for several minutes and then went quiet. Some of the men began to snore loudly. A trainee in the tent next to ours crawled out and went to the trench we had dug and returned, complaining about the cold of the night. All was still. I drifted into sleep, thinking of Mary.

The next morning we got up and took care of the usual morning personal routines. I put on my fatigues outside the tent and also, fresh socks. My feet were in good shape. We were told to break down the camp and then our tents and take them to the trucks waiting for the camp gear. Afterwards we broke out the breakfast C rations and prepared for the march back to the post. "Perhaps the march back will be easier," I said to Archie. "Right. Very funny, Henry." Surprisingly, it was easier. I guess knowing what to expect made the difference. That's not to say it was any less physically demanding, but I believe we were prepared mentally. In any event we got back in a little under 12 hours and were dismissed to our barracks until chow. I turned my extra gear in to supply and then came back to wait for the showers to clear.

Archie and I had discussed the public and open showers. I wasn't comfortable in there, naked and exposed, along with nine other men in like condition. Neither was he. I told Archie, "I don't look down while I'm in there. I soap down with my head in the air. It's hard to wash my lower body with my chin pointing straight up. If I drop my bar of soap, then it becomes almost acrobatic, as I search by feeling around on the floor, briefly glancing down, but mostly while looking at the ceiling. I almost lost my balance recently. That would have been disastrous. Some of the men got a kick out of my trying to be modest, but I can't help it." Bill joined in the conversation. "Shoot guys, it don't bother me none to look around and compare notes, if you git whar I'm comin from," he said with a loud laugh. "Shoot, I come up being bathed with my brothers on the back porch in a wash tub. It ain't no big deal to me!" Those around us laughed out loud. Bill provided comic relief to an otherwise awkward situation, which was welcomed by everyone within earshot.

The time had arrived to complete basic training. We came in as civilians and we would leave as well trained soldiers. It's an amazing change in an individual at every conceivable level. The sergeant told us that we would have a graduation exercise. For the first time we would wear our dress uniforms and form up in companies to perform what is called in the military, a 'Pass in Review' ceremony. After that we would stand down and receive our new orders for advanced training. Most of the men would stay on post to continue their training. I'd be assigned to a new post where I would receive combat medical training. I wasn't sure how that would work, but knew that new orders would be provided to inform me when I could expect to be deployed, how I'd travel and where I would go.

We practiced as companies on the parade field for three days, usually two hours at a time with brief breaks in between. First we were organized into military groupings. We were initially divided into squads of thirty men each. Four squads would group into a platoon and finally, four platoons would form a company. We marched as a battalion, comprised of four companies with a total man count per battalion of one thousand nine hundred twenty men. Some were designated as platoon leaders and each platoon had an accompanying drill sergeant. Flag bearers were placed up front to lead us.

On the first day it was an uncharacteristic event, with a certain level of confusion because of the efforts to organize us in ranks by height. The drill sergeants were very impatient as we shuffled about trying to find the right places to stand. "You people remind me of chickens in a barnyard. Shape up in there and be quick about it. We don't have all day for this!" When each company was finally formed up and was reviewed by the sergeants, company-by-company, we were told to remember our positions and that they would remain the same until the parade was completed. To test us, we were ordered to fall out and gather on the side of the field and then fall back into our designated positions. Thankfully, this resulted in a successful regrouping, with all personnel in their correct places. "Good! Now tomorrow we will give you instructions on how to conduct a 'Pass in Review' and then we will practice. You are dismissed to your barracks until going to chow. At 1800 hours you can go to mail call and then return to barracks, so that your sergeants can talk to you. Fall out!"

When I got back everyone had gathered on the first floor and the sergeant was standing at the door, waiting for the rest of us to arrive. No one was called to attention and most were milling about and talking. "All right, settle down. I want to give you some pointers on 'Passing in Review'. Gather around and those in front sit on the floor. Now listen up because this is important. There will be brass in the grandstand and so I want you crisp and sharp at all times. What you do out there is not just an indicator of your level of training. It is tradition. How you conduct yourself will not only display your level of training, but also will be a reflection of your pride in the U.S. Army. Take some extra time at night before the event to clean your brass and spit shine your dress shoes. Learn how to tie a military knot. Get a buddy and check each other out."

He paused as if struggling for the right words. "I've done my job with you men. I've been tough on you and yelled, prodded and insulted you. You have good reason not to like me, but that is ok with me, because I am not looking for your approval. I am looking for trainees that I've transformed into soldiers. I've tried to teach you skills that may save your lives someday. Remember what you have learned here. You will be better men because of it. Oh yes, and one more thing. Take a salt tablet before you march. Also remember when standing at attention for long periods, do not lock your knees, but keep them flexible. If you faint you will lie there and the columns will march over you; understood?" "Yes, sergeant."

"I could tell you that you have done well here, will make good soldiers and that I am proud of the way you have turned out. But I'll not do that." With that he dismissed us. As he turned to leave, to a man we all stood at attention and remained still, facing him. As he walked out some noticed that he was smiling.

On the second and third days, we practiced moving past the reviewing stand and around the field in a circle, and back to the point of beginning. As we began to Pass in Review we received the command, "Eyes, right!" Then when we cleared the stand, "Front!" We stood at attention for extended periods of time until our company stepped out. Every move was made with precision. I thought by the end of the third day we had become a cohesive unit and extremely smart as we marched around the field.

"The exercise will take place in the morning at 1100 hours sharp. You will be on the field no later than 1000 hours, and ready to go. 'Dismissed', and we were released until the next morning. There was an air of excitement back at the barracks. We worked on our uniforms, shoes and brass. The toes of the shoes were so polished and spit shined that they reflected images and the brass, with Brasso and elbow grease, glittered.

I went to mail call later and got three letters. Back at the barracks I opened and read Mary's first.

Dearest Henry,

I've been counting the days and know you are about to finish there. Am I right? Do you know what is next? I am anxious to hear from you, so you can catch me up.

School is really going well. I am making good grades and really like my classes.

Football season has started and I went to a game with my girlfriends. We won! I really don't understand what they are doing out there. I just cheer when everybody else does. You will have to explain it all to me when you get home.

I love you and miss you so. What do you hear from your parents and Old Man?

Please write to me soon.

I Love you,

Mary

The second letter from my parents caught me up on all the local news. Mother said they were regularly attending church and that I was asked about at almost every service. It seems that more of my friends had joined up since I left, and all the families missed their boys. Mother formed a group of women that were meeting weekly to support each other and to keep up with events concerning the war effort. Rationing of certain goods and commodities began in May and the families in Mark Hill were acquiring ration books and tokens to use to purchase limited quantities of designated supplies. The military had priority needs for certain goods, and some items were already in short supply.

Hello Henry,

I would really like to see an M-1 and fire one. You said that you scored as a sharpshooter. That is very good. You do realize that your training is very important to your survival in combat. But I really don't need to tell you that, Henry.

Even though your training with weapons is important, as a medic you will not carry one. Medics are only permitted their use in defense of their patients or themselves in a combat situation. I hope you never have to make that decision.

Even though the war seems to be ebbing and waning in our fight, I believe we will prevail. This country loves freedom and our enemies want to enslave or annihilate us. Those who think we should try to appease the enemy are deceiving themselves. Which prompts me to forewarn you Henry. There will be those who consider choosing to be a medic is somehow failing to do your duty for your country. Some will want to know if you are a conscientious objector and others will accuse you of cowardice. I know your reasoning but feel that you should be prepared for the criticism and scorn that will come. It will only be when one of them is wounded and shouting 'Medic!' that you will be admired and even considered heroic.

Enjoy your graduation and parade. It is a special time and actually, quite moving.

Respectfully,
Old Man

As I've often wondered, how does Old Man know so much about the military? My suspicion is that he may have had first hand experience, but prefers to remain silent on his identity and his past. I wish I knew, but I respect him so much that I've never pried, and never will.

The day had finally arrived. As we entered the parade field in our formation we heard the band playing marches. All the flags were posted and flapping in a mild breeze and the sun was brightly shining. Up in the reviewing stand were officers of various ranks, up to and including the Commandant of Fort Jackson, a one-star General. There were a few women sitting alone and many families present as well.

We took our places and went to Parade Rest. A sense of pride welled within me. I now felt a part of something bigger than myself. I believe that my experience that day was one of the most impressive of my life. The General addressed us with a congratulatory speech. Unit captains were recognized and dignitaries and guests were introduced.

"Attention." "Pass In Review!" We began to march, with the color guard leading the way and the band following. The band played several marching songs that day, including many Sousa pieces. As each company reached the reviewing stand, the command "Eyes, Right!" was executed, which was maintained until the stand was cleared. "Front!" Heads smartly snapped to the front. Then we were dismissed and hats flew into the air in celebration. Guests and the soldiers mingled and visited with one another. There was much joy and elation that day.

The rest of the day we spent time visiting and talking about the events of the day and our futures. We were allowed to show the visitors our barracks and other points of interest on the Post. Orders for advanced training assignments were forthcoming, but for now, we were able to relax. Some walked the Post while others stayed in the barracks. It was strange not to have to be in a certain place at a specified time to be trained in a particular way. Free time was uncomfortable to me. But I will say that I used the time to do mostly nothing at all.

At the canteen that night three of the drill sergeants sat at a table in deep conversation. They were thinking back on this class of trainees. "They always look and act the same when they first get off the bus at the reception. I'd call them lost and bewildered, scared and unsure, and mostly, well, civilians." The other two nodded in agreement. "You know, what we do is really odd. We take boys and make men. I mean, remember the first morning on the field trying to teach them simple calisthenics. 'Which one is my right?' they would wonder. It is unbelievable how uncoordinated some of them are. The shape these kids are in when we get them is pitiful. But then slowly, and I mean slowly, they seem to get the hang of it. Some catch on fairly quickly to the training. Others are not so bright and have to be prodded like cows. I wonder sometimes if they understand the training at all."

Another joined in, "Man, I laughed so hard my sides hurt at the grenade range when you gave that kid his second grenade." "Don't remind me," he said with a big grin. "I don't know what I was thinking. He just kind of charmed me and I lost control for a second." "I wish I had a picture of the look on your face. You stood there, with your jaw hanging down, watching that thing fly out there for, I guess about seventy yards or so, and hit that tree. Man, tree bark went everywhere!" "I tell you what I think. If he wasn't such a redneck, I think some college would do fine with him as a quarterback." The men laughed and sat quietly for a minute.

"It's tough to think where these soldiers are going and what they will see." They continued to sit in silence, thinking about what was just said. "Does that get to you?" They were not smiling now. Finally one of them shook his head and spoke for all. "It does. And many more will be coming, and we will be doing this over and over again. I know we do the best we can to prepare them. Maybe some will get through combat because we did our jobs well." With that they rose, shook hands and left for the night.

The next day orders were posted on the company bulletin board. Most would remain on post for advanced training. I would be going to Camp Barkeley in Abilene, Texas.

CHAPTER TEN

The trip took over twenty hours. As the bus rolled west, the scenery gradually changed from forests and rolling hills to sandy plains with fewer trees. I wondered if I'd ever again, see or hear from Archie and Bill. We developed a close friendship while at Fort Jackson. However, I had a sense it was because we were sharing experiences day by day but had little else in common. It's so hard to be close to a person after such a short period of time. I'll always remember our friendship and hope and pray that they come through the war safely and live out their lives in peace.

I thought of Dad and Mom. Dad is my friend and encourager, as well as my Father. As I grew up under his guidance, we grew closer. I noticed that the older I got the smarter he became. I think we shared friendship, love and respect, all wrapped up together. Mother holds a special place in my heart. She continually nurtured me and sustained me as I grew. She was my teacher, nurturer, comforter and encourager. She never failed to tell me when those times of challenge in my life came, to strive to do my very best. I love both my parents dearly.

Old Man and I are truly bonded and share a special relationship. We've always been sympathetic to each other's needs. When we met at the county home, we were drawn to each other immediately and developed a trust and respect for each other over time. I can close my eyes and see him sitting across from me, slowly rocking in his chair, with those piercing eyes searching my mind as if to find some common ground and impart wisdom. I believe that as I spent time with him growing up and learning life lessons, we became as one person in many ways. Our relationship was somehow symbiotic, each being a part of one another and dependent on each other, always benefiting from our close friendship. I find it easy to say that I love him, and I realize that he loves me, too. I am no believer in fate or accident in these matters. I think we are all part of a Divine plan that our Maker has prepared for us. Our meeting and growing together was no accident.

I thought of Mary and yearned to see her. I've heard that absence makes the heart grow fonder. But, I believe that my absence from her isn't good for me. I tried to think of our future together but the present kept getting in the way. I was going to go into combat, and relatively soon. My life would be placed out there on the field where many would die. I've got to prepare myself to face that. I thought of the tree of long ago and what Old Man told me about facing up to my fears. That experience is a comfort to me even now. But I know that, even though fresh in my memory, I'd have to learn all over again to reach down within myself and find the strength I would need to face what surely lies ahead. Thoughts of my love and devotion to Mary would help.

Camp Barkeley was a Medical Replacement Training Center. The base was newly built and was situated near Abilene, Texas. Trainees would be prepared for combat medical situations and upon completion, would be assigned to medical units for deployment.

The bus pulled up to the Army Reception Center and military personnel met us there and directed us inside. I anticipated that this would be a continuation of the basic training I had just finished. That was not the case. I received my housing assignment and list of instructions. Then all the trainees there in the room were directed outside.

We met our new sergeant and he escorted us to our new quarters. The atmosphere was totally different. We settled into the barracks and met our platoon leader and were advised to get our gear in order, pick our bunks and we would eat at noon. That afternoon we attended an orientation class and were advised that our advanced training would begin the next day. The absence of harassment, screaming and stress was a pleasant change. I later learned that the training would be just as intensive. We would work in classroom settings and in the field. Our basic first aid training was adequate but we would learn much more about a variety of medical situations while here. The importance of what we would learn was mentioned several times during the session. The term, "life or death situations", was used over and over. It was obvious that over the next several weeks we were still subject to military orders, military time and close attention to duty and performance.

As classroom instruction began it became apparent that we could be assigned to a variety of duties. The Army system could place a trained medic with a combat unit at the platoon and squad level, or to an aid station. Further from the front lines others could be assigned to medical clearing companies, and then possibly to an evacuation hospital. Next in the chain were general hospitals and eventually, if required, back to the States or back to duty in the field. This progression began on the front lines and then in a chain back away from the front, depending on the severity of the injury and the level of treatment required. Upon completion of training Medical corpsmen would be given a rank designation of "68W10" (commonly called Whiskeys in combat), whose primary duty was to treat the wounded.

The second day I was in advanced first aid class. We were learning bandaging techniques and practicing on one another. My partners name was Fred. "My name is Henry Jimson. You want to be my partner?" "Sure, I'm Fred Guenther." That was the extent of our conversation. We learned the various types of bandage applications for the next hour. That night at chow I saw Fred sitting alone and so I joined him. "How are you Fred? Mind if I join you?" He nodded and continued eating. I sat and ate with him in silence. He finished before me and as he stood he said, "Well, I enjoyed eating with you. Hope to see you again sometime." "That would be great," I replied and he left. Fred intrigued me. I liked him but I couldn't figure why. He was a big guy, six feet tall and about two hundred pounds I'd guess. I thought he might have German roots. I decided I'd make an effort to get to know him better and spend some time with him.

I suppose we had hospital ward training because we might be placed in that setting. I was not prepared for what we learned over the next week. One day we received a lecture on caring for convalescing patients. How does one take vital signs? How do you turn a patient and make a bed with the patient still in it? How does one function as an aide to a doctor? Did I mention handling bedpans? But the highlight of the day was the technique of giving a fellow trainee an enema. Roll over on your left side with knees bent and left arm extended. Apply vaseline to the end and insert it several inches into the rectum and place the bag on an arm attached to a stand a couple of feet above the poor patient. Open the valve and listen to your patient asking if you are enjoying yourself and shouting are you finished yet. As if this was not mortifying enough, we then had to swap roles and get what we gave. It was not my finest hour or my favorite lesson.

We learned about types of injections and how to give them. Practice was done with syringes filled with a saline solution. First needles were stuck in oranges because they told us the orange and human flesh had a similar tension. Then we paired up and gave each other intramuscalar shots. We would draw a saline solution into the vial and then push the plunger slightly to clear any air trapped in it. We wiped the area to be injected with alcohol cotton swabs and then we inserted the needle and pulled the plunger to see if we drew blood from a blood vessel and, if so, we retracted the needle slightly and tried again. Next we thrust the needle into the arm in a steady, fluid motion and upon penetrating the muscle, we pushed the contents of the vial into the patient.

I went first. My partner watched me prepare to give the shot with great interest. He looked at me in disbelief just before I stuck him and said, "Hey man, you ain't gonna stick that thing in me are you? Don't you hurt me!" I told him I was sorry but I had to. Well, things have a way of working out and he got his revenge on me. To make matters even more unbearable, we had to do the procedure twice more just beneath the skin and into a blood vessel.

It was a very long day for us. The class time was completed with an activity I thought was impossible to accomplish. The Instructor said we would now learn to inject ourselves in the upper leg muscle. That sounds easy enough until you hold the needle just about three inches above your leg and attempt to stick yourself with the needle and administer the injection. Three times I lifted my arm and thrust it toward my leg, only to stop an inch or two away and freeze. The instructor came and hovered over me and said, "Jimson, you inject yourself and you do it now!" "Yes, Sir," and I did. Of course it did not hurt nearly as much as I had imagined and I'd never hesitate to do it in the future. But the mind is a powerful force when it advises you not to intentionally and voluntarily inflict pain on yourself. It had been an interesting day.

After several more weeks of classroom instruction we entered into a new phase of training. Several days were spent on fields learning how to erect and break down large tents. The tents and accompanying gear were pulled off the trucks and unfolded on the ground. We continued by climbing under the tents to place center poles into grommets and side poles around the perimeter of the tents in like manner. We pulled the tents outward as men underneath brought the center poles to an upright position and then the side poles were tied off with rope anchored into the ground with stakes by others. There were many tents for various purposes and the end result was a fully functional field hospital. We then reversed the procedure.

After the initial training we loaded into a convoy of trucks and went into the field. When the trucks stopped we were expected to unload the field hospital and set it up. Each of the men had a particular duty in the process. We were timed from beginning of setup to completion. After a short break, we broke the tents down, loaded them on the trucks and moved several miles. Upon arrival the operation was repeated and we were timed again. This drill was repeated at least six times the first day. By the end of the day the time to setup had reduced by at least half. After that we ate in the mess tent, took showers, which were part of the facilities and bedded down for the night in the personnel tents. We stayed in the field with the same daily routine for five days. By the time we returned to base we were well trained and well prepared to set up the field hospital for operation in short order. I'll admit to a feeling of pride in what we had accomplished and more than a little amazed at how efficient we had become as a unit. At the end of our training regimen we were soldiers, ready for combat in a fully functional field hospital.

Later, Fred and I were walking back from our last class to the barracks, and I asked him if he had any idea when and where we would be deployed. "We will probably go overseas," he said and continued, "What do you think?" "We will probably go somewhere across the Atlantic. I heard that a lot of big troop convoys were going now and that things were heating up in Africa. Germans were fighting Americans and the British out in the desert, mostly in tanks. Of course there are ground troops in the middle of it too." Fred nodded.

CHAPTER ELEVEN

We got our orders two days later to report to Virginia for embarkation. They would tell us our destination when at sea. Fred and I would ship out together and be going to the same place. "I hope we serve together, Jimson." I thought to myself that Fred, in his quiet way, had grown to like me and the feeling was mutual.

I wrote letters to everyone that night to tell them we were going overseas and did not know where yet. I told them all not to worry about me. My training had been very thorough and that I was well prepared to take care of myself and perform my duties. I spent some time in writing to Mary. There was no small talk. I told her that I loved her with all my heart and soul and couldn't wait to return, marry and begin our family together. I pleaded with her not to worry for my safety. I also asked her to pray for me and for the men around me that we would be covered by the Grace of God and enabled to find inner strength to perform our duties well.

Old Man,

We ship out from Virginia in a week. I believe we will go to Africa, but have no way of knowing for sure. I've tried to reflect on our many conversations together. I greatly respect your uncanny ability to understand me. Your advice has never disappointed me.

I'll take you with me wherever I happen to go. I'll talk to you even when you are not there. You do the same for me please. I covet your thoughts for me.

I live for the day of my return when we can once again sit across from one another and share my experiences. Please continue taking care of yourself. Read books and listen to the radio. Keep up with the news of the war. I look forward to hearing your thoughts also when I return.

With deepest regards,
Henry

We arrived in Newport News, Virginia and quartered there to await our departure. We still did not know of our destination. Fred and I were assigned to duty together and I guess we would serve in the same unit. Two days later we boarded a converted luxury liner that had been stripped and redone to transport combat servicemen across the Atlantic. It looked like we would be spending Christmas on the high seas.

We left in the middle of the night. It was pitch dark, foggy and with no moon to provide light. We ran silently out of the harbor and into open water. One of the seamen that I had just met told me that this was necessary to avoid spies on land and submarines at sea. There had already been sinkings reported of ships in convoys that made the crossing. I had given absolutely no consideration to the possibility that we could be sunk before we reached our destination. Therefore, I paid close attention to the instructions we received in the event we were torpedoed and ordered to abandon ship. We quickly settled into a rather monotonous routine and even though we had duties on board, there was plenty of free time to roam the ship and talk with the other men onboard with us. Our quarters were below decks, where double-decker, narrow bunks had been constructed. They were not comfortable and very narrow. Railings had been added to keep us in the bunks in rough seas. We ate in shifts in small areas set aside for us. Most of the time we spent topside for the fresh air.

I had heard that if the weather held we would be across in two to three weeks. We sailed in a convoy of some forty-five ships of various types, but all carrying troops and supplies. We had a destroyer escort but learned that many convoys making the crossing did not. One morning Fred and I were alone on the aft deck, watching the propellers throwing up a considerable wake. The dark waters swirled behind us as we proceeded to the east. Gulls were flying overhead and would dive down low and near us to see if we had anything to throw to them. The sky was a deep blue with small puffy clouds floating near the horizon in the distance. The wind was very brisk and we had our winter gear on. "What do you think of the open sea Fred?" "It goes on forever." I asked him if he had ever been at sea before. "No, we had a lake near us in Oklahoma but no boat; just for swimming." "Which part of Oklahoma are you from?" I asked. "Shawnee, but nobody knows where that is. It's East of Oklahoma City." We stood there in silence for several more minutes. "You are from the South?" "Yes," I answered. "I was raised in a little town called Mark Hill, Georgia. My family lives on a farm and my Dad works at a cotton gin." He thought about that for a little and then said, "You talk funny so I figured you were from the South."

General Quarters sounded and we rushed to our assigned stations and put on life vests. "What is going on," someone shouted. Then the convoy began to change course and start zigzag maneuvers. The destroyers began to run ahead and away from the convoy at flank speed. "They must have spotted a submarine," another observed. The smoke stacks of the ships were billowing thick dark smoke and the waves were lashing against the sides. Our ship was shuddering as the engines revved up to speed. It was a frightening experience. Suddenly one of the destroyers laid down a pattern of depth charges off the convoy's port and the water exploded into high plumes of seawater and the sound of the explosions made a thumping noise. As quickly as it started it was over. We altered course and resumed normal speed to the east and the destroyers pulled back into their escort positions. Several minutes later we were ordered to stand down. We never found out if it was a submarine or a false alarm. I preferred the latter.

That night in our quarters the incident was the only subject of conversation. I just listened as the men talked. "I never thought I might get torpedoed when I joined the Army." Nervous laughter ensued. "I wish now they had given us swimming lessons in basic. I can't swim worth a lick." "You can't swim. Where you from?" "South Dakota. No swimming there." More laughter. "Anyone ever see a submarine?" "I saw pictures before but not the real thing. How big are they and how many torpedoes can they shoot?" "Well I think they are big enough and can sink a ship with one well placed hit." There were several minutes of silence, which was broken by the clanging bells signaling General Quarters once again. We quickly gathered our survival gear and scurried topside to our stations. It was pitch-black dark and a moonless night. We heard the destroyers' staccato blast of sirens, growing louder with each sounding as they moved about in the darkness.

Just then the horizon lit up from a blast in the distance, followed by several violent explosions. Now one could see the ship near the perimeter of the convoy ablaze in the night. We all stood there on the starboard side, gazing silently at the ship as it slowly disappeared from sight. It was over before many realized what had just happened. I expected the convoy to stop but it did not, because to do so would place everyone at risk. Depth charges were discharging with regularity now and the destroyers were moving about helter-skelter in search of the submarine. There were in all likelihood many of them. One of the men had some knowledge about the submarines and shared it with us. He related that they traveled in what were called 'wolf packs' and proved very effective at disrupting convoys early on in the war. Many ships carrying supplies to Britain were sunk in the first years of the war. But the subs had an achilles heel. The wolf packs had to communicate by radio and also, they were required to surface periodically to recharge their batteries and get fresh air.

As we proceeded on in the night we eventually stood down and returned to our quarters, got in the bunks and attempted to sleep. I tried not to think of the men on that ship. It was a long and fearful night. We had no further attacks.

The time was again filled with daily routine onboard the ship. I especially looked forward to the exercise topside in the mornings. I enjoyed it because my mind was focused on the activity and away from thinking of the danger that we constantly faced.

On day twenty-two, a coastline appeared on the horizon. Everyone rushed topside and watched as the details of the coast came into view. "Where are we?" Fred asked. "I am not sure but it may be England." Eventually we saw the docks and maneuvered in and moored the ship. That day we were told we would stay on the ship as it took on additional supplies needed to continue our journey. No one was allowed off the ship for any reason. It was obvious as we watched workers on the docks and heard them talking that we were in England. One of them shouted up to us. "Where you bound for Yanks?" "Who wants to know? The King?" He responded, "You bloody well better believe he knows. I bet you are going to kill Germans. Good show lads. They bombed our great homeland during the Blitz so give it to them double, I say."

The next day near nightfall, we once again sailed out to sea and turned to the South. We learned that night that we were bound for somewhere in North Africa and would be at sea another couple of weeks.

Fred and I noted that we had acquired our 'sea legs', but there were still some of the men that spent time at the railing throwing up and looking very sickly. They learned soon enough to always do so with the wind at their back or else it would come back in their face, which only made their condition much worse. At first I really felt bad for these fellows, but I admit to seeing a certain amount of humor in it. Fred said I had a weird sense of humor. We were nearing the end of our second week. We put in at Casablanca and the next afternoon we went through the straits of Gibraltar and entered into the Mediterranean Sea. We passed by a very large mountain on our port side. The seamen called it "The Rock of Gibraltar". It was quite a sight to behold, seeming bigger than life and very much out of place.

As we neared the end of our voyage those of us in the Medical Corps received word that we would be put ashore near Oran, Algeria in North Africa and would be attached to a field evacuation hospital. It was already up and running and they were waiting for us. The hospital had a large patient load, which had steadily increased during the latest North Africa campaign, and they had great need for new men and replacements. The medics offloaded in a group and were immediately directed to quarters and issued uniforms and supplies. There were fifty of us, including Fred and myself. We bunked together, cleaned up and ate. That night we were given assignments to serve within the hospital and also in the field, assisting with incoming wounded combatants.

Our combat experiences had begun. At 0500 I ate and then reported to the post surgery ward. "My name is Henry Jimson, Sir," I said, as the Doctor, a nurse and I began going from bed to bed. The doctor was checking charts and talking to the patients lying in their beds. There were about twenty beds in the ward and they were all occupied. When we finished, the doctor introduced me to the nurse on duty, gave her instructions, and then he left. The men were in the hospital for a variety of reasons, some combat related and some for other medical problems. The nurse suggested that I go to each bed again and let the patients know my name. "For those who are awake or conscious, carry on small talk with them. Do not ask them what happened to them or anything concerning their experiences in the field. Ask them questions like where they are from and do they miss home and the like. Above all be a good listener. Don't discuss their medical condition or prognosis. Remember, you are not a doctor and one of your many duties is to put these men at ease and take their minds off the war. I'll assign you tasks and if you have questions then please ask me. There are no stupid questions in my book. Don't worry about catching on to the routine in here. You will catch on soon enough. If at anytime you lose it, don't let the men see you. Go outside if you have to throw up. Remember your training and pay attention. You will do fine if you do that." As she turned to leave she continued, "Now at 1100 hours I want you to take vitals on each patient and enter them on the charts." "Yes nurse," I acknowledged, and began going from bed to bed, meeting and briefly talking to those patients who were awake. I looked at each chart to see what their problems were and for insight on how I could best care for them.

"Good morning. I just wanted to let you know I'll be taking care of you. If you need anything at all just call me and I'll see what I can do to help." The responses ranged from a nod to long conversations. Most asked about home and where I trained and how I got over here. "Where you from?" "Mark Hill, Georgia." "What were things like at home when you left?" "Do you hear anything about how we are doing in the Pacific? "Do you have a girl back home?" "Yes I do." "Tell me all about her!" "I got married two days before I left. I really miss her. We don't get much mail over here. I did get a letter last week." He showed me the letter that he pulled out from under his pillow and then smelled it. "It smells like her you know." His eyes misted and he said, "I sure will be glad to get home and see her." "I know you will."

"Medic, I need something for pain." "Give me a minute," as I went to the nurse's station. She went to his bed, checked his chart and administered a dose of morphine. "Thanks." "Don't mention it, Honey. Now, get some sleep." Within minutes he was asleep. I took vitals as instructed and then settled in for the rest of the day.

During the next couple of weeks I got to know most of the patients and staff. I grew comfortable with my duties and tried to be helpful when a need arose. "I'm hungry." "I think I am going to throw up." "I need to go to the bathroom." I produced a bedpan and took care of the need. "I can't sleep." A sedative was given. "I need to roll over. Can you help me?" "Do you have anything I can read?" "When can I get out of here?" "I need to talk to the doctor. Now!" Some of the requests were incidental and others more serious. I tried to give them all equal attention.

And then I was caught completely off guard and shocked at what I heard and saw. One of the men had to undergo an emergency appendectomy almost a month ago according to his chart. He had developed multiple infections over that time. His surgical site had reddened, bloated and continued to fester. The staff became concerned that the site was not healing. The doctors had to reopen his stitches and leave him open to watch for the possibility of gangrene setting in. He was examined and monitored twice daily and lived on pain medication and fever control. One day while I was on duty a doctor I had not seen before came in for rounds. When we arrived at this man's bed the doctor looked at his chart and then lifted the covering gauze and started to probe the wound with his fingers. "Stop right there! I have been in this bed for over a month and have been seeing doctors coming and going, looking at me and working on me. I don't get any better, only worse. I don't want to die. I think you people are trying to kill me! You are not sterile! Don't even think about sticking your hand in there without scrubbing up first. Do you understand me?" The nurse and I glanced at each other in shock, and waited for the response from the doctor that we knew was coming. I thought to myself that this could be the first step toward court marshal and dishonorable discharge.

With the tirade completed, the doctor stepped back away from the bed. He turned and whispered to the nurse and then went to the pre-op room. In about five minutes he came back and leaned over the man, face to face and spoke softly to him. "I want to apologize to you. Although your outburst was unnecessary you were absolutely right. I was negligent and could have further infected you. I am so sorry. Will you forgive me?" "Yes, Sir. I'm sorry too. It is just that I don't get any better and I'm real sick. I don't want to die this way." Those in the beds nearby were watching intently to see what was going to happen next. "I want this man to be well cared for while he is in here. He will get better and I'll see to it. He is a good soldier and a fighter."

He turned to the nurse and me and said, "See that this soldier is closely monitored. I want him irrigated three times a day and fresh dressings applied after each time. Continue his medication and give him whatever he needs to make him comfortable. He has been through a lot and we are going to see to it that he gets better soon." The nurse and I responded simultaneously, "Yes, Sir!" I was very moved by that encounter. In that brief time, I came to respect that patient and that doctor and took on a whole new attitude as I continued on, caring for the sick and combat wounded.

Fred was assigned to a ward for treatment of soldiers with psychiatric problems. Even though he had been there for the same length of time as I had at my assignment, he decided to open up to me for the first time when I got in that night. "Henry, I hope you are doing better than me in your job." "What's the problem Fred?" I never heard Fred talk that much before. He began, "Well, for starters, there is very little that can be done for these fellows. I have tried to figure out what is going on in their heads. It's tough. My head nurse tried to explain it all to me so I'd know what to expect. These guys are really in bad shape." He paused and we sat in silence for several minutes. I waited for him because it was obvious that he needed to talk about it. "One of them told me that if you were in a tank and you saw a German tank coming, then he said to me, 'Get out of your tank really fast. You don't have much time. They will blow up your tank and it will catch on fire. If you don't get out you will burn, just like in hell. You need to get out of the tank'." Fred stared at me. "Some just sit up in their beds for hours and stare. It is a blank stare like nobody is in there. Those never say a word. They won't talk to you and don't seem to hear you. Others have imaginary people they mutter to under their breath. There is nobody there but they talk anyway. This goes on for hours sometimes. Then there are those who suddenly scream and warn you that you are about to die and that you should run and cover and be very still. The worst are those who just lie there in a fetal position and keep saying, 'I want to go home now. Please let me out of here. I need to talk to my Mother now. Please help me get out of here'." Fred reached up to his face and wiped his eyes. "Sorry man. It's just really hard." I went over to him and put my arm around his shoulder, sat there on his bunk and did not say a word. After a brief time he got up and said he was going to turn in. Lights went out. In the darkness I heard, "Thanks, Henry." I had trouble sleeping that night.

As time passed the numbers of incoming wounded began to slack off a little. You never knew how many at a time would be brought in for care. We were rotated from assignments and spent a considerable amount of time receiving the wounded, applying first aid as needed and using litters to move the wounded as directed. On occasion we assisted in applying temporary bandaging, splints to stabilize, and tourniquets to control bleeding until doctors took over. As we became more proficient we performed triage on wounded personnel when doctors were occupied elsewhere or when shorthanded. The months passed quickly and we settled into a fairly hectic routine. Some of the soldiers we cared for returned to duty, others were sent back to hospital ships and general hospitals and some were sent back to the States with serious medical injuries. Some died of their serious wounds. The hospital was very active with periods of extreme activity, separated by times of relative quiet.

CHAPTER TWELVE

It was about the middle of June 1943, when we began to hear scuttlebutt that something big was going to happen soon. Some speculated that we were going into Italy while others believed that Sicily would be our next push. Everyone at the hospital thought we would go also. The battles against the Axis powers were over and the Allies now controlled North Africa. Consequently, battle injuries had dropped dramatically. So it would make sense to move on where we might be needed.

Meanwhile back in Mark Hill news of the war kept coming in sporadically and without much detail, both from the newspapers, radio broadcasts and newsreel reports at the movies. Henry's parents now knew he was overseas, somewhere in Europe or Africa, but did not know exactly where. More and more men were being drafted or joining as others returned home, either as wounded or as casualties of war. Mr. Spencer had some additional information not privy to the general public and tried to keep the families informed. Because deaths were usually announced by telegram, waiting for the mail was always hard and when received, a great burden was lifted when no notices were received. This was a never ending routine and always stressful. Mr. Jimson was very busy at the gin. He couldn't keep up with the demand for cotton from the military and worked long hours trying his best to help the war effort with supplies of cotton.

Each time he saw Mose the questions were the same. "Mr. Jimson, heard anything from Mr. Henry? Where do you think he is? I sure miss that boy and want you to know that me and mine pray for him every night at supper time." "Thank you Mose. I know that Henry covets your prayers. You and I both know that prayers are so important and that God is watching over him right now." "Yes, Sir, I know that."

"Mother, how are you doing?" Mr. Jimson asked that night after supper. "I've been sewing some things and mending. I've been cleaning the house more than usual for a good while now. I notice when I see people in town that none of my friends ask about Henry. I often sit with my Bible and read it for hours. I try to come up with new ideas for meals. I watch you come in worn out and go to bed early. I go to church alone sometimes and just sit in there by myself and try to hear God. I love you dearly and you know that I do. But I am not doing very well."

Mary had just finished her classes for the day and as she walked across the campus she thought of Henry. She wondered where he was and what he might be doing. Her mind raced, searching for the possibilities. She verbalized aloud, "I wonder how he is mentally. He is very sensitive to others. I hope and pray that he has seen little death. He told me about how serving in the Medical Corps would be a fulfilling experience. He liked the idea of helping people much better than killing. I wish I could meet his friends and ask them about him. It is hard not hearing from him for so long."

She saw the Chapel up ahead and went in alone, as she had become accustomed to doing. She sat on the back row and let the solitude soak into her soul. She always left there at peace and so looked forward to the experience. It was very quiet and she was alone. The sun shown through the stained glass and colors danced among the pews. It was beautiful and, somehow, spiritual as well. She spoke aloud, "God, I miss Henry. You know how much I love him. My spirit is troubled because of the danger he may be facing. Please hover over him and protect him from danger. Guide each of his steps that he may not fall in dangerous places. Surround him with true friends and comrades. Give him, I pray, a sure knowledge that You are but a thought or prayer from him at all times. May he put all of his hope and trust in You alone and seek your face in times of the turmoil of war. Let him feel my presence Lord and find comfort. And above all, if it be within Your will, I ask that he be returned to me whole in body and mind. Thank you Lord for hearing my prayer. I love you. Amen." A few minutes later Mary rose and left the Chapel. She was smiling and her steps were sure.

Old Man was in the library most of the morning, finished his task and prepared to leave to go to the administrator's office. He had been occupied with preparations for his eventual death. He finished a letter to Henry, and also another to the administrator of the county home. He sealed them both and wrote across the front of each, 'To be opened at the time of my demise'. The first letter, addressed to the administrator, contained instructions on the disposition of the large, locked metal box which the old man had deposited with the home when he first appeared there, to be held in the home's on-premises safe until his death. The administrator was to deliver Henry's letter and the box to him or to his Father in the event that Henry was deceased. The letter addressed to Henry contained a holographic will. The will had been hand-written and witnessed the previous month. It also noted the location of the key to the box, which was secreted within the room he occupied. The box had not been opened since Old Man had entered the home some twenty years ago. The administrator saw that the old man was very somber. He took the two sealed letters from Old Man and asked, "Is there anything else you need me to do, Sir?" He thought briefly and said in response, "If I die before he comes, you might tell Henry that I thought of him often and that I loved him as a Son." "I will do that for you, Old Man."

With that done, Old Man went outside and walked up the hill to the tree. He sat at the base of the tree. His thoughts recalled all of the times he spent with the boy and the wonderful bond that had developed between them. The afternoon sun was warm and there was a light breeze floating across the hill and through the branches of the tree. Old Man dozed off, his mind on Henry and his safety. He had a revelation as he slept beneath the tree. He envisioned that Henry was about to face peril and his very life was about to be placed at dreadful risk.

Meanwhile, back in Oran, Africa, Henry and Fred went up the gang-plank of the docked ship together. They boarded, laden down with full combat gear. There were many ships in the water and each in turn, took on men, supplies and equipment. The wharfs were fully occupied and a beehive of activity. The troops had been told the night before that they were going to the Island of Sicily and could expect German and Italian forces, waiting there. Everyone, through company commanders and platoon leaders, was given instructions on what to do upon landing. Fred and I would be a part of the field evacuation hospital and it would be set up at or near the beachhead.

That evening the Officer in Charge addressed us on board our ship. "You men have served well at the hospital and will continue your duties as before. But your circumstances will be very different now. You will be required to receive the hospital gear and set it up as directed. There will be much confusion. Listen to your superiors and do as they say. We will be flexible in our decisions concerning the timing of setup and the final chosen location of this unit. Expect to come under fire and be ready to act quickly to protect yourselves and to accomplish your mission. We will not be in the first wave. The beachhead will have to be established before we come in. I expect that the wounded will quickly follow.

I can now tell you that we will be a part of an overall mission, code-named 'Operation Husky'. I am told that this is a combined effort of American and British forces. There will be over 2000 ships involved. Our objective is to take the island and use it to our advantage. This will be no cakewalk, but you men have received the best training and on the job experience that the Army has to offer. I wish you Godspeed as you accomplish your mission." With that he introduced a Chaplain and we had a prayer time and then dismissed.

"What are you thinking about Henry?" "I am going to write letters to everyone back in the States. I am going to tell them that we are all going on a little mission, but to not worry. Do you think they will know back home about 'Operation Husky' and that we will be involved? I think Old Man will figure it out. He is the most intuitive person I have ever known." Fred walked over to his bunk and jumped up and into it and settled for a few winks. "I guess I need to write my parents too. Just in case something bad happens they will have something from me." I thought and then said, "Nothing is going to happen to us. We will cover each other's backs. Ok?" "You can count on that Henry."

It was July 9, 1943 and about 1200 hours as the ships slipped out of port. The winds had picked up and the seas were getting rougher. We rounded the jetty and headed out to sea. Sicily was ten to twelve hours away.

CHAPTER THIRTEEN

Many ships had assembled in the open waters. The winds were blowing gale force by now. Dawn would break in about three hours and we lay at anchor, waiting. Our destroyer escort was impressive and provided much comfort as we crossed the Atlantic. But off our bow we could make out ghostlike images of naval ships that were considerably bigger. At about the time the sky started to gray in the early dawn hours, our war began suddenly with the thundering of the big guns of those ghostly ships. We could hear the reports almost immediately and within minutes we heard explosions and simultaneous fireballs lighting up the horizon and revealing the shores of Sicily. Large troop ships with combat units were ahead of the gun ships; waiting for the barrage to cease so that they could land troops onshore. We stood along the rails of the deck and watched in awe and wonder at the power of the big guns. By now we could see what I would call a great armada of many different types of military ships on all sides of us. Our ship had now become a part of something much bigger. Within the hour smaller vessels began to snake toward the shore. Planes were flying overhead now, I suppose from bases in Africa, and began to drop bombs, fire rockets and strafe the mountains with machine gun fire into the towering hills fronting the beaches. Fire was being returned from the mountains in the interior but their range seemed limited to the beaches and just beyond into the seas around the landing sites.

As the time passed, smoke began to accumulate and the scene blurred. Because sound travels over water so well, we could even hear small arms reports in addition to the thunder of the big guns. I thought that we should now have men on the beaches and equipment being deposited there as well, even though the enemy artillery was continuing to pound the area where they were landing. It did not appear that much progress was being made to get off the beaches. I was sure that other medics were now on shore and setting up Aid Stations to provide emergency treatment to the wounded. We began to notice landing craft ferrying from the shore to a hospital ship offshore and then returning. They were transporting wounded for further treatment.

The day passed and night fell. The constant shelling never ceased. We could hear aircraft flying overhead and over the mountains and into the distance. We later learned that paratroopers were being dropped behind enemy lines to attack from the rear.

The next day we offloaded onto LSTs (naval vessels for transporting troops and equipment) and were taken to the shore. Trucks that had been brought ashore during the night were used to load and transport the hospital equipment. We moved as a unit inland about two miles to a secure area and established the evacuation hospital. Our perimeter was established and protected by combat troops and we began to receive wounded almost immediately.

How was this battle progressing? If one were able to hover over the island to observe, the scene was seemingly chaotic. But, there was also a pattern developing below. Lines that separated opposing forces were now fluid, moving back and forth. Flanking maneuvers were constantly being employed. The Italian forces put up less resistance to the advancing forces. Some of the German forces were well-seasoned veterans but many of the Axis forces had little or no combat experiences. Most of the British troops had been in battle in North Africa and were good soldiers. As the days ticked by, there were a growing number of POW's. Many of the Axis forces surrendered or were captured. There was a competitive spirit among the commands of the British and American forces. At times forward progress could be measured in yards, while at other times miles could be traversed without sight of the enemy.

Major highways and towns inland were objectives. Ports and landing strips were targeted early to obtain an advantage and to enhance the allied effective application of strategy. The idea was to inflict maximum damage on the Germans and Italians and to cut off their escape from the island by way of the Port of Messina. Their route of escape would be some two miles across the Straits of Messina to the western shore of Italy.

But there was more to the overview than the grand strategies at work here. There were the experiences of the combat soldiers. Those who were first on the beaches saw stiff resistance, close combat and many casualties. The terrain was rather flat to the West, but became increasingly mountain-ous as the troops moved eastward. This afforded the enemy a high ground advantage and effective cover as the allies approached in relatively, open spaces. At the eastern end of the island was Mount Etna, an active volcano standing over 10,000 feet in elevation and near Messina. The area was heavily fortified and defended because of its strategic location. But, foot soldiers were not so much concerned with these facts. They were more concerned with their next step, and where the enemy might be waiting. Fear was a constant companion, and survival depended on their wits and good fortune.

Henry and Fred were litter bearers, shuttling wounded into the hospi-tal and returning for more. Medics would bring in the wounded by ambu-lance or on the back of jeeps and sometimes walking wounded would show up out of nowhere for help. Some of the wounds were horrific. We saw compound fractures with bones protruding from the skin. Many were bleeding or coming in with transfusions in place. Those unfortunate to be near blasts or grenades were lacerated and in some cases, with limbs shat-tered or blown away by the force of the blast.

There is a saying that 'war is hell'. That is an inadequate description. It is altogether madness and indiscriminate as to its choice of victims. It seems to be a living, evil presence that devours its combatants without feel-ing. Death lurks, ever present in combat, looking for its next soul to take and destroy. One cannot define it in human terms.

Madmen plan their wars and participate in them for some imagined goal of conquest. And when it terminates, one can look back and wonder why it ever happened. It is ultimately, depending on one's point of reference, a battle of forces of evil against the forces of good. But it is obvious, that even though the cause be just and the victory worth the cost, it is still madness and altogether evil. The human condition often seems, as its goal, bent on self-destruction and often times is very adept at accomplishing just that end.

I am exhausted by it all and weary of the misery and death all around. I wish to sleep now and somehow escape this horror. That was not to be.

Word came down that there had been a considerable loss of life at the front and replacements, including two medics, were needed. Fred and I were chosen to join a platoon to bring it back up to strength and so, we were transported by jeep to the front to join a platoon there and each of us attached to a squad, now engaged in combat. The platoon had been fighting for almost a week now and under constant fire. The terrain was mountainous and the Germans were up the mountain and firing down on us. Several times over the past few days the platoon had tried to move from their cover but had to retreat back. They were zeroed in on us and we couldn't move. Surely our forces would come up and help us. The sergeant had a radioman and he was finally able to contact forces further back. We gave them our position on the road by co-ordinates and they were able to lay down fire on the mountain. But the Germans were dug in well and we saw no movement. Dark fell on us and we tried once again to move, this time with success. Perhaps the Germans retreated when their position came under shell attack. A radio message came back to us and this time the news was not good. Our position had been flanked and now we had Germans to our front and rear. We decided to leave the road and go south in hopes that we could avoid detection and meet up with our troops. We stopped several times because we heard German voices nearby. I remained down, flat on my stomach to wait for the all clear.

I awoke the next morning with a start. Everyone was gone and I was alone. I stood and then dropped quickly. A German Panzer unit was moving along in a field not three hundred yards away. There were ground troops and a tank as well. I also saw two howitzers on mechanized platforms, motoring along. I don't believe they saw me but to avoid detection, I began crawling toward an outcrop some one hundred yards away to better hide myself. I pulled myself up and behind the outcrop and watched as they disappeared in the distance.

"Can you help me?" I almost jumped out of my skin and whirled around to see who had just said that. It was a German soldier. He was sitting on the ground and leaning on a boulder. His rifle was next to him and he had grenades strapped to his belt. I turned to run but he spoke in a weak voice. "I need you to help me." I stopped. "Are you going to kill me?" I asked. "I am a medic and you should not kill me." He tried to get up but fell back to the ground and said, "I have been shot in the gut and I hurt really bad. Can you do anything for me medic?" I leaned down next to him and pulled a morphine syrette out of my bag and injected him in the stomach. "What was that," he asked. "Morphine. It will kick in after about twenty minutes. Lie still and let me look at you." I pulled his shirt farther back and saw that he had been shot just below his rib cage. I think the bullet went through him but I did not want to move him to see. He was bleeding slowly and I was sure that major organs were damaged. Next I sprinkled sulfa powder over and into the wound and then made a compress. "I want you to hold this in place and apply as much pressure as you can stand to control the bleeding." He pushed and winced but was able to do as I said. It did not look good for him. He had a grayish color and was clammy to the touch. I believe he was in early stages of shock and would probably lose consciousness soon. I decided to stay with him until dark and then try to find my platoon. It was out the question to attempt to move him.

We sat there in silence as I reflected on what I had just done. This was a German soldier and my enemy. But he was a human being and suffering. I did not have a real choice. He looked at me and said, "You did not have to fix me. I thank you very much American soldier." "You can call me Henry. How is it that you speak such fluent English?" "We were taught English at my school and I liked the sound of it and studied it very much," he replied. "How old are you?" He looked like a very young boy to me. "I am just now seventeen and I've been a soldier for only six months." He reached up into a pocket and it startled me. "What are you doing?" "I want you to see my picture," as he handed me a small, tattered photo. It had obviously been in his pocket for some time. I looked at it and saw the boy and two older people. They were standing on a stairway in front of a small house. They were smiling. "That is my Mama and Papa there and I look at them a lot." He took the photo back and stared at it and smiled, then returned it to his pocket and placed his hand over it for several seconds. Tears were welling up in his eyes. "I don't like this war. It is foolishness. I would like for it to be over. Thank you for taking care of me." He slipped into a sleep like state for several minutes and then he jumped with a start. "Your morphine has made me sleepy. I feel a little better. Do you think I'll die soon?" I did not want to answer him so I stood and walked away a few feet to determine the direction I'd travel in a few hours. I turned back to assure him that he would be all right and his people would find him. He was dead and slumped over onto the ground. I checked his pulse and his pupils. He was gone and I grieved for this boy, who did not want to be in this war.

Incoming shells whistled loudly as they passed overhead. The explosion rocked the ground very close to where Henry stood and threw up a great cloud of dirt and debris many feet into the air. Henry had heard the whistling of the shell and that was his last perception. He did not have time to duck or cover. The concussion of the blast lifted him high into the air, twisted him and dropped him directly onto the dead soldier. He landed face down. One of his arms was broken and his right leg was twisted back behind his body in an unnatural position. Blood was coming out of his mouth and his ears. He had shrapnel wounds to the head and upper torso. His aid pack had been ripped from his body, and his helmet as well, and they were thrown a good distance away from him. It was over in seconds and now it was deathly quiet.

Henry's platoon had moved out that morning back on the road and advanced about two miles, only to come under fire once again from German forces up on the mountain in front of them. They were firing machine guns and lobbing mortar rounds at them with regularity. The platoon had good cover, but was unable to advance. After several hours an artillery company was contacted and they began to fire as directed. It was the first shell fired that hit Henry's position. It was at that same time that Fred had noticed that Henry was missing. "Has anyone seen Jimson? I don't see him." "We must have lost him in the dark last night," the sergeant responded. "Sergeant, I want to go back to find him. Can I?" "Son, that is a good way to get separated yourself and killed." "Sergeant, he is my best friend. I'll find him and bring him back here. I promise you that I will," Fred said with desperation in his voice. The sergeant considered the request and then said, "You get back here by nightfall with Jimson, you hear me. We need you medics with us. We will wait for you until dark and then we pull out with or without you. Understood?" "Yes, sergeant," and with that Fred went back in the direction they had come.

There are some things that defy explanation. Several miles back, Fred left cover near the road and started south, thinking that Henry may have done the same. He saw the outcrop in the distance and went toward it. What he saw next put fear in his heart. There were two bodies lying on each other. One was an American and one a German. At first Fred thought as he approached the bodies that they had attacked one another. He did not think either was alive. He was just a few yards away when he saw the red cross armband on the shirt. He went around the body to the front and it was Henry. "Henry, My Lord, are you dead?" he said, not expecting an answer. He leaned down and felt Henry's carotid artery and there was a very faint and erratic pulse. "You are alive." Fred gently straightened Henry's leg and arm. He checked for any other breaks and moved his neck very slightly for any sign of neck injury. He looked at his pupils and they were dilated. He saw evidence of bleeding at the ears and mouth. "Henry, you're in bad shape and I have to move you now." In his haste to check Henry he had completely forgotten the German. He saw immediately that he was dead. Fred couldn't figure out what had happened here at first. Then he saw the crater that the shell had carved out of the earth and it became clear to him. "You lucky to be alive Henry. Don't you die on me now."

With that, Fred got on his stomach on the ground and rolled Henry over on his back, wrapped his arms around his neck and stood with Henry secured on his back. He was heavy, deadweight. Fred wondered if he could do this. "I hope I don't injure him any by moving him," and with that he started walking back to his platoon. It was a Herculean feat and required all the stamina and strength that Fred could muster. "I have got to save you Henry. We are going to make it." He was afraid to stop for fear that he would be unable to pull Henry up again and continue. He worried about the Germans and what an easy target they were there on the road. It was almost dark when he saw his men. "Look sergeant, there they come. He made it!" They ran to meet them, and took Henry off Fred's back and placed him on the ground. Fred collapsed to the ground as well. The sergeant looked at Henry and then at Fred and shook his head. "Guenther, how far did you carry this man?" "I don't know. Most of the day, I guess." Well son, your friend here is in bad shape. He appears to me to be comatose but he is alive. You saved your friend today Guenther." "I hope so, sergeant."

They called in an ambulance. Several Americans companies were approaching them along the road now and were not receiving any resistance.

The shelling had caused the Germans to retreat. Fred and others carried Henry on a litter to the ambulance, helped load him on it and then Fred knelt beside Henry and whispered in his ear. "Henry, I know you probably don't hear me. Don't you die on me. I worked hard to get you here. I'll see you again someday. I think they are going to take you home now."

CHAPTER FOURTEEN

Six hours separated the time when Henry was injured and Old Man felt a shudder course through his body. He reached for the wall in the hall to steady himself. He was on his way to the library when it happened. He regained his balance and went into the library and sat down. His mind was racing. "Perhaps it was a stroke," he thought aloud as he felt his pulse. His mind turned to Henry. "Something has happened to Henry," as he tried to understand the disturbance welling up inside himself. Old Man closed his eyes and concentrated on Henry. Several minutes passed and the feeling subsided. An attendant had come into the library, saw the old man there with his eyes closed and brow furrowed. "Old Man, you ok? You look like you seen a ghost or something!" "I was just thinking of Henry and hoping that he was safe. You know he is in the war don't you?"

"Now Old Man, everybody around here knows that. I don't need to tell you we all love that boy and sure wish he could get back home now and without no trouble coming on him." She paused and asked, "Can I get you anything? Maybe a big glass of sweet, iced tea to settle you." "Thank you. That would be nice." Old Man's thoughts were on Henry for most of the day and his sleep that night was fitful.

Mr. and Mrs. Jimson were on their front porch about the same time. Mrs. Jimson suddenly felt a disturbance in her spirit. "Don't be alarmed, but I have a strange feeling that Henry may be in trouble. It is just a feeling that Mothers often get about their children. You know what I mean?" He nodded and continued to rock in his chair and watch as a car passed on the main road and disappeared in the distance.

Mary felt a sudden urge to go to the Chapel and did so. She sat and prayed for Henry as never before. She sensed an inexplicable disturbance within herself as she prayed for his safety, his return and for their future together.

As Fred's platoon, which had now rejoined their company, marched along the road to Messina, Mount Etna came into view. It towered over the landscape and was an impressive sight. "I wonder how many Germans and Italians are up there waiting on us? Scuttlebutt has it that they have all left and gone to Italy. I hope so." The radioman was on his radio and said, "I just heard that Mussolini got arrested and is no longer in charge." "Man that is great. Maybe they will all give up now and we can go home." "Not likely. I think we're going to chase the Germans out of Italy instead."

Henry had been moved to the rear lines at the beachhead, and then directly to the evacuation hospital for evaluation. When his fractures had been set and transfusions to replace the lost blood had been administered, it was determined to get him onto a hospital ship offshore and to specialists. He remained unconscious and in a comatose state. He was totally unresponsive. The ship was due for rotation out of the battle zone and so, sailed to Casablanca and then to England with a full load of combat wounded to transfer there to a general hospital.

They placed Henry in a ward and assigned a nurse to attend to him and several others who were shell-shocked or wounded like Henry. He was being feed intravenously with a feeding tube and was constantly being monitored for any change in his condition. His position in the bed was changed often to prevent the development of bedsores. During the third week there the nurse began to notice that his pupils were moving under his closed eyelids, but only infrequently and with no other visible response. He had been comatose for almost six weeks now and the doctors were not certain that he would ever regain consciousness. Even if he did, his prognosis for full recovery was guarded at best. Upon inquiry one day by the nurse, the Doctor stated, "We don't know a lot about these cases. Some do come back, but most don't. At some point it makes very little medical sense to maintain their lives. We are not there yet." He told the nurse to stay objective about the whole thing and hopefully, they may see some improvement soon.

Morning rounds were just beginning. The doctor and nurse were four beds away, attending to a patient. "I'm thirsty." The nurse looked up to see who had just spoken. "Look Doctor, look, his eyes are open!" She left the doctor and ran to Henry's bedside. He looked up at her and began to talk. "Can I get a drink of water? Where am I? What day is this? Who are you? How did I get in this bed? Am I alive or dreaming?" The nurse bent down and grabbed his neck in an embrace and held on to him tightly. She whispered in his ear, "Slow down soldier. You're just fine and you are in a hospital in England. You've been out for awhile." She released him and stood back up. Henry's eyes were wide now and the scene he beheld as he began to look around bewildered him. By this time the doctor was there and was checking him over. "Just relax now, son. You have been out for a long time, but you are going to be fine. We've been taking good care of you. Welcome back from wherever you have been." The doctor later confided in the nurse. "Do you believe in miracles? I believe you and I have witnessed one today. I am not a religious man but I believe some higher power has been in control of this situation and this boy is indeed fortunate. Sometimes I really like my job." "Me too, Doctor," she said with a smile. Henry's condition continued to improve. "I remember the blast and that is all. How was I found?" Nobody knew the answer to that. The nurse said, "I think your guardian angel found you."

During the next two weeks Henry showed steady improvement, except for recurring, severe headaches, and periodic flashbacks. The doctor was not sure when, if ever, the headaches would cease, but they could be controlled with medication. He also noted that the patient's vision had been blurred but that too would probably pass with time. Except for the broken leg and arm, Henry seemed fine. There was no damage to internal organs. The doctor said that was also a miracle. He had not heard from anyone back home and wondered if anyone knew where he was.

Later that week a military courier came to Henry with papers. "Got some good news for you, Jimson. You have been evaluated by a board of physicians and assessed with a medical disability sufficient to grant you an honorable discharge. You will be going home soon." With that said he handed Henry the papers and left. The nurse came over and gave Henry another hug. "You are a very fortunate man Henry Jimson. Who will be waiting for you when you get home? Is she a looker?" "Her name is Mary. We are going to be married as soon as I get back. She is indeed a looker," he replied with a big grin and laugh. "I wish I were going home too, but I'm needed here. This job has its advantages and you have been one of them for me," she replied.

CHAPTER FIFTEEN

Henry was transported back to the States via military aircraft, with a refueling layover in Greenland. When he arrived back in the States, he hopped another military transport bound for Fort Benning, Georgia. From there he took a bus back to Mark Hill. He was carrying his gear in his duffle bag as he walked up the driveway with only a slight limp to show for his close call with death. What a glorious sight home is, he thought.

His Father had just stepped out of the house and saw Henry coming down the drive. "Mother, come here a minute." "I'm cleaning the kitchen. I'll be there in a minute," she responded. "No Mother, you come now," he said in a loud, commanding voice. "What could be so important that it couldn't wait?" She stepped through the screen door and on to the porch with Father. "Who is that?" Then suddenly she bolted and started running down the drive to the man coming up the drive. "Oh, my God! Henry!" She grabbed her son into her arms. He dropped his bag and she swung him around in a circle. She stopped and held him back away from herself to look into his eyes. She and Henry were now crying. She grabbed him again and they stood there in the driveway in an embrace that only a mother and a son could generate. "My prayers have been answered! Thank you Lord! Praise God from whom all blessings flow!" "Hello, Mother. I love you." Father sat down in a rocking chair and took the scene in with a heart full of joy and thanksgiving. He was laughing and crying at the same time. This is so good, he thought.

Mary was home for the summer. Henry went straight to the phone as soon as he could. "Will it be all right if I call Mary now?" "Call her now, Henry." The phone rang in the Blyth household and Mary answered it. Her Mother and Father were both at home and in the next room. "Hello." The voice on the other end said, "Mary." Henry repeated himself. "Hello, Mary." Henry heard no voice but instead, a dull thud. Several seconds later Mr. Blyth was on the phone. "Hello, who is speaking?" "It is Henry, Mr. Blyth." A moment of silence ensued and then, "Henry, is it really you? Thank God. Henry, Mary is on the floor. She apparently has fainted." Mr. Blyth called to his wife. "Bring me a cold rag. Mary has fainted." She was already coming with one and leaned over Mary and patted her head with the dishrag. Mary came to, jumped to her feet and grabbed the phone. "Henry, is it really you?" "It is really me. I love you. Please don't faint again." They talked for over an hour and made plans for her to come to Mark Hill as soon as possible.

Henry spent time with his parents that evening, explaining all the events leading up to his coming home. "As best as I can tell, the shell blast that could have killed me was from friendly fire. My platoon was pinned down just off a road and the Germans were dug in on a mountain just off of and on the other side of the road. They were firing down on the platoons position and so they called in fire from our howitzers. Apparently the coordinates were off to begin with and the first shell fell considerably short of target. A correction was then ordered and the shelling was then on target. The first shell was the one that almost got me. I learned this while in the hospital in England after I came to."

The next morning the mailman delivered a letter addressed to me. It was covered with imprints and had apparently been forwarded and redirected multiple times, and finally arrived to our address. I opened it and it was from Fred. He wanted to know how I was and if I had fully recovered.

He related how he had gotten permission to go back for me. He made light of the fact that he found and carried me back to the platoon. An ambulance got me there and took me back for medical treatment. He said he was worried about me because I was in pretty bad shape and hoped that I received the letter. Now I had the full picture of how I came to be in that hospital in England when I came to. Fred had saved my life.

That morning I ate and cleaned up and then I went to the county home to see Old Man. I knocked on his door. "Come." There he was in the rocking chair and there was my straight back chair facing him. He looked up and said, "Good to see you Henry. Sit down. Now start with where you were when you received your wounds." " I was in an invasion force on Sicily. How did you know I was wounded? Did someone tell you?" "No, but one day on my way to the library I felt it." He continued, "Now don't leave anything out. Start with your crossing the Atlantic." He leaned toward me in the rocker and I spent the better part of two hours relating my experiences to him. He would stop me on occasion and ask for more detail.

When I told him about the shell that almost killed me and that my friend rescued me, he again stopped me. "It was the quiet one wasn't it?" "His name is Fred Guenther. I did not think at first that he might be the one. As time went by I began to notice how quiet he was and that he talked very little. We became very close and served together as medics. Yes, he was the one."

"Where is Mary?" " She is coming soon and I'll bring her to see you." "When is the wedding?" he asked. "The sooner the better," I replied. "Henry, I've been very tired lately and think I'll go to bed now. As soon as Mary arrives, come back with her. I want to talk with her again. It is so good to see you. I am very relieved that you are safe and happy that I can be with you now. Goodbye." With that, I rose from my chair and shook his hand. He seemed weaker now because his grip was not as strong. He went to his bed as I walked out.

As I walked toward the exit the black attendant stopped me. "Mr. Henry, you sure a sight for sore eyes. It seems like you been gone a long time and we missed your face around here. You know that Old Man was miserable when you left. He read the newspapers every chance he got to keep up with news. At times I declare that he was looking for your name in there.

"He had a spell a little while back and we thought something was catching up with him. But now I think it was because he missed you so bad. You sure are a sight to behold and I praise God you back too. I don't want you to worry none, Mr. Henry, but I think that Old Man is failing fast. We don't know how old he really is, but he ain't no spring chicken is he. You need to see him every chance you get now. I can tell about these things, so listen to what I'm telling you." "I promise you I will." "Sure good to see you Mr. Henry."

I spent the next day stopping by to see Mose, Mr. Spencer and the usual crowd at the drug store. They all wanted to hear about my experiences while in training and in combat in Africa and Sicily. When I finished one of my friends said, "When are you going to tie the knot now that you are a civilian again?" "I'm not sure when, but pretty soon. Mary will be here tomorrow and we will probably nail a date down." "She sure is pretty Henry," the waitress said. "Bring her by if you get a chance."

I slept hard that night and woke up early the next morning feeling as if I had been drugged. Mary came in the family car by herself and pulled in about noon. I waited on the front porch as she got out of the car. "What took you so long?" I asked, smiling. "Come here right now, Henry Jimson," as she stood outside the car with the door still open. I slowly walked down the steps and approached her smiling all the while, and she smiled back and then said, "Henry, you have lost weight." With that and the flirting over, she ran into my arms and kissed me so hard that I fell back a step and almost went to the ground. "But that's all right, I like skinny men," she said, and then kissed me hard again and grabbed my waist with her arms and pulled me tight against her body. My head began to swim and I got dizzy as the passion rose up within me. When she released me from her kiss I said, "Let's go get married right now!" "Nothing would please me more dearest, but our parents would never forgive us. Mother started planning as soon as I hung up the phone." "When, then?" I asked anxiously. "Let's talk tonight. First I want to get my luggage inside and talk to your folks." She coyly said to me, "Will we be sharing your bedroom tonight?" "You are driving me crazy, Mary Blyth!" and I kissed her with so much passion that I saw colors flashing before my closed eyes.

It was a wonderful night of eating together, planning our future, speaking of the wedding plans and learning of Henry's many experiences overseas. Mary said later on the porch, after his parents had gone to bed, "Henry, I love your parents. They are so special. I can tell that they love me too, perhaps even like their own daughter." "You are the daughter they never had you know," I responded. "Come sit here on my lap and tell me again how much you love me." She eased slowly down into my lap and leaned her head back against mine. I could smell her perfume as it wafted all around my head. Her body was warm and soft to the touch. I rocked back and forth in a slow and steady rhythm and she joined in the rocking motion. We sat there transfixed with the presence of each other molding into one body and one motion. "Henry, I love you with all my heart and soul. I could not live without you. God has answered my every prayer and now here we are together. I promise you that I will be yours forever and will honor you and adore you and worship you as long as I shall live." We sat there, rocking and sharing until it was very late.

The next morning we went to see Old Man. As we entered the room, Old Man rose and, as before, reached for Mary's hand, kissed it and this time he embraced her and kissed her cheek. "Mary, we have been so long separated because of Henry's absence, but now all is right with the world. Come and talk to me. I would linger here awhile, to be smitten with your wit and charm." "Why Old Man, you are indeed one possessing a silver tongue and you simply sweep me off my feet with your elegance. I think you were quite the ladies man in times past. I see the evidence of it in your eyes and in your manner today." With that, we all broke into laughter together and had a wonderful time, visiting and thinking of the future.

Mary had to go home the next day. "I'll call your Mother, Henry, and she and my Mother will discuss our wedding plans. We will understand them much better than you will, I can assure you. What do men know of weddings anyway? Your part is pretty complicated. You say, 'I do' and then you kiss me. And then you carry me away to your castle on a white stallion." Her laugh was like a beautiful song that penetrated and thrilled my very heart. She pulled slowly away. We waved to one another until she left the driveway and disappeared. I could hardly bear her leaving.

I made time to see Old Man every day. We spoke at length about my continuing education at the university. "What do you think you want to do with your life, Henry?" "I've had time to give that a lot of thought. After getting my undergraduate degree, I believe I'll enroll in medical school or perhaps law school. I have great admiration for those professions. I like the idea of serving the needs of others. The doctors and nurses around me in the Medical Corps were very professional. They seemed to be serving a grander purpose in life. I believe that there is much gratification in serving others. I'd like to be a part of that. I don't personally know any lawyers but intend conferring with a few before I decide. What do you think?" "I think you will be excellent at whatever you attempt, Henry."

"Do you think you will have children? I know you and Mary have discussed it." "We definitely will, Sir. We would like to have three and perhaps four. Whatever God blesses us with will be fine. I plan on naming a boy if we have one, 'Old Man'. What do you think of that?" "I think that people will be convinced that you have lost your senses. Perhaps circumstances will give you a good name for the boy," he said with an air of mystery. I was somewhat puzzled by his statement.

"Will you handle the arrangements for my funeral, Henry?" "Are you planning on dying soon, Old Man? Why you still have all your hair and don't appear to me to be anywhere near ready for the grim reaper to visit you." He smiled. "I agree, but will you?" "You know I will. Just write down your instructions for what you want and I'll see to it."

"If you will leave now Henry. I would like to be alone for awhile." I rose from the chair and said goodbye and left him.

CHAPTER SIXTEEN

Monday morning I was at the gin visiting with Mose and the foreman when my Dad called to me from his office. "Henry, come in here for a minute please." "Is anything wrong?" I asked the question as I moved toward him, but I knew the answer. I had a sense of dread welling up within me. I entered the office and he closed the door. "It is Old Man, Henry. They called here after calling the house. They say he is really bad and that he is asking for you repeatedly. Take the truck and go, Henry."

I raced along the highway and as I turned into the county home grounds I saw the administrator standing on the steps. "I am glad you are here, Henry. Go now and see him. He is in his room. Hurry." I opened the door without knocking. The room was rather dark because the overhead light was off. The light from the window was sufficient. He was in his rocker. I noticed that he had his suit on. It surprised me to see him dressed so formally. His hair was pulled to the back, combed and parted neatly. His shoes had been shined and he was clean-shaven. I took my usual place in the chair opposite him. He lifted his head slightly and he smiled. Then he locked his eyes on mine and they did not leave me. He remained silent. He reached his hand out and took my hand and placed it on his knee. "How are you, Old Man?" "I am well, Henry. How are you? I will see you again someday. I know that in my heart." "Yes, Sir." He released me with his eyes and looked at the tree out the window. "Remember the tree, Henry?" "Yes, Sir and I always will." I turned my head and looked out the window, too. Then he spoke in a whisper, "No fear, walking through the shadow." His grip on my hand relaxed and then released. I looked back. His head had slumped forward to his chest. He was slowly sliding down in the rocker. I jumped to catch his fall. I reached around and picked him up as a baby is lifted up. I held him close to my chest. He was very light. I walked over to his bed and gently placed him there with his head on his pillow. I moved him near to the wall and then lay down next to him. I pulled his hand to my chest and held it gently. I began to sob quietly and my whole body was shaking, as if I were shivering from the cold. I looked over to see a smile on his face. I reached over and pulled his eyelids shut. "Rest now, Old Man."

The administrator looked in the open doorway and saw us there on the bed. He shook his head sadly and then quietly slipped away to leave us alone again. I thought to talk to God then. I asked Him to receive Old Man into his bosom and grant him peace, grace and eternal happiness in His presence. I thought that now I would no longer be a whole person. That with the Old Man's passing a void had been created within me, never to be filled again. I was part of Old Man and Old Man was part of me. And now death had suddenly separated us, one from the other. I continued to cry and feel the emptiness of it all. I'm not sure how long I lay there. It must have been for an hour. I revisited every experience that I had shared with him. I thought of his wisdom and insight and how he nurtured me as I grew. I remembered his penetrating eyes and his many counsels with me. I grieved there in the bed, next to my friend.

Finally I rose, covered the old man's body and face and left. As I walked back to the front, the black attendant looked at me with tears in her eyes. "Did he pass, Mr. Henry?" "He has gone to his Maker now," I replied. "Glory to God, Mr. Henry."

The administrator stopped me and expressed his sorrow at Old Man's passing. "I am so glad you were with him, Henry. Would you step into my office for just a minute? He had two envelopes in his hand, one of which had been opened. He showed his letter to me and I read it. He then handed me the other sealed envelope addressed to me and also gave me a large gray metal lock box. It appeared very old. "When Old Man first came to us, he requested that we place the box in our safe and we did. It has been there ever since and has never been removed from the safe until today. As you see by my letter, he wanted it delivered to you along with your letter."

"Thank you Sir. He recently asked me to handle his funeral arrangements and that he would provide me with instructions." "Yes, I forgot. He gave them to me to deliver to you. Here they are." He reached in his desk, retrieved them and gave them to me. They were one page long and penned by the Old Man. "I'll be in touch with you tomorrow. What will you do now?" "I've called the coroner. We will take care of the body and will be ready for your instructions."

I drove back to my home very slowly. I tried to clear my head to prepare for what I was to do for Old Man. I told my parents and they were so sorry for his death and were a great comfort to me that night. We sat in silence on the front porch and they only spoke if I asked a question or made some comment. I appreciated that. I did not open my letter that night. I just couldn't do it. I put it under my pillow and the box under my bed. I looked over the instructions and then went to sleep.

The next morning I opened the letter. It was addressed to me and as I read it I could see him writing it. He said that because I was reading the letter that he was dead and he wanted me not to think of the death but rather, of how our lives were enriched by knowing each other. He told me that he was at peace with the prospect of dying. He did not fear death and considered it as a journey from life to a much better place. He looked confidently to the peace and joy that is promised to a believer. He wanted me to know with a certainty that he was just such a believer and was fully aware that it is not about the works a person performs, but about the faith that a person has.

I also found his last will, leaving what few possessions he had to me.

He stated that the box contained his treasures and some money to take care of his burial expenses, and he trusted that I would handle the contents of the box as he himself would, if still alive.

He closed by telling me the location of the key to the box, hidden in his room. He said he would pay me the highest compliment he could think of, being that I represented the son he never had and the only true friend that he ever knew. He wished Mary and I a long, happy and prosperous life together. In closing, he stated his love for me.

That day I called the administrator of the home to tell him of my plans. I then went by the funeral home and made arrangements for him to be buried and for paying the costs involved. I suggested a Saturday morning service and he said that would be no problem for the home. Then I talked to our Pastor, Reverend Hill and he said it would be an honor to have Old Man buried in the Methodist Church Cemetery and that he would announce the Saturday funeral at the Wednesday night service. My Dad, Mr. Spencer, Mose and Mr. Johnson agreed to be pallbearers. Old Man wanted me to say a few words before the casket was lowered. Next, I visited a stonemason who prepared headstones. He agreed to prepare the marker and I told him I'd give him the inscription for it tomorrow.

With all the arrangements complete I then went back to the county home and found the key. I went back to my home, pulled the box from under the bed and opened it. What I saw in there caused my emotions to run rampant. I was amazed at the contents. I had always wondered about Old Man's secret past life, before his coming to the county home. And now I had the facts of his past life revealed to me through just a few objects that were in there. The envelope marked 'for my burial expenses' contained $500.00 dollars. Then I saw a very old photograph depicting a very young boy, a man and a woman standing in front of a modest home. On the back was inscribed, "Mother, Father and William at age four.

There were two remaining items. One was what appeared to be a jewelry case, covered in velvet and lined in gold trim. There was also a folder lying under the case. In the case I found a Purple Heart medal. I had seen one before and knew what it meant to have one. Under that was another medal. It was attached to a blue ribbon, and a part of the ribbon was a ribbon face with thirteen stars displayed on it. The ribbon appeared to be for placing the medal around one's neck. The medal itself was gold. It was clasped by two rings attached to a rectangular gold bar on which was perched a gold eagle with what appeared to be olive branches in it's talons. On the bar was written the word 'valor'. The attached five-pointed star was surrounded by a green colored wreath. There was a figure of what appeared to be a helmeted head in the center of the star. I was clueless as to the identity of this medal and why Old Man had it until I read the citation contained in the folder. The document was executed by The President of the United States in the name of the Congress and was identified as a Medal of Honor. Suddenly I realized what I had in my hand. It was The Congressional Medal of Honor. I had never seen one before and realized how rare it was to receive one. The recipient was identified as Sergeant First Class William Andrews Stone. It documented his bravery in the rescue, on three separate occasions, of men who were seriously wounded and incapacitated during the charge up San Juan Hill in Cuba. It further stated that Sergeant Stone exhibited extraordinary bravery by placing himself in mortal danger of death by his actions that day. He was shot by enemy rifle fire and fell three times. It further stated that on each occasion he got up and continued to pull the three men off the hill, one by one and thereby, saved their lives.

Also in the folder was a newspaper clipping dated in 1900 that recounted his war experiences, his Medal of Honor award and his many extended stays in a veteran's hospital. It went on to say that he had complications from his wounds and suffered with recurring episodes of malaria. Those patients who knew him said that he withdrew over time and became anti-social in his behavior and began to avoid those around him. He had adopted a solitary lifestyle and many considered him mentally unstable. Others believed he had become paranoid, as he did not seem to trust anyone. He often refused to give his name when requested and while at the hospital, became a recluse, refusing to speak to doctors, nurses and fellow patients. The article closed by saying that he disappeared from the hospital during the night and, in spite of an extensive search for him by the authorities, could not be found. His physical description was given and help from the general public was solicited in locating him.

It all now became clear to me. He chose to enter the county home as a means of hiding from his past. I wondered how long he was out and wandering before he came here. I reasoned that he would never identify himself for fear that he would be found and become an object of curiosity and criticism. Even though he committed no crime, he was a fugitive from the society that once honored him for his bravery. Perhaps he was paranoid, for reasons not obvious to me. He coveted his privacy so much that he became an invisible man. He did that very well. He managed to hide for most of the rest of his life until now. I would reveal his identity to no one. I felt I owed that to him.

I talked to Mary for over an hour. I told her not to come. I would tell her all about the service later. She reluctantly agreed. I would see her back in school soon.

Saturday morning a small group gathered at the graveside. His instructions stated that he wanted no church service, a closed casket, the black attendant from the home singing a couple of hymns which the old man had chosen, and a few words from me. He told me to keep it simple and I determined to honor his request. At my direction the funeral director placed the metal box containing all its contents, except for the money, in the casket and upon his chest. The headstone was finished and in place at the head of the grave. It stated as follows: "Here lies Old Man. He was my friend. Died September 1944. 'No fear, walking through the shadow'."

Just then, I saw Mary walking to the graveside and standing there quietly. She came anyway.

The attendant from the home then sang the two songs he wanted. First she sang, 'Crossing over Jordan' and then 'In the Sweet Bye and Bye'. This black woman had a beautiful voice. When she finished those in attendance applauded and Mose shouted 'Hallelujah'. Somehow, even at a funeral, it all seemed to be appropriate.

I then spoke. "This man was my friend. He walked with me through my childhood and helped me become a man. He gave and gave but expected nothing in return. His wisdom enlightened my soul. He enjoyed my company and I cherished his. We shared all our thoughts, hopes and dreams together. I will miss him so very much.

I am confident that he is in the loving arms of our Lord and Savior this very day. I look forward to seeing him again in the sweet bye and bye. A part of me lies in that grave with him. I say to you all here today that, over the course of the time we shared, our two lives became as one life. What more can one ask of a friend? He gave his very life to me and for me."

With that the casket was lowered into the ground. Mary and I left together.

EPILOGUE

During the period of time from old man's death in 1944 to the present time, being 1954, these friends of mine are all still clearly in my thoughts.

I believe that Old Man is enjoying Heaven, even now.

Mose is still working, part time now at the cotton gin and we stay in touch.

My mother and father are still on the old home place, and will be there until they pass on. They still enjoy good health and our family visits them as often as possible. They love the grandchildren.

Mr. Spencer finished his duties at the draft board and retired to his farm, where he raises a few cattle.

Archie went home and then to college on the GI bill to become a medical doctor.

Bill is back in Alabama. He was a walk-on at the university, and is playing football as a quarterback. The university really wanted his talents and so, tailor-made a curriculum just for him.

Fred was with the Army during the invasion of Italy. He was killed during the battle for Monte Cassino. I really miss him and wish he had survived the war. Each time I think of him, I am reminded of the "quiet one" Old Man often spoke of.

The Second World War ended with the surrender of the Axis powers and shortly after the dropping of the atomic bomb on Hiroshima and Na-gasaki in August of 1945.

Mary and I got married soon after Old Man's funeral and returned to the university to finish our undergraduate degrees. I graduated from law school in 1950 and Mary and I settled on the Mississippi gulf coast, where I now practice law. We have three children, one boy and two girls. We named the boy William Andrews Jimson. Old Man would have been very pleased.

ABOUT THE AUTHOR

Charles and wife, Elizabeth Pitcher
50th wedding anniversay. May 2012

It has been my long time desire to write a book. It is done now and the result is a fiction novel, entitled *Two Lives One Life*. I determined not to use profanity, pornography, immorality or lewd behavior to sell this book.I believe it stands on its own merit. In my opinion it is suitable reading for all ages and honors my Christian belief system. I sincerely desire that you enjoy the book and believe that you will.

I am a Christian by the Grace of God, husband of a beautiful wife, and happily married for 50 years. We have been blessed with three daughters and thirteen grandchildren; the joy of our lives! I am a retired lawyer from Pascagoula, Ms., having practiced law for 26 years. My wife and I now reside in Cumming, Ga. I am also a citizen of the United States of America and proud to be so.

Made in the USA
Charleston, SC
08 February 2014